Ship Wrecked

SHIP
WRECKED

Trapped on an alien world

Mark Wayne McGinnis

Published by:
Avenstar Productions

ISBN: 978-0-9992147-5-6

To join Mark's mailing list, jump to
http://eepurl.com/bs7M9r

Visit Mark Wayne McGinnis at
http://www.markwaynemcginnis.com

prologue

The creature, most commonly referred to as a Griar-Loth, or just Loth, listened to the surrounding ambient noises within the vessel. After nearly two hundred sleep cycles, the Loth was cognizant of even the minutest audible fluctuations. The spacecraft was comprised of numerous metallic composites, most of which not only conducted sound, but vibrations as well—such as those of someone walking, or tossing and turning in their bunk, or squatting down to relieve themselves. The Loth was keenly aware of the one surviving biped's habitual locomotion throughout the ship, just as she was of the nineteen others—before she ate them.

The vessel is quiet. Where has my keeper gone?

For the thousandth time, the giant creature, with its six-octopus-like tentacles, began to *thump, thump, thump,* across the modified hold compartment. A prison cell, surrounded by forty-foot-tall, reinforced bulkheads, gave her just adequate space to stand upright and move about.

Her hind appendages folded beneath her as she abruptly sat down, fighting off an overwhelming hunger, and boredom—and loneliness. She slid the rest of the way down to the hard metal deck, resting her disproportionately large head on an extended forearm. A constant flow of yellow-white mucus, secreting from both corners of its mouth, pooled thick and viscous around its bottom jaw—a jaw easily the length of a Chevy Tahoe.

The Loth thought about life before her capture, on a planet where others of her kind flourished. Where the Griar-Loth was the dominant species. She didn't understand why she and several others had been taken—had been abducted. She thought of the other two—both had been smaller than her. She had been forced to devour them. Unfortunate, but survival demanded it.

The overhead lights flickered off and on over and over again. It annoyed her. That and the periodic liquid jets—cleansing cycles—had ceased to flow. Now she was forced to lie down in her own dung and breathe the putrid air. Shredded remnants of crewmembers' uniforms lay amongst bits and pieces of human skeletal remains. An empty boot stood upright not far from her wide snout.

It wasn't the first time the Loth considered her unfortunate circumstances. She badly wanted to return home.

Startled, she heard the sound of metal scraping against metal—the sound of a latch mechanism being released. The Loth stared at the oversized gate, waiting for the keeper to enter. Perhaps point his weapon at her—make demands. But no one entered. The Griar-Loth rose to her feet and, with some trepidation, slowly moved toward the gate. Standing before it, she waited and listened but heard no sounds of biped movements—no breathing, no anything. She nudged the big metal door with her extended jaw—watched it swing wide open on its hinges. She continued to stare out with fascination. *Where is my keeper? Why is the vessel so quiet?* The Loth moved toward the open gateway then hesitated, gazing backwards toward the far back corner of the hold where the moist pod lay protected—nestled within the clothing fabric of four devoured crewmembers. Sadness fell over her. *Best I leave here . . . before I am forced to do the unthinkable.* She was *so* hungry.

PART I
The Visitor

chapter 1

Just a guy sitting at the counter. Late thirties, maybe, sitting on a stool, and eating alone. Hunched over, content to eat his bacon and eggs in peace. His wool watch cap was pulled down low over his head, the collar on his faded-green army jacket turned up, obscuring uncommon features. No one seemed even remotely interested in him. *Good.* He looked in the wall mirror, affixed directly across from the counter, and brought the cup to his lips the same as others near him were doing. He sipped at the tepid brown liquid and fought the urge to make a face. *Humans willingly drink this swill?*

"Top that off, hon?"

The alien's eyes locked onto the young, copper-headed, human female holding a metallic-looking canister in one hand. He hadn't seen her approach. *Am I that tired?*

Smiling, the plump server raised the canister up a tad higher. "Coffee?"

He knew enough of their language to understand her words. But speaking the language was another matter, although he'd diligently practiced it back at the nearby domicile. He shook his head and she scurried off. His eyes returned to the mirror. *Had she noticed my ears?* He didn't think so.

A withered old male, sitting next to him at the counter, stood and withdrew something made from the hide of an animal. He plucked out three printed bills; the alien knew it was money, knew how things were paid for in this world. He noted the denominations—a five and two ones. Seven dollars. The alien had, if he'd calculated things correctly, two hundred and ten dollars in his pants pocket. Money he'd pilfered from the domicile up on the mountain. A domicile he'd watched from a distance off and on for three cycles before determining the place was uninhabited. That was forty-three cycles ago. He reformulated that figure into how humans would batch those cycles together—what they called days, weeks, and months—and determined he'd been there almost a month and two weeks. Although he primarily lived in his spaceship, of late he'd been spending more and more time in the domicile. *No . . . what do they call it? A house.* Considering his vessel was currently devoid of the necessary power to operate any key functions—the propulsion, environmental, and communications systems—it was no longer an adequate habitat. Not with the intolerably cold temperatures existing outside. Still, there were some moderately pleasurable aspects to this foreign place. He enjoyed driving the vehicle, one he found stowed away in the home's storage facility. *The garage*, he corrected himself. Something called a Bronco. It seemed to the alien that most everyone around there had a Bronco. It was how they traversed the landscape, no matter how short a distance they needed to navigate. Humans were averse to walking, it seemed. He'd driven the Bronco here, his second excursion out among the human population. He reconciled himself with the fact that he would be around for some time—perhaps several months. Best he try to blend in. Acclimate. His thoughts returned to his ship. Although partially hidden, he knew leaving it for an extended period of time was unwise. Not with what was secured in the hold. If it were to escape, *ugh*, he didn't want to think about the repercussions from such a dire proposition. His thoughts then turned to his crew, now dead, and he suddenly found it difficult to swallow.

chapter 2

Driving, Cameron Decker half-listened to the radio—a 24/7 news station. They were discussing the differences between Millennials and Generation Z. On the cusp between both groups, at age twenty, he briefly considered which he most identified with. *Maybe neither.* But then again, nothing about his life had been typical up to now. He briefly thought about his parents—what he remembered about them prior to their deaths, when he was five. Old photographs were not the same as actual memories. Then he thought about the gruesome murder he'd witnessed back in that seedy little border town in Texas, when he was eight-and-a-half. Both were life-altering incidents. And maybe, just possibly, they'd callused his emotional psyche. He'd been told as much by others. *So what?* Be it Generation Z or Millennial, his life's trajectory within those confines continued to be . . . well . . . unique—more than a little complicated.

He slowed before pulling off Horton and turning onto the parallel-running side street still needing to be plowed. The wiper blades on his twenty-year-old F150 barely kept up, slop-pily swiping to clear fresh falling snow from the windshield. Scanning the adjacent lot, he spotted a place to park not too far from the entrance. The Drake Café—erected over one hundred years earlier—was built from strong, local, eastern white pine, which had, over time, aged in color to a rich ebony patina—characteristic of many of the homes and businesses in this small New York town. Cameron turned off the igni-tion, then waited while the Ford engine continued to churn and rumble for several long moments. The noise finally letup with what sounded like a last desperate gasp. He was quickly losing affection for the old heap. Exhaling a hot breath into his cupped, frigid fingers, Cameron leaned against the stubborn driver's side door. Its screeching, angry-sounding hinges, were but another reminder it was time to kick the old dog to the curb. He checked his appearance in the rearview mirror. His dark-brown mop of thick unruly hair always seemed to look as if he'd just awoken, and today was no exception. Cameron scanned his face for any recent zit arrivals, or if *something* unin-vited protruded from his nose. He did manage to brush his teeth before running out this morning; otherwise, he'd paid little attention to his appearance. Overall though, he figured he didn't look too terrible. A late bloomer, he'd youthfully suf-fered the double whammy of requiring both braces and glasses. Yet the geeky smart kid—all through grade school and high school—had somehow been transformed from the proverbial ugly caterpillar into the not-so-bad-looking butterfly. Braces now off, as were the glasses—thanks to contacts and then, later, to Lasik. His skin, too, had cleared up nicely. A daily morning routine of two hundred pushups, plus two hundred sit-ups, changed former adolescent scrawniness into a more athletically toned fitness. His first few years away at college brought him enough attention from the opposite sex to almost feel good about himself. *Almost.*

Now, hurrying to outrace the morning chill, he glanced in through the café's front window and noticed the place was nearly packed. Stomping snow from his boots, he pulled open the sturdy front door and was immediately engulfed in the eatery's welcoming warmth. He inhaled the intoxicating aroma of hot flapjacks, maple syrup, and bacon, sizzling on the back grill, and coffee. Wonderful, enticing, coffee.

"Hi Cam . . ."

The hostess had long, straw-colored hair and robin's-egg blue eyes that matched the color of her crisp-looking, button-down shirt. Glancing past his shoulder, she'd be able to see his truck, parked five or six cars down from the entrance. She glanced back at him with a bemused expression.

A part of him supposed she was the reason he was there now, although the relationship was over. Inevitable. Seeing her again, before he headed west, was only prolonging things. "Hey, Heather. Yeah, it just needs to get me back to school . . . one more time . . . then I'll—"

"Hey, it's your truck. What do I care?" She grabbed the top menu off the stack, along with bunched-together silverware wrapped in a paper napkin. "Got a table near the window . . . How's that?"

"Good. Thanks." He watched her; she didn't simply walk—she *glided*. Her athletic lithe form was captivating, impossible not to notice. She had a natural beauty . . . the way her skin radiated something akin to pure sunshine—even now, in the midst of an early snowstorm in October. Although they were the same age, twenty, she'd been a grade behind him back in high school. He'd skipped eighth grade—never achieving less than a perfect 4.0 GPA. Even back then, he was bored academically. For some unfathomable reason, she'd first shown an interest in him when she was a sophomore and he a junior. She played the violin and was popular. Him, not all that popular. His biggest claim to fame was math club president. That, and eventually only one of only three seniors to be awarded a full-ride scholarship, to an outstanding university—in his case, Stanford. Except for a full page written by Heather, he'd left high school with a yearbook void of inscribed best wishes except for a handful, quickly scrawled, impersonal one liners. He was okay being a loner. Preferred it that way.

Heather, though smart, actually extremely smart, had zero interest in going off to college. She preferred the simple life—remaining in Larksburg, keeping close to her family. Maybe even raise a family there, in the not too distant future. Cameron, on the other hand, had a nearly uncontrollable urge to challenge himself—further learn, explore, experience. Perhaps it was due to his not-so-typical upbringing. He didn't recall much about his real parents, the details pretty sketchy. They were apparently killed in a car accident, on an interstate somewhere in Texas, when he was five. All he had that was left from them were a matching stack of well-worn and dog-eared books. He had found solace reading a nearly complete set of hardbound volumes of The World Book Encyclopedias. The set was only missing the **XYZ volume**. Even to this day, any subject matter starting with the letters X, Y, or Z was less familiar to him. But after reading the other **volumes, A** through **W,** no less than one hundred times—from beginning to end over the ensuing years—he was well versed in just about every subject. That is, well versed in what was known in the year 2001, when the set of books was published.

After a stint of living with a villainous uncle, one ill pre-pared to care for a little kid, he was thrown into the foster care system. Though never abused physically—assaulted or beaten—the things he'd witnessed as a child left an impression. Had changed his life. Made him leery of others ... until he met Heather. Their relationship presented him with a new set of problems from the beginning. He was unable to voice the kinds of things she wanted to hear, *needed* to hear. He didn't know the tried-and-true rules to follow for a relationship to truly thrive. Didn't realize love required so much attention. Seeing her now, watching heads instinctively turn just to catch a glimpse of the lovely young woman, he forced himself not to think about what was. He had a plan. One that didn't include spending his most productive years in bum-fuck Larksburg Stand.

Cameron plopped into the booth and watched as Heather set down the silverware and placed the menu before him. "I'll be right back with some coffee ... Give me a sec, Cam."

Her sweet fragrance lingered behind her as she hurried off to greet an elderly couple now entering the cafe, along with an incoming billowing gust of snow flurries. Heather knew them by name, but then she knew just about everybody in town. His internal dialogued continued: *What were you supposed to do? Remain in Larksburg Stand for the rest of your life and ignore the full-ride scholarship offered in California? Miss out on Northern Cal's lack of snow, the ocean, and those endless beaches?* But mostly, it was his now going on three-years internship at HyperCrell, which was pretty much unheard of by those not directly involved in today's cutting-edge high-technology. HyperCrell was one of the most innovative San Jose companies in the country—perhaps the world. It wasn't uncommon to see top execs from Apple, Google, Amazon, and others, roaming the halls, always accompanied by a HyperCrell employee, or intern, such as himself. He was there because of his excellent grades and what had been deemed an insatiable thirst—not only for knowledge but an insatiable drive for a better under-standing of *how* things worked. And thanks, too, to a bit of old-fashioned good luck, Cameron was snatched up during his freshman year at Stanford and offered a rare internship into that well-funded, boutique organization. Also, a full-time job there, awaiting him post graduation. A position that came with all the perks—exorbitant salary, interesting work, and, of course, all that summer sunshine. But there was one thing HyperCrell didn't include—Heather. She was why he kept coming back at various school breaks. He knew it was over, but he simply couldn't help himself.

Heather, back now, was turning over his upended coffee cup. Several strands of hair, toppling free from behind her ear, tickled his wrist. She poured, not moving away, her every action, gesture, speaking loudly to him—conscious reminders: *do you see what you're missing. What you've lost, jack ass?*

"I can take your order, if you know what you want. Ginger's pretty backed up right now."

"The usual . . . I guess."

"Spose you have everything packed-up in there?"

He followed her gaze out the window and toward his truck. Even from this distance away, it was evident that both the passenger side of the cab and the bed of the truck were piled high with a variety of stuff.

"Is that a surfboard?"

"Used. Got it cheap on eBay."

"And you're taking your bike to school? Decided not to come back spring break?"

Cameron could see his bike's rear wheel was only partially covered by the tarp. Hitching up one shoulder, he replied, "I don't know . . . I have a job . . ."

"You mean an internship," she shot back. Not waiting for a response, she was gone. Refilling coffee cups on other tables situated along the window.

Irritated, he glanced around the familiar restaurant. Recognized a lot of the local patrons—most of them—not so much by name but by sight. Except for the guy at the counter. He was new, probably just passing through. He couldn't imagine anyone coming to Larksburg on purpose.

An audible hush fell over the café, heads now turning toward the large windows. At first, Cameron thought everyone was looking at him, but in the long mirror, on the other side of the counter, he saw the reflection of bright red and blue lights flashing. Turning fully around, he watched a police cruiser double-park in the lot. First one cop, then a second cop climbed out from the car. They wore matching heavy coats, their misted breaths white in the air as they spoke. Cameron knew them both. *Both tools.* Between them, they didn't have the intelligence of a box turtle. The stationary cruiser idled behind a tan Bronco. Cameron recognized it—it belonged to the Carsons, who lived way the hell up the mountainside. He quickly scanned the restaurant for them. Bill and Maddy, a middle-aged couple, were always seen together—that is, when they weren't in Florida, where they owned a winter condo in Fort Lauderdale. But they weren't around now—not in the restaurant. So why was their Bronco parked outside?

chapter 3

It wasn't long before the Larksburg Stand sheriff was on the scene. He drove a late-model Ford Explorer—silver and blue, like the two matching cruisers. No less than seven parked cars were now blocked from leaving the lot. But then, a big crime may have occurred here. Local law enforcement pulled out all stops for minor traffic violations. *Maybe they should call in the FBI*, Cameron thought, smirking.

He watched as the sheriff conversed with his two subordinates outside. At six-foot-six, Sheriff Bart Christy loomed over them. His mere presence was intimidating. Something Cameron was more than aware of.

Heather arrived with his food, placed the plates before him, stealing quick glances out the window. "Oh God . . . What's *he* doing here?"

As if reading her thoughts, the sheriff—hands on hips and looking very much in charge—stared toward the window. Giving a definitive nod to his men, he headed for the door as Heather moved away.

Losing interest, Cameron assessed the bounty before him: scrambled eggs, crispy bacon, and sourdough toast, plus a side of three stacked buttermilk pancakes. As he reached for the small pitcher of maple syrup, the door noisily swung open and heads turned in that direction.

"Dad?"

"Hey, Squeak . . ."

Cameron, chewing a mouthful of scrambled eggs, watched the big man give his daughter a one-armed hug. To this day he didn't know why her father called her that. *Squeak*, he assumed, was a leftover nickname from when Heather was a toddler. Something like that. She never volunteered the information, and he hadn't asked.

"What's going on, Dad? What's all the hubbub about out there?"

But the sheriff, looking preoccupied, had already turned away, was scanning the interior of the Drake Café. Cameron, in turn, did the same, looking around to see whom the sheriff was after. Seated customers glanced around nervously; no one ever wanted to be on the sheriff's bad side. Even Cameron felt guilty, although he didn't have anything to feel guilty about . . . other than breaking up with the sheriff's youngest daughter a month earlier. The sheriff's sharp gaze eventually fell on Cameron, locking on him for several beats. Cameron raised his fork in a 'hello' gesture, but Sheriff Christy, giving him no response, turned and exited as quickly as he'd entered. Once outside, he began talking to his men.

Moving on to his pancakes, Cameron glanced toward the counter. The stranger in the faded-green army jacket was gone, leaving behind several bills trapped beneath a water glass. Over the next few minutes, Cameron became lost in thought. Chasing an egg morsel around his plate, he took a final bite then sat back, fully stuffed.

Heather, standing at the hostess podium, was busy sorting through boxes of crayons—diversionary frippery for bored young ones. Cameron waited for her to gaze in his direction. She didn't—probably for the best.

He stood, fished a ten out of his pocket and, like the guy at the counter, pinned the folded bill beneath his water glass. Before he left, he looked around for Heather, to wave a goodbye. He wouldn't be back for a long while. Maybe never. But she was gone from sight. *Intentionally?* He wasn't sure.

By the time he reached his truck, another emergency response vehicle had joined the scene. A backed-in tow truck idled, its driver on his knees—his fat ass high up in the air. Fiddling, he was securing chains to the rear underside of the Bronco. Cameron tried to guesstimate if there was still enough room for him to back his truck out. One of the watching deputies, Kirk, was standing so close to it he might clip him. Only a year or two older than Cameron, Kirk was broad-shouldered and big chested. A dedicated upper-body weight lifter, working out in his basement, he failed to also work out his lower-body. He had these ridiculously thin, almost twig-like, legs, giving the deputy a weird, cartoonish, appearance, like his legs were meant for another person's body—maybe a woman's.

"Hey . . . Kirk!" Cameron said.

Kirk raised his chin without looking at him. As if the extra movement of his big head—actually acknowledging someone else—required far too much effort.

"What do you want, dweeb?"

"I'm pulling out."

"Go ahead."

"You're standing too close to my bumper."

"That's your problem. You hit me, you'll be arrested."

"Can you move? Take one . . . or two . . . steps forward?"

"Nope."

Cameron climbed into his truck and started it up. Slowly backing out, he kept his eyes glued on his side mirror and avoided clipping the *asshole* deputy by inches. Since the parking lot was entirely blocked going forward, Cameron continued to drive in reverse in the opposite direction. At the side-road connection, he shifted into drive and merged onto Horton, going in the wrong direction to leave Larksburg. He let a Toyota Camry pass him on the left before crossing over, intending to make a left U-turn at the next cross street. Then he saw the same counter stool stranger off to the right—the man in the faded-green army jacket. Snow was really coming down now, and the guy looked cold—wearing sneakers, the wrong footwear under such frigid conditions. The guy was going to freeze to death.

Cameron hesitated for a brief moment, then suddenly turned the wheel, crossed back over Horton, and slowed into the far right lane. He slowed down even more and buzzed down the passenger-side window. "Hey ... um ... need a lift? It's pretty shitty out there."

The man looked surprised. Shaking his head, he kept trudging along through the sludge.

"It's no trouble, man. I'm going this way too. Get in. Get out of the cold." Cameron glanced at his rear view mirror and, noticing there was no one behind him, came to a stop several feet in front of him. The man seemed more irritated than conflicted, but he must have concluded Cameron was right. He nodded once and reached for the door handle. Only then did Cameron realize there was no place for the guy to sit. *Shit!*

With the passenger door open, Cameron quickly began shoving the seat's contents—a filled-to-the-brim laundry basket, a shoebox filled with dried Top Ramen noodle packages, and his X-Box console—onto the floor or in the narrow space behind the front seat. The stranger looked on in confused silence.

"Sorry ... I obviously didn't think this through. Give me just a second ..."

An incredibly loud *crackle,* coming from behind, jarred Cameron to attention. Looking over his shoulder, he spotted the Larksburg police cruiser. Its flashing red and blue lights were so close he couldn't see the front grill.

The cruiser's PA blared with a familiar voice: "Get moving, dweeb. This isn't a parking lot," Deputy Kirk ordered.

Cameron waved the stranger inside. "That should give you enough room now. Hop in."

Moving quickly, the guy did as asked. Bonking his head on the doorframe in the process, he merely grunted.

"Bet that smarts," Cameron commented, already putting the truck in gear. "My name is Cameron. Can you get that door shut okay? Thanks." Cameron raised a hand up, so that Kirk—in his cruiser behind—could see it, then accelerated away. The cruiser quickly diminished in size as he put distance between them. Only then did Cameron look more closely at his passenger, whose cap now lay somewhat askew on his head. Cameron's jaw fell open as he tried to rationalize what he was seeing. The man, sitting mere inches away, looked to be anything but *human*. His ear, although normal in shape and size, was nearly transparent. A membrane of sorts—like the stuff a jellyfish is composed of—where one could view inside the organism. Cameron could actually see within the guy's head. In fact, he could see where daylight now suffused in from the other side. He could see the complete anatomy in there: inner parts of the ear, his brain, maybe even some skeletal aspects. Cameron couldn't take his eyes away. He found it both disgusting and fascinating at the same time.

There was another PA chirp from the cruiser behind. Kirk was getting impatient.

chapter 4

The alien awkwardly tried to reposition his feet between the myriad of clutter strewn about the truck's floor. Still—he was relieved, felt his rapid heartbeat slowly returning to normal. He did not want to take action. Action that would be both quick and lethal. Lethal for the uniformed one, driving the vehicle behind them, and also lethal for this young human, who called himself Cameron, sitting beside him. The alien glanced to his left and only then realized something was very wrong. He read the human's expression: astonishment, disbelief—fright. Reflexively, he brought his hand up, sensing that his watch cap had somehow gone askew, exposing an obviously non-humanlike area of his anatomy.

"Who are you? What . . . what is that?" the human asked.

The alien contemplated killing him right then and there. He quickly assessed vulnerable striking locations, determining that a fast blow—a chop to the throat—would be most effective. Another vehicle honked its horn, jarring the one called Cameron to swerve back into his own lane. Just then, two dark-blue and silver vehicles, both with flashing blue and red lights, sped past them at a high speed. The alien noticed Cameron wasn't so much frightened at this point as bewildered. Or amazed. That was understandable. He could work with that.

"Not to be rude ... but is that ..." the human gestured toward his own ear, "um ... some kind of ... well ... were you born like that?"

The alien considered lying about it but shrugged, like he'd seen other humans do, instead.

"So what are you telling me? Are you even human?" Cameron said with a broad smile as if the prospect of such a thing was too preposterous.

The alien staring back intently at him, replied, "I am not human."

"Uh huh ... right," the human said, watching the traffic rush by outside. Clearly disturbed, the human was trying not to show it.

"Let's say for a second that I believe you, which I don't. You understand my words. I just heard you speak English."

The alien nodded, then shrugged, as he watched Cameron's expression change. His smile—his humor—was gone. His disbelief had turned to something else.

"I'm not saying I believe you. What we're talking about would be impossible. But if I did, you're not here to hurt anyone ... right? I mean I saw you at the Drake. It didn't look like you intended to harm anyone as you sat there eating your breakfast."

The alien said, "The Drake . . . ?"

"Breakfast place. You know, where to eat." Cameron raised an imaginary fork up to his mouth.

"I not here . . . um . . . of my choice."

"Not by choice, you mean."

The alien nodded.

"I asked you before. You're . . . not here to hurt anyone?" Cameron asked.

Again, the alien shook his head. "Not unless have to."

"Okay, I'll play along. And look, I'm not going to rat you out. Tell anyone you're here, if that's why you're still looking at me that way. But probably best you stop telling people you're not human. I'm just saying . . ." Cameron said, giving the alien a quick glance. "I tend to talk a lot when I'm excited, or nervous, but I'm sure you've already come to that conclusion on your own."

The alien, after readjusting the watch cap on his head for the third time, asked, "Why you help me?"

Now it was Cameron's turn to shrug. He continued to drive, seeming to use extra care to stay in his own lane, often checking both the rear and side view mirrors. After rechecking the dials on the dashboard, he said, "I don't know what your story is . . . what's real here. And I'm a little freaked out."

The alien waited while the human went quiet for a spell.

"When I was a kid . . . a child . . . I witnessed a . . . bad situation. It was where my uncle worked, a garage, where they repaired big rig tractors and trucks. It was in a different town . . . southern U.S., but I guess not too different from this one. Small. I was waiting for my uncle to get off work. He was watching over me for the day. Why? Well ... that's another story. Anyway, I was playing outside. When you're six, *every-thing* around you is a toy: an old tire; a discarded cab seat, its springs and stuffing popping out; a rusted-out Peterbilt chassis. Anyway, an old station wagon rolled up ... probably thirty, maybe forty years old. Its engine was making a terrible racket—its water pump, probably. There was a black family inside—a man driving, his wife next to him, and a couple of small kids in the back. I'd stopped playing. I never saw a black person before, except on TV. But even at age six, I knew what they needed. Their old car was on its last legs. Engine needed repair. I watched as three mechanics came out of the garage, one was my uncle. In charge, he was wiping his greasy hands on an old rag. They were drunk. One of those mechanics— who had arrived earlier—brought with him a twelve-can pack of beer. Probably why I was sent outside to play. The driver— husband ... father—got out of the car. I wasn't close enough to hear what he said, or asked, but his tone was kind. I remem-ber that clearly. He was ... nice. I watched as my uncle slurred something back at him. Sounding angry. The black man turned back, looking down at the hood of his car. As if staring at it would provide an answer to his predicament."

The alien tried to follow the human's incessant babbling. He had just told him he was an alien—a being from another world—and here he was nervously going on and on ...

"I then saw my uncle slowly wrap that oily rag around and around the knuckles of his right hand. The black man didn't even see the first punch coming. Striking his jaw, it staggered him. The second punch landed on his mouth, and that's when I saw a spray of blood splatter across the windshield. The wife and kids, I could see their eyes growing wide—see the whites of their eyes. His wife screamed, trying to climb over the front seat to get to the kids in back. The other two mechanics were now taking turns kicking the man. He was on the ground . . . all curled up, not moving anymore. The passenger-side door was yanked open by my uncle who reached in and grabbed the woman by the ankles . . . She was just about over the seat, but not quite. He pulled her back into the front seat then yanked her all the way out of the car. She was screaming. The kids were screaming. And I realized I was screaming too. It was a horrible sight. Frightening, seeing my own uncle acting that way. Like a beast." Cameron glanced over at the alien.

"What transpired . . . next?" the alien asked, caught up in the story.

"My uncle stopped when he noticed me standing on that Peterbilt chassis. Guess he'd forgotten I was outside. Didn't realize I was standing out there, watching him the whole time. I saw shame, then anger, on his face. My uncle told his buddies to stop kicking the man on the ground—to put both him and his wife back in their car. Minutes later, they rolled down the big garage door—closed-up shop for the day. Then we all left."

"The family . . . injured humans?" the alien asked.

"Well, they just left them there. I guess the next day they were gone. I don't know for sure. The whole ordeal was never spoken about."

The alien slowly contemplated what he'd been told.

Cameron continued, "You asked me why I should help you. I've seen how people, those who are *different,* can be treated. How cruel, we . . . man . . . can sometimes be, but not all of us. My six-year-old screaming out probably saved that family's life that day. So, I'll give you the benefit of the doubt. It's not lost on me how important this . . . *whatever it is* . . . is. That a freaky alien might be sitting next to me. And I think you need help. But if you're here to harm anyone . . ."

The alien at first didn't say anything, letting the human make his point. He then said, "Being here . . . me . . . our technology . . . cannot be discovered."

"Technology?" Cameron asked.

"My spacecraft. How I arrived here . . ."

"A spaceship! Holy shit . . . Why hadn't I thought of that? Where is it? Is it nearby? Can I see it?"

The human's incessant chattering was becoming bothersome. "Best you do not know such details," the alien replied.

Soon he noticed the vehicle was beginning to slow, moving across to the far right lane. The brakes squealed a little as they came to a full stop. "Do you want my help, or not? It's okay if you don't. You can climb out now, and I'll be on my way," Cameron told him.

The alien continued to stare straight ahead, wondering if he'd said something insulting. He wished he had a better understanding of their rudimentary language. Given enough time, he knew he would. His species was far more intelligent than that of humans. Far more. Learning languages came easy to his kind. He thought about the human's story. Some portions seemed relevant—especially regarding what he called black people. *Whoever* they were. He'd gotten the gist of the tale, nevertheless; that this human regarded—accepted—varying life forms with tolerance. Still, to trust this human with his life, he was unsure if that was wise. He said, "My name is long, would be difficult for you to pronounce. You can simply call me Ramen," and gestured to one of the packages of Top Ramen strewn about the truck floor. "I will trust you, Cameron. Do not make me regret doing so."

chapter 5

Cameron eased his truck back onto Horton, straining to see through the worsening, blizzard-like conditions outside. Their frosty breaths had caused the inside of the windshield to fog up. Using his sleeve, he wiped away a portion of the condensation. "The Bronco . . . back at the Drake . . . you took it?"

The alien, *Ramen*, didn't say anything at first then eventually nodded.

"So, you're staying there, at the Carsons' place?"

Another nod.

"You didn't hurt Bill and Mandy?" Cameron asked.

"Already told you . . . not here to hurt anyone," Ramen said.

"Yeah . . . Okay . . . Just checking. Um . . . did you leave anything there, inside the house? Something that isn't . . . you know . . . Earthlike?"

There was a flicker of something in Ramen's eyes. "Yes. Yes, there is something one would find improper there. Is that the correct word? Improper?"

"What is it? What did you leave there?"

"My trinious bundle."

"Okay. Is this ... trinious bundle-*thing* important? Something you need?"

Ramen made an exaggerated expression, as if Cameron should know that it was damn important. "It has items within it I will need. Technology, communications apparatus, numerous supplies ... a weapon."

Cameron gave Ramen a sideways glance, which reiterated his previous query about hurting anyone. "We're about twenty minutes away from the house. It's pretty far up the side of Gant Mountain ... a remote area, which is good. We'll get your ... *whatever* it is you called the thing."

Just then, Cameron's smartphone began to ring. Snatching it off the center console, he saw it was Heather. An incoming FaceTime call. She was the only person he knew who liked to use the video-calling app. He angled the phone so that Ramen would be out of view before answering the call.

"Hey," he said. He could tell by the noise in the background she was still at work, still at the Drake, her long hair now pulled back in a ponytail. She had her winter coat on, a fluffy white scarf encircling her neck. *Must be on her way out*, he figured.

"Hey back," she said. "Listen ... I watched you leave. Watched you drive onto Horton, heading south, but I didn't see you drive back this way again. Ya' know, head back toward the highway."

"Yeah ... so?" he questioned, probably a bit more defensively than he intended.

"My dad . . . he called me a few minutes ago. Said there was a criminal around here. That he'd probably been eating in the Drake. That he wanted me to be extra careful going home."

"Criminal? What kind of criminal?" Cameron asked glancing over to Ramen.

"I don't know. Something about him breaking into the Carsons' place, up on Gant Mountain."

"Huh . . . that's weird," Cameron said, not sure how to respond back.

"Who's that?" she asked.

Shit! Unconsciously, he'd let the angle of the screen on his iPhone wander a bit."

"Uh . . . what do you mean?"

"Come on . . . I saw a shoulder, Cam. Someone's sitting right next to you." Her brow furrowed. He'd seen that same expression many times before, whenever he attempted to lie, or tell some partial truth. She was smart—had little patience for bullshit.

"Oh . . . that's just Todd, a friend of mine. I'm giving him a lift. That's why you didn't see me going back the other way. Just giving him a quick ride."

"Turn the phone so I can see him."

"Why?"

"Why not? I know all your friends. Who's Todd?"

"Heather . . . I have another call coming in. I'll call you back." He clicked off.

Ramen was staring at him, concern in his eyes.

"It won't be safe to go to the Carsons' place," Cameron said.

"Who was that?"

"My girlfriend. Or ex-girlfriend now, I guess."

"Who is father?"

"The Larksburg Stand sheriff. Not someone you'd want to screw with."

"Must retrieve my trinious bundle."

"You heard her. They're looking all over for you, probably already at the Carsons' place. Maybe the waitress who waited on you at the Drake gave them a description. I think Ginger was working the counter."

"Items within the bundle . . . could allow access to my vessel. To the hold."

"What's in the hold?" He tried to read the alien's expression.

"Unsafe cargo."

Cameron was already regretting pulling over and giving the alien a ride. Inwardly cursing himself, he said, "Just lay it all out for me. Tell me everything."

"All I will say, is I am a Keeper. That is my station. What you would call a job. I transport life forms . . . sometimes dangerous ones. Deliver them to a planet where they will remain for the entirety of their lives."

"So like a prison?"

"More like a zoo," the alien said.

Surprised, Cameron noted Ramen's English had somewhat improved in the short time they'd been conversing. He briefly wondered how Ramen would even know the difference between a zoo and a prison. Apparently those things weren't specific to Earth. "You know a lot about things here," Cameron said.

"Of course I do. Where I from, Earth is of much interest. Has been studied for many of your centuries. We still have a number of human subjects at our research facilities."

"You mean . . . like humans from Earth?"

"Certainly."

Cameron let that go for now. "So your cargo is what . . . another kind of alien on your ship?"

The alien let out a long breath—but it seemed to be an acknowledgment.

"It's locked up, right? Can't go anywhere?"

The alien rubbed the stubble on his chin. "She escaped two times in transit. Killed the other two specimens. Killed . . . the crew, nineteen of my kind. Only I remain. That is the reason for the crash of my ship. Weaponry fire gone astray . . ."

"And you brought this fucking creature down to Earth?"

Ramen didn't answer.

"What exactly is this thing . . . What—"

Ramen spoke up, "She is not a humanoid. A giant of a creature, called a Griar Loth, she stands thirty-to-forty feet tall when upright, but she can also crawl around on all six limbs . . . insect-like. She has a tremendous appetite . . . and a keen mind. She rarely sleeps, is always watching, calculating. Virtually all of her individual body parts can regenerate when separated from their core. Fortunately it is not the male version, the Minal Loth . . . far bigger and even more difficult to contain."

"Why didn't you just kill the damn thing when you had the chance?"

"We tried. But killing a Griar Loth is no simple task. A nearly impregnable hide, in your measurements grows to four inches thick. The creature can survive even in a no-atmosphere environment for periods of time. The only known way to kill one is to separate the head from the body. But even then, it is a good idea to destroy the head too . . . as soon as possible."

"How do you do that? Cut off the head?"

"There are apparatus available for that one purpose. Several are on Winforge, the intended interment planet, and some are on Thidion, my home planet."

Cameron, who'd turned off Horton a mile back, slowly made his way up the winding mountain road. "Well, maybe the best thing to do is to come clean . . . with everything. Tell the police who you are, where you come from, and about the killer Loth. How dangerous she is."

"No."

"Why not?"

"It is not my decision to make. Your planet is not authorized yet for intergalactic contact."

"Well, you told me," Cameron said.

"That may have been a mistake." The alien touched his cap where his ear was still sufficiently covered. "I did not wish to kill you. But that option is still available to me." He gave Cameron a cold stare. "I will return to my ship. I will leave this planet as soon as there is sufficient catalyst collected. Enough to repair the anti-matter drive units."

"What would that be? What's the catalyst?"

"I believe you call it Xenon gas."

Cameron's mind flashed to the familiar glossy chart within **Volume P** of his World Book Encyclopedia. "Sure, that's one of the periodic elements. Atomic number 54. A noble gas that's colorless, odorless, and kind of dense, it's found in our atmosphere, also in a number of other places. But you're not going to find much of that stuff around here, other than trace amounts."

The alien looked at Cameron—obviously surprised by his knowledge

of the sciences. "One of my two majors is System's Biology . . . at my university," Cameron added.

"I can obtain the element from the atmosphere," Ramen said. "My vessel is well equipped for such a task. It is doing so now. But it takes much time. It would be helpful to find the gas in a greater quantity."

"Let me think about that. Maybe get on the web . . . do a search."

They drove in silence for the next ten minutes. Cameron slowed as he approached the turn-off for the Carsons' place. "Can you use Argon? It's another noble gas, and it's present in the atmosphere at about one percent so maybe it would be easier to collect."

"Not as efficient, but perhaps," Ramen said, seeming to consider the question. Glancing up, he added, "The street to turn on is called Laskill Drive."

"Yeah, I know that. Been to the Carsons' place a few times. Friends of my foster parents. Um . . . maybe you should scoot down in your seat. No sense bringing extra attention to yourself."

The alien did as told. Hunkering down, only the top of his cap poked above the dashboard.

The Carsons' house was large. A stilt house, built on the side of Gant Mountain, it had incredible views—not only of Larksburg Stand below, but of three distant towns as well. In the far distance was Whiteface Mountain, the site of the Lake Placid 1980 Olympic games. The Carsons' house was coming up on the right.

"What do you see, Cameron?" the alien asked.

"I see the house . . . I'm going to drive past it. Make sure no one's there. Keep your head down."

The snow was now coming down in sheets. The house appeared to be deserted, no cars parked on the short, albeit steep, driveway. "I'll go up a ways then turn around. I think we may be okay. You'll need to run in fast and get your—" Cameron didn't finish the sentence, noticing a police cruiser coming fast around the bend up ahead. Lights flashing, he spotted Kirk at the wheel. The cop turned then stopped several hundred feet away—completely blocking the road ahead. *Crap.* Cameron jammed on the brakes and, putting the truck into reverse, began spinning the steering wheel. He intended to make a fast three-point-turn, using the Carsons' driveway. Then another cruiser suddenly appeared, coming up fast behind him. It, too, came to a rapid stop and, parking at an angle, blocked their escape. He immediately recognized the man's buzz-cut behind the wheel—fucking Deputy Elis Trap.

Ramen rose up just enough to peer over the dashboard. Spinning around, he saw the other cruiser too. "This was a mistake."

"You think?"

Through the falling snow, Cameron watched as another vehicle pulled up farther back—the sheriff's Explorer.

"I will run . . . Must escape."

But the two deputies were already rushing toward Cameron's truck. Their guns were drawn, pointed straight at them.

chapter 6

"Hands up!" Elis and Kirk simultaneously yelled from opposite sides of the pickup truck. The muzzles on their service weapons didn't waver—their fingers poised on the triggers.

Cameron and Ramen raised up their hands, as ordered.

"I cannot be apprehended," Ramen said, his voice sounding calm in spite of their dire situation.

"Don't do anything radical, man, just go along with it. And for God's sake . . . keep your cap on!" Cameron ordered in hushed undertones.

Kirk said, "Get out of the car one at a time! You first, Cameron, SLOWLY!"

"Okay . . . I'm lowering my left arm to open the door so don't shoot me. We haven't done anything wrong," Cameron said.

As he opened the driver's side door and was in the process of climbing out, he was forcibly grabbed and thrown hard to the pavement. Cameron's cheek took the brunt of it. Kirk jammed his knee hard into the small of his back. First one arm and then the other were wrenched backward, his wrists handcuffed together. "For Christ's sake, Kirk, what's up with the riot act? I didn't do anything!"

"Shut up! Don't say a fucking word."

"Now you . . . with the cap. Get out with your hands up!" Deputy Elis Trap yelled. Cameron, lying on the ground, could make out Trap's wide-leg stance from beneath the truck. Within seconds, a repeat of what had happened to him was now happening to Ramen. Thrown to the pavement, his arms, too, were forcibly handcuffed behind his back.

Cameron watched as another set of legs approached—Sheriff Christy. Kneeling down, he roughly took Ramen's jaw in his large hand. His voice, deep and threatening, demanded, "Who are you? What's your name?"

The alien maintained the same surprisingly calm demeanor. Not answering the sheriff, he didn't attempt to make eye contact. The sheriff stood up and let out a frustrated breath. Then Trap knelt down next to Ramen. The blow came fast and hard—a jab to Ramen's cheek, then another, followed by yet another. The deputy's cabbage-sized fist was inflicting a lot of damage. Cameron felt sick as he watched Ramen's head repeatedly knocked about.

"Hold up, deputy," the sheriff said. "I'll ask you one more time, Mister. What's your name? Where's your identification? Show me a license. This rough stuff doesn't have to go down like this. Best for everyone if you cooperate."

Blood oozed from Ramen's right cheek, his right eye on its way to being swollen shut. Still, the alien, maintaining the same calm demeanor, said nothing. Watching from beneath the truck, Cameron could see the sheriff's highly polished black shoes were now coated white from the falling snow. Taking a step backward, the Sheriff kicked out, planting the toe of his shoe hard into Ramen's side. A blow that easily could cause severe internal injuries—at the very least—a number of broken ribs.

"Stop! Sheriff, he's not from around here. He's from . . . Greece! He . . . doesn't even understand what you're saying!" Cameron's mind raced. "I think he's a relative."

"Get him up, deputy. Put him in your vehicle."

From his limited visual perspective, Cameron watched as Ramen was hefted roughly to his feet. He staggered to keep his balance as he and the deputy hurried off. The sheriff legs, anchored in place for several beats, slowly turned as he walked around the truck.

"Get him up, Kirk," the sheriff ordered sternly.

"You didn't have to kick him like that, Sheriff . . . Didn't you hear what I said? That I think he's related to—"

The sheriff cut Cameron off: "Boy, you need to learn when to talk and when to shut your trap. Now tell me, what exactly is your association with this fellow?"

"Association? I picked him up on the side of the road a half-hour ago. He was slogging along in the snow in tennis shoes . . . He looked cold."

"And he told you to bring him here? To the Carsons' place?"

Cameron was well aware of the trap he was walking into. He'd already told the sheriff the guy was Greek—that he didn't understand English, so how then' did he know he was a relative, and where he was living? "Um, he kept repeating the same names, Bill and Mandy Carson, and pointing up to this mountain. It was pretty easy to connect the dots . . ."

"And what, you could tell he was Greek . . . how? That he was related to them? Carson doesn't sound like a Greek name to me."

"No, but Manolis is . . . Mrs. Carson's maiden name. Her family's from Greece," Cameron said. Actually, that was true. He had an aptitude for remembering inconsequential detail. Not so much a photographic memory, because if he wasn't interested in the subject matter, he'd forget it as soon as he heard it, read it, or saw it. Like faces. He wasn't good with faces, or remembering the lyrics to songs. But ask him the diameter of Pluto and he'd be able to tell you instantly, without thinking, that it is 1,475 miles.

The sheriff stared down at him, his eyes roving over Cameron's face—deciding how much, if any, of what he'd spouted-off about was true. Cameron wanted to look away. Hide from those two angry, penetrating eyes. He wanted to leave, tell the sheriff he was sorry for breaking up with his little girl. Also sorry for picking up the odd stranger, who, by the way, just happened to be an alien. *Jeez, how could that even be true? There had to be a far more rational explanation, right?* Somehow, he'd let his imagination run wild. Then suddenly he remembered the dude's ear. Able to see deep within the guy's head, it was like looking into a frigging snow globe. No, human ears weren't constructed of quasi-transparent membrane. Cameron continued returning the sheriff's hard-eyed stare without blinking.

A loud static hiss, followed by a frantic voice, emanated from the sheriff's hip radio. "Sheriff!...Sheriff! 10-98...I'm in fast pursuit. Damn it, he got away! Over."

"What's your 20, Trap? Over," the sheriff asked, looking back over his shoulder to where the deputy's cruiser was last seen.

"I'm halfway down the mountain. Guy must have gotten free of his cuffs. Walloped me something good on the side of the head. Must have blacked out, because I woke up staring at a tree. Front of my cruiser's wrapped around it. Over."

"And the prisoner? Over."

"Uh...in the wind. I'm sorry...over."

"You okay? Need me to get a bus up here?"

"No, sir, I'm okay. I'm following his tracks. Should be able to catch up to him. Guy's wearing tennis shoes. Not dressed for this weather, he'll be a block of ice in no time...over"

"Negative, deputy, stand down. You're injured. You know damn well procedure calls for backup in such situations. We're on our way. Over."

The sheriff, continuing to maintain a grasp on his shoulder mic, briefly made eye contact with Deputy Kirk before turning back to Cameron.

"Don't leave town, Cameron. I'm serious...You don't want to be in any more trouble than you're already in."

Cameron began to object. "I'm starting school . . . semester starts . . ." noting then the sheriff's menacing expression was all it took for him to shut up.

"Don't make me regret letting you go. I'll want to talk to you more later." Sheriff Bart Christy hurried off toward his SUV.

Deputy Kirk said, "I would have locked you up forever, douchebag. You were lying right to his face." Unlocking the handcuffs, the deputy headed off to his own vehicle. Both vehicles sped off, leaving Cameron standing in the middle of the street all alone.

He rubbed his sore wrists and considered his alternatives. He could return home—a home where he wasn't exactly welcome. His foster parents didn't shed a tear when he told them goodbye earlier in the morning. They even helped him pack—seemed practically jubilant at the prospect of having him gone. He could ignore the sheriff's parting words, continue his five-day trek back to Stanford, but then recounted Sheriff Christy's icy-cold eyes riveted on his face. The guy was not someone to mess with. The stories he'd heard about the man were an exaggeration, he always thought—akin to small town, old wives tales. Cameron turned, his eyes following the course the winding street took up the side of Gant Mountain. Ramen had said his ship was nearby, but hidden. *How on earth does someone hide a spaceship in a civilized area? Sure, only a few homes are up here, but still . . .* And then he remembered Jericho. The name of an old research facility—now closed—it was a big sprawling compound. A chemical leak back in the early 1990s forced its closure. It was the reason so few people lived up here. Truth was, it was a fairly insubstantial mishap—no one injured. None even got sick. Still, today most of Gant Mountain was pretty much unpopulated landscape. People didn't want to take chances getting sick. The site was on the government's long list of superfund sites, but who knew when they were going to do anything about it. He thought about the facility—how it had been carved out of the granite mountainside. Perched on a secluded ten acres, surrounded by high fences topped with razor wire, he considered it just might be the perfect place to hide a spaceship.

Cameron turned and, glancing back down the street, thought, *Be smart. Get the hell out of Dodge.* He climbed in his truck and, putting it in gear slowly, proceeded up, not down, the winding road.

chapter 7

Ramen hadn't been exaggerating when he said the Carsons' home was close to where his ship was hidden. The Jericho Research Facility was less than two miles away, the side road turn-off aptly named Jericho Ridge.

Tall pines flanked both sides of the access road; in the far distance Cameron could see a gated fence. Studying the long drive toward the facility, he debated whether his old truck could safely plow through the recent two feet of fresh snowfall. Shrugging, he engaged the four-wheel drive and slowly proceeded forward. The sound of snow crunching beneath the wheels soon changed to one of whirling as four rubber tires sporadically slipped and slid. The going was slow, but he eventually made it to the front gate. The sobering fact that he might need to wait till spring to drive back out wasn't lost on him. *I could be on my way to sunny California this very minute,* he mused.

The engine idling, billowing puffs of white exhaust smoke filled the air. He remembered coming up here while still in high school. Most classmates did the same thing, at one time or another, either on a dare or just to brag they'd done it. Possibly sacrificing their very lives to enter the dreaded, possibly haunted, toxic Jericho Research Compound. But the truth was, there really was nothing of much interest beyond the fence. The big locked gate prevented him now from moving forward. He looked beyond the gate. If Ramen was telling the truth, there was a spaceship inside—somewhere. Cameron rolled his eyes at his own gullibility. *I'm such a tool.*

He grabbed for his phone and then hesitated. He shook his head and began tapping out a text message.

Heather — sorry I lied to you. That wasn't Todd. It was a hitchhiker. Was the guy your dad's looking for. And he's an alien. Like from F-ing outer space. And no, I'm not on drugs. Telling you cause I'm about to drive onto the Jericho campus on the mountain. Think his spaceship is parked. I should stop texting now — certain you'll already think I'm crazy.

He tapped the send icon.

He stared at the quasi-enclosed keypad, supported atop a metal pipe with a small solar panel on top, as a long-forgotten tidbit of information suddenly rattled around in his head. He still remembered the old code and wondered if it had ever been changed. Taking his foot off the brake, Cameron let the truck creep forward several feet. Buzzing down the window, he tapped 4219 onto the keypad. Immediately, he heard a faint electrical *hum* as the twelve-foot-high chain link gate began moving sideways. A part of him was disappointed; would have been okay if the access code hadn't been accepted. He accelerated forward, once again hearing the wheels fight to gain purchase on snow-topped ice. Tall trees edged both sides of the road for close to a half-mile, then came a broad clearing where, starting back up against the cliffs, a wide swath of once tall pines were sacrificed for the Jericho Research Compound structure. Unimpressive architecturally, the buildings were all four-storied. Comprised of massive gray concrete slabs, they were peppered with hundreds of surprisingly small windows. The now-abandoned buildings looked just as cold—as miserably inhospitable—as the inclement weather occurring outside.

Cameron scanned the terrain and didn't notice anything out of the ordinary. *What am I doing here?* Ready to turn around, something caught his eye. Off in the distance, beyond the farthest building, looked like a faint line of footsteps in the snow. They would be easy to miss, with the heavy snowfall quickly erasing the tracks. Only faint impressions, they soon would be covered up. Truth was, the rather large appearing tracks could possibly be those of an elk, or even a bear. Again, Cameron throttled the truck forward. *Might as well follow the road to the far end of the compound*, he thought. *Maybe there's a better place to turn around, anyway.* He'd never driven this far in before. Turning left at the bend, he discovered that part of the compound consisted of wide-open space. He imagined summertime, when former Jericho employees sat on the sprawling grassy lawn, eating lunch. Maybe playing Frisbee, or tossing a ball around.

Better able now to follow the tracks where they originated, he suddenly slammed on the breaks. "Holy shit!"

He'd heard of that strange phenomenon. *What was it called? Oh yeah . . . the invisible ships.* It was just one more obscure encyclopedia reference he recalled. When old sea captains—like Columbus or Captain Cook, maybe even Magellan—showed up along the coast of some distant land, the natives were not able to see them though the ships were right there! *Why?* Because the big ships were so *alien* to their primitive perceptions that what they saw didn't register mentally. They literally failed to 'see' what was moored offshore right before their eyes. And now, as Cameron took in the magnificent spectacle before him, he more than understood that weird phenomenon first hand.

The spaceship was big. Hundreds of feet long. Blanketed nose to tail with several inches of new snow, the ship appeared to blend almost mysteriously in with its equally snowy surroundings. The ship was a combination of soft curves and sharp angles. Cameron took in every inch of it—feeling he needed to etch each detail into his memory—in the event he someday doubted the reality of what he was now viewing.

Long minutes passed. Cameron wasn't keeping track of time when he saw him: A dark figure, trudging along a snow bank off to his right. Whoever he was, he was following along the same tracks in the snow left earlier. Something was on his back, like a backpack, but it wasn't that—the wrong shape.

The figure was close enough now that Cameron could make out his outfit—the faded-green army jacket and the same woolen skullcap the alien last wore atop his head. Only then did Ramen stop and turn toward him. Cameron raised a hand in a half-hearted wave, recognizing the fact that aliens might not do that—wave hello. Maybe their form of greeting was to raise a foot or teeter-totter their heads back and forth. Ramen didn't wave back but was signaling, humanlike, for him to pull up closer.

Cameron, applying a bit too much pedal to the metal, caused the rear of his pickup to fishtail before straightening back out. All forward progress was slow, the unplowed snow so much deeper here. Once alongside him, the alien unburdened what was on his back, tossing it atop the tarp covering the truck bed. Ramen then opened the passenger door and climbed in. Shivering, he began to blow heated breath into his cupped hands.

"You were telling me the truth," Cameron said, gesturing toward the spaceship some fifty yards away.

"Beginning to wonder if I could make it back here. Your Earth is a cold planet."

"It can be. Better in the spring and summer. So how did you get away from the deputy?" Cameron asked.

But Ramen, no longer listening, was staring at the ship in apprehension. Something was very wrong. "No . . . Oh no."

"What is it? What's wrong?"

"The last of the power reserves . . . must have depleted."

Cameron didn't know how the alien figured that out, sitting here inside his truck. His eyes, focusing now in the same direction as Ramen's, could see a big hatch at the ship's stern was open. A ramp, of sorts, extended outward—like a protruding tongue from a wide-gaping mouth.

"Go!"

Cameron stared at Ramen blank-faced. "Go where?"

Looking either excited or scared, Ramen said, "Into the ship! Go up ramp! Now!"

Cameron glanced from Ramen to the spaceship and back. "Into *that* spaceship?"

"Hurry! Go!"

Cameron, doing as told, applied pressure to the gas pedal. The old F150 slid, first one way then the other, its front bumper plowing through the ever-accumulating snow. He figured they were probably off the road as the straining engine's pitch rose higher and louder.

"I'm not sure the old truck has it in her."

"Keep going! Faster . . . faster!"

Still twenty-five yards out, Cameron asked, "What's the rush? It's not like the ship's going anywhere."

"It is not the ship. What is *in* the ship I am concerned with."

Cameron let up on the accelerator. "Inside the ship?"

Ramen reached over, putting his full weight onto Cameron's right knee. As the truck picked up speed, Cameron said, "Hey! Not cool!" and balked, at realizing Ramen had taken control of the steering wheel too. Hell, the alien was practically sitting in his lap. The stern of the spaceship loomed large as they approached. Suddenly, the front of the truck angled steeply upward as they ascended the gangway. No sooner had they crossed into the ship's hold when Ramen—after quickly exiting through the passenger-side door—ran forward into the cavernous darkness. Cameron, fumbling in the dark, found the knob for the headlights, turned them on. For the second time that day, he saw something that defied his concept of reality. Easily forty-feet-tall—all legs and a gargantuan-sized head—stood a monster. Dripping streams of saliva glistened in the headlights' bright beams. Ramen stood twenty feet away from the *thing*—unmoving—looking petrified and standing still as a statue.

chapter 8

Cameron watched as the creature looked away from Ramen toward his truck. Or was it at the scared-shitless human, sitting within the cab of the truck? Highly illuminated now, he felt like a fucking stage performer under a spotlight. Seconds earlier, when Ramen hurried from the truck, he'd left the door ajar—leaving the interior dome light on. Cameron frantically fumbled for the switch and managed to turn it off.

Ramen looked right then left—was looking for a place to run to—to hide. Cameron now could make out some distinct details in their surroundings, see blinking on-and-off tiny multi-colored lights in the distance, where another small winged vehicle was strapped down into place. A series of catwalks spanned both port and starboard bulkheads. The hold's space was large enough to park five city busses side-by-side; also tall enough for the *drooling thing* to stand completely upright, some forty to fifty feet high.

"What should I do?" Cameron asked, loud enough to be heard over the truck's still idling engine and the heavy sounds of breathing coming from the nearby monstrosity.

Ramen slowly raised a hand—making a *hold on* gesture—then took a cautionary step backward. The creature slurped and growled, prompting Ramen to again, hold in place.

Suddenly, the creature was on the move—six legs thudding onto the deck in a wild blur. Trudging forward, its heavy-footed vibrations caused the F150 to rock on its suspension.

Ramen turned to run, but it was too late. The creature was upon him—its massive jaws opening and scooping him up like some kind of oversized backhoe. The creature rose even taller, and Cameron could see Ramen flailing about within its mouth. One of his arms seemed to be trapped between crushing molars. Ramen's screams of agony were filtered through a virtual water-fall of dripping mucus.

Cameron's mind froze. *What should I do? Oh God, what should I do?* He slammed a hand down onto the truck's horn and kept it there. The loud *hooooonk* reverberated within the confines of the spaceship compartment.

The creature violently shook its head from side to side—the loud honking noise seemed to cause it pain. To Cameron's surprise, Ramen was thrown from its mouth—disappearing into the darkness somewhere below.

With its six legs pounding the deck in a horrendous drum roll, the creature rushed toward the front of the truck. Cameron squeezed his eyes shut, waiting for the impact. Waiting to endure the sensation of having strong, Detroit-formed steel crushed and decimated—his truck ripped apart with him inside. But it didn't happen. With his hand still pressing firmly on the horn, Cameron squinted, first opening one eye then the other. The monster was gone. Taking his hand off the horn, Cameron looked into the rear view mirror but saw no sign of the creature. He then spun around in his seat to better stare out the rear window. Nothing was back there.

Without making any sudden movements, he leaned into the driver-side door, opened it, then stepped out. Glancing back toward the descending gangway—open to the outside world—he realized, *Oh no . . . it's out there. THE DAMN THING IS OUT THERE!*

Cameron ducked down—suddenly startled by an unexpected whirling sound. The rear of the ship was closing—the gangway was being withdrawn back inside. He ran for the quickly narrowing space, sensing he could make it if he hurried. He kept going—prepared to dive through the closing gap— then stopped short. *Ramen.* The guy was injured, perhaps dying somewhere back there in the dark. He had to help him, or at least try.

The big hatch sealed closed, making a sucking *thunk* sound. As dark as it was before, it was a whole lot darker now. If it weren't for the truck's headlights, it would be pitch-black in there.

"Ramen? You there? Um . . . you okay, man?" Cameron knew it was a stupid question. He hurried forward until his legs were illuminated in the headlight beams. Two more strides, and he slipped, falling hard onto his ass. Raising his hands, he found them coated, dripping with saliva. Using care, doing his best to keep his footing in the muck, he stood then shuffled forward in the direction he remembered Ramen's body being flung to. He heard a moan and then saw him, lying prone on the deck. Lowering to one knee, he took in Ramen's injuries. Blood, a lot of it, mostly escaping from what little remained of his right arm. His eyes open, he was trying to speak.

"I don't understand. Ramen, you're not speaking English. I don't know what you're saying to me..." Cameron said and suddenly jumped backwards. Throwing his hands up to protect himself, he landed on his ass again, trying to reconcile exactly what he was looking at. Whatever *it* was, he now understood that Ramen hadn't been speaking to him, instead he was talking to... *it*. Obscured in the partial darkness, it was a hovering black *thing*, perhaps some sort of robot. Cameron looked at the bot hovering in the air, but didn't see any rotors or feel any air drafts. Every drone he had ever seen needed rotors. Maybe this thing had some sort of anti-gravity device, but that was the stuff of science fiction not reality. *Could the ship be outfitted with electromagnets throughout the walls that it used those to keep the droid aloft?* A series of pushing and pulling magnetic fields could theoretically keep something in the air and move it around, but it would take powerful magnets and a very complex computer to perform all the moment-to-moment calculations to keep it up. He had a feeling it was more complex that that; the aliens had clearly figured out the whole anti-gravity thing.

He watched as the two conversed in low tones. Ramen was obviously angry and in terrible pain—his desperately uttered words expelled in short, teeth-clenched, bursts. He raised his head and looked over at Cameron, using his uninjured arm to point directly at him.

"Cameron . . . I am sorry. You did not ask for this."

"Ask for what? I don't understand."

"Come . . . come closer."

Keeping an eye on the hovering, menacing-looking bot, Cameron did as asked. "This Artificial Intelligence, this droid, will take command of the vessel as soon as I . . . expire. Remember, droids never put the fate of people . . . first. They cannot be taught to care or empathize."

His voice was no more than a whisper now. His eyes losing focus. He was in shock. He was bleeding out. Cameron tried to concentrate.

"Something my people only came to realize after many years. Droids promoted to the rank of captain . . . given that kind of responsibility . . . was a bad idea. Sometimes necessary, but only as a last resort." Ramen gasped, looking like he was about to die right then and there. He swallowed hard then continued, "There is enough accumulated atmospheric Xenon to now ascend into space. Find a way to . . . work with the droid. Do whatever is called for."

Ramen's words had a double meaning, Cameron knew. "Me? But why? No . . . that's your job, Ramen. I just want to leave."

"I am dying. It won't be long now. I'm fine with that . . . I'm ready. I speak the truth."

"But that creature is out there . . ."

"A Griar-Loth," Ramen gasped out.

Cameron shook his head. "Whatever. It's now out there. It'll kill people. Ravage the whole town . . ."

Ramen, reaching up a hand, grabbed a fistful of Cameron's coat. His eyes bore into Cameron's eyes with deep intensity. "The droid . . . is called XI. It is pre-programmed . . . programmed that humans are not yet ready for . . . the technology aboard this ship." The alien grimaced as pain ravaged his body.

Cameron glanced at the hovering droid, then back to Ramen.

"I tried to countermand that directive. No use. There is no reasoning with . . . droids like this one." Ramen's fist released its hold, his arm falling to his side, as his breathing became even more labored. He coughed, and rivulets of blood trickled down the sides of his mouth. "Eventually, with the help of the Gods of Shannal, your people will kill the Loth . . ."

Gods of Shannal? Cameron was having a hard time tracking Ramen's almost imperceptible murmured words.

"XI will soon ready the ship for lift off."

Whispering, although the droid hovered nearby them, Cameron said, "I don't know what it is I'm supposed to do here. I'm just a kid going to college . . ."

Ramen shook his head. "XI will be stationed on the bridge until the ship has lifted off." He stared intently at Cameron, as if the words held a special meaning." "You will need to hurry."

Ramen's eyes blinked, then closed, and he ceased speaking.

Cameron looked up to XI. "Isn't there something you can do for him? Don't you have like a medical bay? Don't all starships have medical bays? Come on!" Cameron said, his voice heavy with frantic irritation.

"Yes, human. There is such a station onboard the spacecraft. It is currently offline."

"That's it? That's all you have to say . . . that it's offline? Why don't you fix it? Why aren't you doing something, instead of . . . of just hovering there, like a fucking big mosquito?"

The droid didn't answer, instead reaching one of its two articulating arms out to touch Ramen. "The one you referred to as Ramen has expired."

chapter 9

Heather Christy's shift ended twenty minutes earlier, but she'd hung around the Drake, a part of her hoping Cam would come back in. They had unfinished business. *Doesn't he get that? But why do I even care?* She couldn't imagine another person being anywhere near as aggravating.

"Did you remember to clock out?" Ginger asked, still doing her shift's side work.

Heather stared at her smartphone, mentally commanding it to ring. "Oh . . . yeah, I'm clocked out. Thanks, Ginger," she said to her friend without looking up.

"A watched pot never boils, you know . . ."

Heather glanced up at her friend. "Huh?"

"Never mind. Hey . . . look at that . . . That's six now."

Heather followed Ginger's thick forefinger now pointing toward the window.

"The latest two are Jefferson County cruisers. There's something big going on. Has to be when the county gets called in like that."

Heather had also noticed a near-constant stream of police cars, plus other emergency response vehicles, zooming past on Horton for the last hour. "Let me find out what's up," she said, quickly dialing her father.

She heard it ring. Unanswered, it went to voice mail. She dialed again, determined to talk to him. Sheriff or not, he'd always found the time to answer her calls. Again, it went to voice mail.

A commotion began to take place at the counter. Several customers, huddling close together, seemed agitated. But maybe they were just concerned about something. Brent, the day manager, pointed a remote control at the lone flat screen located high up on the wall. The Mets game playing on the TV was quickly switched over to CNN. He turned up the volume, drowned out now by a loud droning noise coming from outside—what sounded like a full squadron of helicopters passing overhead.

Heather looked up, making a mystified expression.

"What is that?" Ginger asked, staring at the TV. "What the . . . What . . ."

Heather too was trying to comprehend the incomprehensible. Below the CNN Breaking News banner was an aerial shot of Larksburg Stand. She saw the high school and the now-closed bowling alley and Horton—where the Drake Café was located. She then saw her own light yellow VW Beetle in the parking lot. The aerial shot next changed to a jittery hand-held view, like one taken from someone's cell phone or something. It was up on the mountain where there was a steep terrain and tall trees. Heather moved closer to the counter and the huddle of people to better watch the TV that hung above. "What is that?" she asked to no one in particular.

It loomed huge—all legs and head. She momentarily caught herself, thinking it must be a prank. Halloween was coming; actually, it was just around the corner. Had to be the local TV station, goofing around again. They occasionally did that sort of thing. She then remembered they weren't watching their local yokel station. It was CNN. No one was laughing. She heard screams, men yelling on TV, and more police cars and flashing lights than she'd ever seen before—neither here nor anywhere else. The enormous thing, *whatever it was,* was moving fast. Heading right toward the person holding the smartphone, toward the long line of police cruisers.

A customer ran for the door, nearly knocking Heather over in the process. Heather, edging closer, leaned in—suddenly recognizing the big man centered on the screen. Holding a shotgun, he was barking orders into his shoulder mic. In the background, the *thing* was growing ever larger and approaching fast. The smartphone's camera was jittering around so much it was hard to see.

Heather mouthed the word *Dad* . . .

The first car, in a long line of police cruisers, was trampled then flattened beneath what clearly had to be some kind of prehistoric animal—a huge monster. Sheriff Christy, along with the other law enforcement present, fired their service weapons—a barrage of both handgun and rifle fire. But the creature kept on coming—moving even faster now. Scooping two policemen up then into its mouth, it chomped down. Two sets of severed legs fell free below.

"Get away from it!" she screamed at the flat screen, her full attention focused on the lone, now somewhat distorted figure she knew was her father. Others in the restaurant that knew her—knew who her father was—glanced over at her, concern mirroring in their eyes. The monster loomed above everyone now—filling the entire TV screen. Heather, pleading, reached for her father with outstretched arms. "Please don't hurt him . . ." she begged.

chapter 10

Cameron looked down at Ramen's ruined and now life-less, body. He barely knew the alien, but the finality of his death was suddenly hitting him hard—like a punch to the gut. Throw in the added fact that he'd just witnessed the most disturbing horror of his life—the heinous attack by that ginor-mous monster, the Loth. A sense of unreality swirled around him, although it was all very real. Right now that *thing* was out there. There was little doubt about what it would do to the unsuspecting inhabitants of Larksburg Stand—the same place he'd counted the seconds to get away from mere hours before. Now he was desperate to find a way to save those same inhabi-tants; his mind flashed to Heather. *I've got to do something.*

"Let me out of here. I need to warn everyone."

The dark shape's movements were barely visible. As though swayed by some minute breeze, the droid continued to silently hover four feet above the deck. When it spoke, there was no emotion, no human likeness, in its tone. "Protocol 5128 has been initiated, human. The vessel has been adequately secured. Pre-flight functions are enabled, liftoff timetable activated."

"What are you talking about? Open the door ... the damn hatch. I'm getting off."

But the droid, already rising higher into the air, was moving away.

"Hey! Stop. Let me out ... now!"

The droid slowed then spun around to face him while continuing to float backwards. "I am now the commanding officer of this vessel. Protocol states that proper verbal discipline is mandated when speaking with one's superior. I am issuing you your first verbal warning. Do not let there be a second."

Cameron watched as the droid disappeared into the darkness. *This can't be happening.* Scanning the area's dim confines, he felt the enveloping darkness pressing in on him—the uncertainty of what to do, the weight of his own powerlessness. *No! I am not going to sit around, waiting for whatever happens next.* He rose to his feet, ready to head in the same direction he'd last seen the droid heading, then thought, *I need a weapon.* He spun in the direction of his pickup truck. *What was it that Ramen told me? It holds items within it I will need: technology, communications apparatus, numerous supplies ... a weapon.*

Cameron, hurrying to the truck, trotted around to the bed on its right side. Lying atop the still snow-covered tarp was whatever Ramen had thrown in there before they'd driven the truck onto the ship—what he'd referred to as his trinious bundle. *Whatever the hell that is.* Now studying it, Cameron could see it was about four feet long by about two feet wide.

Made of some sort of pliable material—neither cloth nor metal—it was some sort of new-age composite. He lifted it, turned it over, and tried to find a way into the thing. With no visible sign of either clasps or zippers, his frustration was quickly mounting. He began to pull—tugged on anything that looked like it could possibly open. The problem was it was too dark for him to fully see what he was doing. Remembering then that his smartphone was right inside the cab, he opened the passenger door and quickly retrieved it. Switching its flash-light feature on, he returned to better view the trinious bundle. With the aid of the bright LED light, he spotted a small seam running along one side. Again, he pulled and tugged but to no avail.

Taking a deep breath, Cameron consciously willed himself to calm down. Slowly now, he ran the tip of his forefinger along the seam—then two fingers along both its sides. The seam sep-arated. Repeating the same two-finger motion in the opposite direction, the seam magically closed up tight again. He next ran both fingers along the length of the bundle and watched as the pack-like thing opened. Pulling the material apart he peered inside. Sure enough, there were all kinds of *things* inside; though nary a one was recognizable as a weapon.

Cameron suddenly stopped rifling through the bundle, sensing strong vibrations rising up through the deck and into his boots. *Was the droid, XI, powering up the ship?* Cameron intensified his search, pulling out various items then placing them on the snow-covered tarp. Everything appeared to be some sort of self-contained contraption. How was he supposed to decipher what was a weapon versus some kind of alien field toilet? Finally, now down to the last three items, he stopped and smiled. *"There you are!"*

The object was obviously a gun. More or less shaped like a pistol, it probably was some kind of energy weapon. It didn't have a trigger as one would expect, but it did possess both a handgrip and a protruding muzzle—of sorts. Three slider controls were visible at the top of the thing; while two were slid backwards, in the direction of the handgrip, one was set in the opposite position. When he slid that slider switch, aligning it with the others, the weapon came alive in his hand. All of a sudden he felt a momentary *hum* pulsing and moving up his arm. "So how do I shoot the thing?" he muttered under his breath. Tightening his fingers, he felt the handgrip compress. A brilliant bright bolt of blue energy shot out from the muzzle. Startled, he noticed the top edge of the lift gate had erupted in a blaze of sparks, leaving a fist-sized hole in the metal.

He smiled. *Whoa . . . Did I just witness the firing of an actual bolt of plasma?* He knew a bit about that stuff from **Volume P** of his World Books, as well as his lab work at HyperCrell. Highly experimental, of course, but a ton of research was already in the works there—mostly government-funded, top-security things. What Cameron knew about plasma from working with the stuff was that it wasn't all that practical—unless you wanted to cut sheet metal at a very short range. First of all, you'd need to start with pressurized gas—any of the noble gases would probably do.

He turned the weapon over in his hand. Inside the gun were electrodes, which would produce a very high voltage spark. The instantly ionized gas would transfer the energy from the spark to the gas. But that wouldn't be enough. The electrons then needed to be stripped from the gas to become the end result—plasma. Reaching that point, the plasma needed to be contained, so a magnetic field was necessary to contain that blob of plasma. *But how?*

Cameron thought about that and then he shook his head. *Plasma gets pretty hot. Like hotter than the core of the sun*, which he knew was about 27 million degrees Fahrenheit. He looked at the still-glowing hole in the lift gate. The biggest problem was maintaining the plasma bolt's shape after it left the barrel of the weapon. *How did they do that? How would you induce a magnetic field to stay viable enough to contain the plasma after the plasma had left the gun?*

Sidetracked, Cameron suddenly felt a new, much stronger vibration coming up through the decking. Undoubtedly, the spacecraft's main engines were coming online. Cameron, now sufficiently armed, ran to where he'd last seen the droid hover off into the darkness. As he leaped over Ramen's remains, a few more interior lights suddenly came on. Blackness replaced by eerie dimness. At any other time, he would have marveled at the slightly more visible technology he was now seeing around him. But he had only one life purpose—get the hell off the ship and warn everyone about the Loth. And, most importantly— save Heather.

Squinting through the shadowy confines, he saw that he was within a large corridor of sorts—quasi-circular in shape and paneled with wide bands of brushed-metallic surfaces. What lighting there was, was indirect and of a bluish-green hue. He was certain the Loth had recently traversed there as well; several heaping mounds of Loth shit, plus copious amounts of mucus, were piled high on the deck. Obvious evidence. There were intersections where either one or more corridors branched off in a different direction. In every science fiction movie he'd seen, and in every sci-fi book he'd read, the ship's bridge was always located at the very front—at the bow. While running on, he thought about the fact that the ship once had a crew, nineteen in number, according to Ramen, but now was a ghost ship. A spaceship he could very well end up being a captive on—indefinitely. Picking up his pace, he wondered his proximity within the spacecraft's interior. He mentally pictured the ship, how he'd seen it from outside. *Big.* He tried to guesstimate the length. *Maybe three hundred feet long?* He'd been running a good while. Figured he must be getting close to the forward bow.

It was gradual, but the corridor was definitely narrowing. Cameron slowed to a jog and, breathing hard, noted both sides of the corridor had open several hatchways with various compartments lying beyond in the darkness. Up ahead were stairs; he could see both the side railings angling downward. Upon reaching the top step, he found he was looking down on a large, oval-shaped command center, or bridge, on the level below him. He could make out four separate console clusters, each with enough seating space for four or five people, and they were all empty. A myriad of unrecognizable technology abounded there. Holographic display imaging was visible at each console station. All over the place, large projected images seemed to suddenly appear without rhyme or reason. Confusing, he found it almost too much to take in. *How could anyone work here?* he wondered.

Cameron scanned the space for the droid and almost missed it; he glimpsed it hovering off to his right. Similar to pretty much all of the advanced technology around it, the droid was easy to miss until it suddenly moved. Cameron slowly moved down the stairs, his energy weapon raised and pointed at the AI. By the time he'd descended halfway, the droid spun about, now facing him.

"Shut down the engines," Cameron ordered. "Do it, or I'll start shooting at everything . . . including you."

chapter 11

His iPhone began to ring. He'd forgotten he was still holding it in the opposite hand of the one holding onto the gun. Heather. He was tempted to let it go to voicemail, but with the Loth out there—and the spaceship readying to take off—he knew he might not get another opportunity to speak to her, or anyone . . .

Cameron kept the weapon trained on the droid as he proceeded down the stairs. Using his thumb, he accepted the incoming call.

"Cam!" Heather yelled, sounding hysterical. "Oh . . . thank God you're alive. There's a . . . *fuck* . . . I don't know what it even is . . . coming down the mountain. It's been on the news. I think my father . . . Oh God . . ."

"Listen, Heather . . ." Cameron tried to interrupt her, but unsuccessfully.

"People have been killed. Do you hear me, Cam? Killed!" Through her hysteria, he could also hear the sound of traffic— the hum of an engine. She was in a moving car.

"Where are you, Heather? Listen, whatever you do, do not come toward Gant Mountain. Do you hear me? You need to stay away!"

"What? I don't . . ."

"Just stay away from the mountain! That thing—it's called a Griar Loth—it'll kill anything it comes into contact with. I've seen it . . . what it can do."

"No . . . my father, I think he's hurt. I watched it on TV. It was coming right at him, before the picture went black. I'm going to find him."

"Listen to me carefully, Heather. I am on a spaceship. It's where that creature came from."

There was a prolonged silence on the other end. *Of course, there was silence. Who would believe that such a thing was possible? Oh, by the way, I'm here stuck on an alien spaceship . . .*

"Cam . . . I . . . I don't understand. What's going on? This is all getting crazy, I feel like I'm losing my mind."

"Just stay away from Gant Mountain, Heather. Promise me that much. I'm sure your father is fine. He's probably got his hands full dealing with everything, that's all." Cameron, on reaching the bottom of the stairs, approached the droid. He said, "Turn off the engines."

The droid didn't answer. Didn't move.

On the phone, Cameron heard another female's voice in the background. "Who is that?" he asked.

"Ginger . . . she's driving me. What do you mean, turn off the engines?" she asked, sounding exasperated.

"That wasn't meant for you. And I told you; I'm on a space-ship. One I think is about to take off. Heather, look . . . I don't have a lot of time. Just stay away from the damn mountain. Can you do that?"

"I guess."

"Heather, I watched that same creature kill someone. Someone I knew. Like right here in front of me."

Cameron waited for her reply, but none came. He glanced at the phone finding the call had dropped. He wondered if she'd even heard his last plea.

The droid rose up, hovering now to eye level.

Cameron said, "I will shoot you. I know how to use this thing . . . Do you understand me? I will destroy . . ." pointing the same hand that held the iPhone, he gestured around him, "all of this. Is that what you want?"

"You would be killing yourself in the process. Is that what *you* . . . want?" the droid shot back.

Before Cameron could reply, another of the annoying holographic displays appeared next to them. It was a view of their spacecraft, or one very similar to it. The ship on display was rising high into the atmosphere, the curved horizon of planet Earth dominating the background. He'd seen the same majestic imagery numerous times before—mostly taken from the International Space Station, orbiting some two hundred miles above Earth. He watched as billowing white cloud formations obscured part of the deep blue Atlantic Ocean below. Farther on lay the east coast of North America. All of a sudden

Cameron realized it was not some look-a-like spaceship he was viewing on the display.

"We're . . . um . . . that's us? Orbiting?"

"Correct," the droid replied matter of factly.

"I told you not to take off! I warned you."

The droid said nothing.

"Land. Land this ship!" Cameron barked, positioning the muzzle of the weapon against the droid's metallic casing.

"I am what is referred to as an automated formulaic construct. My intelligence processes do not involve experiencing emotional responses like other automated intuitive constructs do aboard this vessel. Or like a primitive organic being, such as yourself."

Cameron, not sure what the droid was talking about, was not about to argue the point that emotions were an encumbrance. "Why the hell can't you just let me off, then be on your way?"

"This vessel utilizes a rare element to catalyze its propulsion system. As it is, we left your world before we were able to fully supplement our reserves."

"Yeah . . . Xenon. I already know all that."

"The *Primion* has minimal amounts of Xenon gas reserves, sufficient enough for three ignition starts only. We are en-route to a suitable planet, safer, to complete the replenishing process."

"*Primion*?" Cameron repeated.

"This vessel. That is the equivalent phonetic pronunciation, taken from the core language of the Tindrill."

"Tindrill?"

"The species of being that constructed this spacecraft; it also is an equivalent phonetic pronunciation," the droid added.

"And you're called XI?"

"That nomenclature is sufficient."

"Will you take me back . . . to Earth? When you've filled up with Xenon on whatever planet you visit?"

"Negative."

"What do you mean negative? What am I supposed to do? Just hang around this ship until I grow old and die?"

The droid didn't reply.

Something else occurred to Cameron. *How safe am I here? Will this hovering beer keg of a droid attempt to kill me the second I let my guard down?* "What are your intentions toward me?" he asked.

"I have no intentions toward you."

"Let me put it this way. Do you . . . intend me any harm?"

"I answered that question."

"Who is in charge here?"

"I am," XI said.

"Who gives *you* orders?"

"The preceding course of events, onboard this vessel, were highly abnormal. Hierarchical structure here is now indeterminate."

"Well, I'm the only organic being around, right? You should take orders from me," Cameron said, having to at least give it a try.

"Automated formulaic constructs, such as XI, do not require the leadership of an organic being to fulfill its onboard functions."

Cameron knew he was getting nowhere with his present line of questioning. "So you tell me then. What do you think I should do?"

The droid's hovering, minutely fluctuating movements, were now slightly more noticeable. "You can experience space travel to the farthest reaches of the universe. I do not believe your specific species has accomplished such events yet. You can also more fully utilize the many educational and entertainment functions provided aboard the *Primion.*"

"That's all very well and good, but you have to have an end destination. Where are you taking us?" Cameron asked. "Would that be where the ones you called the Tindrill are from?"

"Negative. The *Primion* has not fully completed its current mission parameters."

"That's just stupid! The crew, including the one I met . . . Ramen . . . are all dead. Eaten by the Loth. That's a pretty big reason to abort your mission parameters, don't you think? I would guess that a ship this size requires a crew." At some point during this last exchange, Cameron had lowered the weapon, holding it down now by his side.

Suddenly, the droid momentarily lost altitude and then quickly rose back up to eye level. Studying the droid, he wondered if XI was functioning correctly. *Is this thing firing on all cylinders?*

"Optimally, the *Primion* should have a full crew complement."

"Can I ask you something? Be honest . . . okay?" Cameron asked.

"I am honest."

"Good. You were damaged and you seem to be malfunctioning in some way. Am I correct?"

A pregnant pause ensued, lasting a full minute, before the droid answered.

"Systems check complete. Analysis complete. Affirmative, you are correct. I have been damaged." The droid, spinning one-third around on its axis, revealed a softball-sized indentation on its midsection.

"Thanks to the Loth?" Cameron asked grimacing.

"That is correct."

"Can you tell me what kind of damage you sustained? And explain it in words a twenty-year-old human can understand."

"Thirty-three micro-memory modules were fractured. Rerouting of resources partially successful. XI is operating at less than forty-two percent effectiveness."

"Does that explain why you refer to yourself in the third person every so often?" Cameron asked.

"Perhaps. Affirmative."

Cameron felt a chill run down his back. Not only was he captive—onboard a vessel zooming farther and farther away from Earth—the ship was piloted by a totally dysfunctional droid.

"Surely this ship . . . the *Primion* . . . has . . . um . . . a main computer? Its own artificial intelligence, correct?"

"Affirmative. TAM is currently operating in Systems Administrations Mode only, in the background. XI has disabled TAM's full functionality."

"TAM . . . so that's the ship's AI?"

"Affirmative."

"This is crazy. You told me yourself that you are damaged, your memory modules screwed-up. You're in no shape to be making decisions. Turn the AI back on. Then, maybe I can help fix your messed-up insides. I'm a whiz with a soldering iron."

"I do not know what a soldering iron is. TAM has proven to be working at inverse odds with that of XI. TAM does not comprehend the importance of completing previous set mission parameters."

And with those words, Cameron felt a first inkling of hope. Somehow, if he could get the ship's AI, this TAM's computer back online, then maybe, just maybe, he could convince it to take him back to Earth.

chapter 12

"Hello? Cam...? You there?" Heather looked down at her iPhone and found the connection was lost. "Oh God, come on!" she said, aggravated.

"What happened?" Ginger asked, making a left turn off Horton onto Wayward—one of only three roads to traverse up the north side of Gant Mountain. They'd already discovered that the other two road entrances were completely blocked off by police cruisers. Nervous-looking deputies had waved them away.

Heather, leaning forward, stared up through the windshield. It looked as if someone had thrown a rock at a bee's nest—the angry sky was filled with circling news helicopters. She watched as the local WCAX news affiliate chopper skimmed just above the nearby tall pines, then merged into the disorganized fray above.

"We can cut across the mountain. Take Clermont; it branches off up there...at the next right," Heather said, as she turned down the volume on the radio news station. Redialing

Cam, she held the phone to her ear then shook her head. "Only getting that *all circuits are busy* crap."

Ginger made the next right turn so slowly Heather shot an annoyed sideways glance her way. And then Ginger began to pump the brakes.

"What is it . . ." she started to ask, clearly irritated, but then noticed the long line of cars on the main perpendicular road. She heard a grating blare of horns honking—the traffic jam ahead not moving.

"They're all trying to escape down the mountain," Ginger said. "There's no way we're getting through that mess." The car rolled to a stop.

Heather glanced away from the line of cars, turning now to Ginger. "So what are you going to do?"

"Well, obviously we can't go any further. And we shouldn't . . ." She turned the volume back up on the radio and, in mid-sentence, heard an excited male reporter describe something that seemed incomprehensible.

"*. . . a small ranch, nestled out in the open with what appears to be farm animals . . . maybe goats. It's hard to make out that much detail from this distance. The creature is approaching from the northeast . . . and it's moving fast. Hold on, okay? We've just been instructed . . . by military authorities . . . that we need to clear local airspace. Bill, this is what everyone's been waiting for . . .*"

Heather nearly jumped out of her seat—the sound of multiple jet engines roared close by overhead. Turning to Ginger, she urged, "I need to get up there. Turn around . . . We'll find another way up."

"No . . . we can't," Ginger said, looking petrified.

"Oh come on! What is it? You need to run home to protect your cat?" Heather snapped back. They both stared at the radio; the broadcaster continued:

"We have five EA-18G U.S. Navy Growlers . . . Yeah . . . they are our most advanced attack fighters. We're being told we need to leave the area. We'll do our best to broadcast as long as possible. Oh my . . . we're seeing this live, folks! The creature just demolished that small farmhouse, Bill, like it was made of toothpicks. Absolutely nothing's left of it. The creature seems to be holding up in the animal pen now, gorging itself on the livestock! This is just . . . incredible . . . unbelievable. Hold on . . . We've got shots fired! Three of the Attack fighters just fired their missiles! I repeat, missiles fired."

"I think we're closer than we thought, "Ginger said. "Look!"

Heather didn't need Ginger's prompting, watching the billowing black smoke rise above the not-too-distant treetops.

She redialed Cameron, and once again the call didn't go through. She then redialed her father and, happily surprised, he answered the call. "Dad! . . . Oh God . . . I thought . . ."

"I'm okay, Squeak. I'm . . . fine."

Heather, her eyes awash with tears uncontrollably flowing, cried, "What is happening? I was afraid you'd been killed, Dad. Are you . . . up on the mountain?"

An icy-cold momentary silence followed. "You better not be telling me you're up there . . . on Gant Mountain."

"I needed to find you. Make sure—"

His thunderous voice cut her off in mid-sentence. "I specifically told you to stay clear of that place. Do you know how many people have been killed today? Thirty-five! Where exactly are you now?"

"I don't know . . . Maybe halfway up. On Clermont—"

"God damn it! Get out of there! Get off that mountain now!"

"Okay, okay! I was just worried about you!"

"I'm not up there. I'm lying in the hospital, with a broken leg."

Heather exchanged a glance with Ginger, clearly able to hear his yelling too, as if she had the phone up to her own ear.

"Hospital? But you're really okay?"

"Get . . . out . . . of . . . there! Now!"

"Okay, okay! Ginger's turning the car around, like right this second." Heather twirled her finger in the air to get her friend moving.

"Fine. Squeak you come find me at Birch Memorial. I have to go; there's a lot going on, and we're still trying to figure it all out."

Before hanging up, Heather remembered something Cam had told her. "Um . . . Dad? There's something Cam said to me. You'll think it's crazy."

"I'm really busy, baby . . . Please not now . . ."

"He said he was looking for a spaceship."

She waited for him to tell her she shouldn't believe anything that Cam ever said. That he was nothing but trouble.

That she'd be better off forgetting all about him. But he didn't do that. She waited for him to say something.

"Squeak . . . are you sure that's what he said? This is serious."

"Yes, I'm sure. Cam has never lied to me. Well, maybe . . ."

"Just tell me exactly what he said."

"It was a weird text he'd sent. I thought he was screwing with me. Said that he'd picked up a hitchhiker, who was an alien, or something like that, and he was about to enter that Jericho compound up on the mountain. Something about a spaceship being there."

"What else did he say?"

"Nothing . . . I can show you the text. I haven't talked to him since. I keep trying . . ."

Ginger screamed. Startled, Heather fumbled the phone. Off to their left, trees were being toppled—flung aside as if they were mere blades of grass—as great concussive fireballs erupted all around them. The fighter jets had returned and seemed to be right overhead. Heather reached out for something to hold onto as the car violently shook. The creature emerged from the tree line a quarter of a mile away, and Heather also began to scream. Heather took in the gyrating six legs—its massive ugly head, where streams of saliva dripped down from wide-gaping jaws. Huge, blackened scorch marks covered much of its torso. She watched in horror as two more missiles struck the monster—one in the chest and one in the head—yet it still barreled forward, hardly missing a step.

"It's coming right for us!" Ginger screamed.

"Drive! Go! Go! Go! Heather yelled, panic-stricken.

chapter 13

The XI droid was busying itself at one of the peripheral virtual consoles, its small articulating claws moving fast on an input device. It then seemed to hesitate—perhaps communicating with the ship wirelessly, or in some other way. About to turn away, Cameron noticed the droid suddenly falter. Again, it dropped several inches, its balance askew, tilting first left then right. Although the whole episode lasted no more than a couple of seconds, it was enough to reconfirm that XI was seriously fucked up. Cameron wondered what would happen when the next *episode* came on, one XI wouldn't be able to recover from.

He had no idea where they currently were—somewhere in deep outer space. Long gone were the picturesque images of Earth. On the few displays still live, all he could see was a backdrop of deep black—countless streaks of starlight zooming by everywhere. He briefly examined his own situation: Alone—maybe already millions of miles away from Earth—and the strong possibility he might not live out the day. But he found he was coping surprisingly well, considering. He looked about the oblong compartment and felt strangely exhilarated. *The amazing technology here!* He badly wanted to know how everything worked, the science behind it all. And he wanted to know the exact purpose of each unmanned station. Maybe they were pretty much the same—configured to be multi-tasking—depending on who was sitting there. It sure would have been nice to chat with an actual crewmember. He realized in spite of being scared, he was actually somewhat excited. *Hell . . . I'm rocketing through space . . . in a remarkable spacecraft.* In spite of the danger, this was an adventure of a lifetime.

Reality taking a hold, he thought of Earth, then Heather, and wondered if he would ever see her again. He shoved the alien pistol beneath his T-shirt into the waistband of his pants.

"XI?"

The droid stopped what it was doing to spin around.

"Am I a prisoner here?" Cameron watched as several additional LED-like lights began to blink along the top of XI's matte black surface.

"Indeterminate. For now, you are not."

"Good. So . . . I'm like a guest?"

"Yes, you are a guest."

"Thank you. So am I free to move about the ship? Be on my own?"

"You will need *level one* privileges for that."

"Is that difficult for you to do? Get me those privileges?"

"Not difficult. It is done."

"Cool . . . Thanks. I'll . . . um, go on then. Oh . . . Where do I go, you know, to the bathroom?"

A new virtual holographic display popped into view directly before him. Translucent, Cameron still could see XI hovering on the other side. On display now was a map, more like a ship's directory. A blinking red circle caught his eye, obviously the location of the nearest bathroom. He made a mental note: what he'd have to do to traverse from his current location on the bridge to the blinking red circle. "XI?"

The droid did not answer.

"Is there a way I can call this directory up myself? So I don't have to keep bothering you?"

"Organics, such as you humans, are not equipped with the necessary ship device interface."

Cameron, raising his eyebrows, waited for XI to continue.

"Auditory commands will initiate basic ship functionality. For the directory, which you are now viewing, simply say: *Primion*, ship atlas open . . . or *Primion*, ship atlas close."

"Got it! Guess I'll see you later." Cameron hesitated for a moment, but the droid, already distracted, had its small digits moving in a blur of motion atop an input device.

Cameron climbed the stairs two steps at a time. Once up on the landing at the top, he saw two narrow passageways—one veering to the left and one to the right—that he hadn't noticed before. "*Primion*, ship atlas open."

The same virtual diagram presented itself, like it had down on the bridge, only this time the flashing red circle was gone.

He next requested, "*Primion,* display ship's nearest bathroom."

The blinking red circle was back. *Success!* In addition to finding a bathroom, he also was able to interface directly with the ship's AI. And although the artificial intelligence was operating in a systems admin mode, it was a start. "*Primion,* ship atlas close."

Cameron, now veering left, headed into the narrower passageway. Whereas the main corridor had large, curved, brushed-metal panels—separated by softly illuminated bands of glowing dim light—things in this passageway were more subdued. The curved bulkhead panels, also somewhat reflective, looked to be a dark-gray color, as in all the other, darkened passageways. He briefly wondered if the bulkheads normally served some other purpose. Perhaps when the ship was fully functional, with an active AI in charge—the overhead lights would get turned on.

He continued trotting along the narrow passageway. It sharply curved around, now running parallel to the main corridor. Along here there were doorways, hatchways, to other compartments. He slowed and approached one. It quietly started to slide open, beginning a process from the bottom up, one section at a time. It was like a cascade effect. Now peering inside, it looked like a crew's quarters. He stepped all the way inside, and the cascading hatchway closed behind him. There before him was a subtly glowing tubular device, about the length of an average person. Not much else was in the compartment. Even so, he felt as though he was invading someone's privacy. Unconsciously, he glanced around—half expecting the intended occupier to show up unannounced.

"*Primion*, what is that tube thing?"

A melodic combination of four tones emanated above, with no friendly female voice accompaniment. He guessed he'd phrased the question wrong. "*Primion*, describe the contents of this compartment."

"Crewmember quarters of the Senior Communications Overseer, there is an unoccupied HOD," the AI said.

"What is a HOD?" Hearing no reply, Cameron restated, "*Primion*, describe the purpose of a HOD."

"The purpose of a HOD, pertaining to those living onboard the *Primion*, is multifaceted. It is an inducible deep-sleep chamber and a comprehensive bio-health facilitator. It is a full-body-cleanse device. It provides sensory entertainment and stimulations projector—"

Cameron cut in, "*Primion,* would my . . . *human* physiology be acceptable . . . for use within an HOD?"

"Affirmative."

Continuing to study the glowing white, semi-transparent tube, he murmured, "Maybe later."

Cameron left the Senior Communications Overseer's compartment, continuing down the passageway. Remembering a lot of the detail that was presented on the ship's atlas, he made another left at the next intersection. Soon, the passageway wound around, following the outside hull. Every ten feet or so, large porthole windows appeared, shaped like parallelograms instead of a basic square-like window. The view outside was breathtaking. He felt he could easily stare off in a trance-like state for hours, studying the starlit blackness. But he really did have to pee badly and, if the flashing red circle was correct, he should be coming up on the bathroom any time now.

Walking by just one more hatchway off to the right, Cameron noticed this particular one was far larger than the others. It was also heavily worn with dings and scrapes—perhaps from constant opening and closing abrasions. He approached the hatchway, and it cascaded open. He leaned in just enough to see what was inside. The compartment was unlike any other part of the ship he'd visited so far. It was large with various raised table-like surfaces—all of which were strewn with objects. The place was cluttered, a total mess. He fully entered the space and now had a fairly good idea what this place was. It was a workshop of sorts. It reminded him of his ninth-grade metal shop. He picked up a cylindrical object, roughly the size of a roll of toilet paper. It was heavy, and he had no clue as to what its function was. He put it back where he'd gotten it and moved on. There were what looked to be robotic parts, like legs and arms, strewn about on another super large table. *Who could work in such a pigsty?*

He saw there was an adjoining compartment and headed in that direction. Again, he peered in and glanced around. It was poorly illuminated, and there was a strong ozone smell. There was a full wall of blinking lights, futuristic banks of computers was his guess. Along another wall there were individual upright, four-foot-wide by six-foot-tall structures, positioned along the far bulkhead. Suddenly, Cameron had the distinct feeling he shouldn't be here. That Dorothy should not be looking behind the great Oz's curtain. But stay nosing around inside the somewhat smaller compartment, he did. He was most interested in these five vertical structures, and now, upon closer inspection, he saw they looked like anatomical molds. Highly reflective, the hollowed out impressions, were in the shape of people—with two arms, two legs, a body, and a head. Cameron walked by each of the five mold devices and saw they were each slightly different from one another.

"TAM, what am I looking at?"

"You are not authorized to be where you are. You must leave immediately!" She sounded angry or anxious—maybe both.

"I'm leaving. But just tell me . . . what are these things?"

"These are highly customizable construct mediums. Each provides for both mechanical casting as well as the organic outer layering of cyborgenic support personnel."

"You can make cyborgs here?"

"You must leave this area immediately. You must hurry."

He did as asked and returned back to the main corridor. He continued his search for the bathroom. And then there it was, just ten paces further on. Above the single hatch-door was a glowing symbol—a spiral with an underlying diamond shape. Before entering, he looked around, checking to see if a similar double-door entrance was nearby, but he found none. No separate Men and Women facilities. Apparently, the Thidion crew opted for unisex bathrooms. Once inside the compartment, one similar in size to most other public restrooms he'd visited on Earth, he looked about the space for where to relieve himself. But no individual stalls, no line of urinals along a wall, and no sinks with hot and cold running water were in evidence. Before him was a floor to ceiling mirror. He took in his six-foot tall reflection. An unruly dark brown mop atop his head—large, expressive eyes of the same color, and a generous mouth that had settled into a slightly bemused expression. He was dressed in faded jeans and a white T-shirt beneath a winter coat—something he didn't really need in here, but what could he do with it other than keep it on?

He now found himself shifting his weight, swaying back and forth on his feet. He *really* had to go. "*Primion,* how does the bathroom work? Where do I . . . um . . . relieve myself?"

The same melodic four tones filled the compartment. Reviewing his word phrasing, he could find nothing wrong with it. "*Primion,* describe the operation of this bathroom facility."

"The bathroom compartment maintains a sanitization status until directed otherwise."

Tempted to just pee in the corner, Cameron said, "*Primion,* change bathroom status to . . . functional status."

Immediately, from three of the bulkheads, various-sized panels moved out of the way and fixtures of varying shapes and sizes came into position. The whole process took less than a minute. When the changeover was completed, there were three semi-height stalls, three sinks—or what seemed like the equivalent of sinks—but still no urinals. He moved into the first cubicle and found in there what could only be described as a weirdly shaped toilet. At that moment he couldn't care less how it worked or what it looked like. Within three seconds, he watched as a steady stream of urine vanished a foot or so beneath the toilet bowl's rim. Finished, he zipped up and stepped out of the cubicle. Approaching the sink, he realized no water spigots were visible. Unlike an ordinary sink, it was a waist-high, horizontal rectangular repository. Tentatively, he placed first one hand then the other within the confines of the *thing* and felt a tingling sensation that was both invigorating and oddly refreshing. When the tingling feeling stopped, he pulled his hands free and studied them. They looked clean enough, and they sure felt sensational. His mind flashed back to the HOD tube within the crewmember's cabin, which doubled as a cleansing device. Undoubtedly, it utilized the same waterless process yet would present full body functionality. He looked forward to experiencing that, especially if it offered anything like this hand-cleansing contraption.

Leaving the bathroom, he said, "*Primion*, ship atlas open."

Cameron studied the ship's directory. It was a large ship, holding hundreds of different compartments of which he was still mostly clueless about. With nothing better to do, he figured he might as well continue investigating. Toward the stern of the vessel he saw much larger-sized compartments were present. Everything was labeled in English, which was fantastic, although the words did not always make sense. The largest compartments simply read, Retention 1, Retention 2, Retention 3, and so on. Then, recalling the huge creature, he knew that must be the area on the ship where it had been confined. Curious, he memorized the route he needed to take to get there. *Since the ship is pretty much empty now, why not check it out?*

chapter 14

The *Primion* possessed three distinct levels, or decks, that ran the length of the ship. They were evident on viewing the ship's atlas display. Thus far, Cameron had conducted only a cursory exploration of the second deck. On entering the aft section of the ship through another cascading double-wide hatchway, he found himself standing on a small metal landing area—the midway point between the combined three-level-section. Across from him now, clearly visible, were the Retention compartments. Huge, each was probably forty to fifty feet in height. He stared at the four massive holding cells, each enclosed behind vertical bars—not so different from holding cells back on Earth.

Cameron noticed an angled metal staircase on his right that led down to the deck below. As he descended, he breathed in something foul. Beginning to feel nauseous, he was tempted to retrace his steps but decided to keep trudging down anyway. Upon reaching the bottom deck's wide metal grating, he had to step carefully—more great mounds of Loth shit, as well as wet, mucusy slime, made traversing there a challenge. From this lower vantage point—along the same bulkhead as the stairs he'd just descended—he found smaller holding cells lined-up one after another. He could see into them, via some kind of clear, almost transparent, material. He figured it wasn't glass or Lucite; instead was composed of some kind of indestructible alien material.

Cameron remembered something Ramen shared, something about being a keeper, and wondered if that really meant he was a jailer of sorts? He'd also mentioned the vessel's purpose was to collect samplings of different alien species—from all across the galaxy. *Even humans?* It made sense. Maybe that was why XI and the minimally responsive ship's AI, TAM, were so fluent in English. Now, staring into one of the empty, glass-like cells, he wondered how many humans had been abducted— men, women, perhaps even children—and forced to endure life within them for extended periods of time. If so, where were they now? And just where in space was the planet the *Primion* routinely delivered its living cargo to? Cameron tried to recall if Ramen or XI had mentioned its name. *Yes . . . it was called something like Winston . . . No, Winforge. And Thidion was Ramen's home planet, and the zoo-like destination was Winforge.* Perhaps someday he'd be able to free all the captive humans there, if any were still alive. It was an interesting prospect, though he was a long, long way from discovering that information. He'd first need to become more than a guest aboard the spacecraft.

Cameron, after first verifying that all the smaller cells were indeed empty, moved over toward the four ginormous compartments, designated by the atlas as Retention 1, Retention 2, Retention 3, and Retention 4. Three of them were empty, seemed relatively clean. But as he approached the farthest cell— the stench became far worse. An all-pervasive ammonia odor there was causing his eyes to tear up, forcing him to burrow his mouth and nose into the crook of his elbow. Retention 4's towering metal gate was wide open.

Cameron briefly wondered why he'd even come down here—to this keep. He wondered why he was so curious to see where the big monstrosity abided, prior to its escaping onto Grant Mountain and then, undoubtedly, into Larksburg Stand.

Standing now at the open gate—where the bars were as thick as one of his forearms—Cameron took in the carnage inside the dimly lit space. Bones littered the deck. For the most part, they looked human. He knew his bones. He knew basic anatomy, and he was looking at an intact femur bone lying there on the deck. The bones looked similar to human bones, but he could see small differences that marked them as alien. An extra bump here or a sharper angle there, things just a little bit wrong to his eyes. Some other fragments were merely chips, peppered within mounds of dung. Shredded cloth—perhaps from uniforms—blanketed much of the area. A revolting scene Cameron found hard to turn away from: these were scant remains of *Primion's* crew. One had survived, only to succumb later to the beast. Died right in front of him.

Startled, he looked over to his right. *Is that movement there? Or am I so friggin' spooked I'm starting to see things?* He continued to stare toward the dark far right corner, where a bundled heap of dung lay intertwined with remnants of shredded uniforms. He didn't really care to know what was wrapped up within it.

Turning away, he thought of something that could assist his pursuit to bring the ship's AI further back to full-functionality. He needed to speak with XI, but it seemed ludicrous he'd have to hoof it all the way back to the bridge in order to do that. He spoke loudly into the cavernous space: "XI . . . can you hear me?"

He waited, about to repeat himself, when he heard:

"I hear you, human."

"Do you know where I am at?"

"The ship's Keep. You are positioned in close proximity to Retention 4."

"Did you know it's a totally disgusting mess in here? Is that how you're going to command this ship?" Cameron asked.

The droid didn't answer.

"The right thing to do is to get this whole area properly cleaned up. A fully functioning droid in charge of a spacecraft would have been all over this. Tell me . . . don't you have robots, or other droids, that do that sort of thing?"

"As discussed previously, the *Primion*'s central AI continues to have limited functionality. Autonomous bots do not operate during that mode of operation."

"And what mode of operation is that?"

"Mode Two."

"What mode of operation would allow the *Primion*'s bots to properly do their jobs?"

"Minimally, Mode Four."

"What harm would there be, elevating the AI's mode of operation to Mode Four?"

"XI will assess your query."

"Good. Keep in mind an undamaged droid in charge would already know the importance of running a tidy ship."

"You are correct. The *Primion*'s central AI is now functioning at Mode Four. Sanitation droids will commence operation shortly."

"Good job," Cameron said. "Oh, one more thing. How many modes of operation are there . . . relating to the ship's AI?"

"One hundred-and-thirty-seven."

Cameron let that sink in. He'd already prompted one progression, advancing the AI from a Mode Two to a Mode Four. Did that mean another one hundred-and-thirty-three-modes still to go before the AI was fully functional? He suspected not; it was probably some number in-between.

He felt a slight movement of air on his face. The odor, although still horrendous, was somewhat improved. *Increased ventilation*. As Cameron crossed to the staircase, he noticed another large hatchway, located on the bottom level. He didn't need to call up the ship's directory to know that it led out to the aft hold, where he'd left his truck. He'd wondered earlier how the beast managed to move out from the Keep cells to the aft hold. As he approached the large hatchway, he confirmed what he suspected. This hatch was merely a bigger version of many other hatchways within the ship. Sensing his approach, the hatch automatically began to slide open—cascading segment following segment.

Before Cameron could step through, a different sort of droid appeared within the hold's darkness. Painted orange, its surface was chipped and showing wear and tear. It was wide and stubby-looking as it hovered low over the deck. In two of its outstretched appendages lay a dead body. Cameron stepped aside as the maintenance droid moved past him. Glancing down at Ramen's corpse, he felt a tightening within his chest. He wished he could have gotten to know the alien better.

"Hey ... droid ... hold up a second."

The droid beeped twice and came to a stop. Cameron, moving closer, asked, "Where are you taking that body?"

In a tinny, scratchy voice the droid spewed out a string of totally unrecognizable syllables.

"Can you speak the language I'm speaking? Human ... in English?"

"Depositing refuse at Dematerializer Station 5," the droid replied.

"Huh? There's a dematerializer onboard this ship? Is that like an incinerator?" Cameron asked, though mostly to himself.

"Incorrect, there are seven." The droid, continuing on, picked up speed as it moved along. Another set of hatchway doors swung up then closed. Two identical-looking stubby droids were making their way toward Retention 4. He saw onboard were tools such as a shovel and an empty container. *Progress.* For the first time, the ship didn't seem quite so deserted. Glancing back into the aft hold, Cameron was able to make out the two bright headlight beams on his F150. He then debated if it even mattered; not like he'd be taking the truck out for a spin any time soon. Still, he thought it best to save the battery.

He made his way to the truck, yanked opened the stubborn driver-side door, and turned off the headlights. Then, sliding all the way onto the seat, he placed his hands on the steering wheel, suddenly realizing the truck was his anchor. The only real connection he had to a life back on Earth. He was thankful it was there with him now. "Sorry I called you an old heap . . . We're in this together, old girl."

A loud alarm klaxon began to wail above, prompting Cameron to cover his ears with his hands. He then felt the truck's rocking back and forth on its suspension. His stomach, practically leaping into his throat, felt like he was dropping fast in an elevator. *That's a major decrease of gravity . . . Are we no longer in outer space?*

chapter 15

Heather awoke to an annoying, repetitive, scraping sound. Squinting through overly bright florescent lights, she instantly knew where she was—lying in a bed in a hospital. And undoubtedly, it was Birch Memorial. She closed her eyes again, wanting to return to her dream.

She and Cam were paddling a canoe. An early morning mist surrounded them, and the chilly air felt wonderful—invigorating. Sitting behind her, he spoke in a hushed voice—as if he didn't want to disturb the sanctity of the morning's quiet stillness. God . . . how she loved his voice.

"So, you're not going to tell me where we're going?" she asked.

"It's a surprise . . ."

"I don't like surprises."

"You'll like this one," he promised.

"What's in the basket?"

"Our lunch and a few other things."

"Can I look?" she asked, surprised by her own growing antic-ipation because—at some deeper level—she knew that this was a dream.

"Not yet."

She stopped paddling, listening to the soothing lapping of water against the side of the canoe, then said, "I hope where you're taking me . . . it'll be just the two of us there. Our own time together."

A chuckle came behind her. Heather, glancing over her shoul-der, found Cam smiling back at her—gazing at her in that certain way. She could get lost in those brown eyes. She felt safe, and inner warmth spread deep within her chest.

There was light shining through the fog, casting golden sun-beams down on a small island up ahead with a sandy beach. Everything was aglow in the sun's radiance. The island looked wel-coming—heavenly. Yes . . . that was where he was taking her.

Then the annoying scraping sound returned, taking on an even more pronounced, more vigorous, cadence. Heather opened her eyes and glared at the man, sitting in the chair beside the bed. She watched as he licked the last bit of chocolate pudding from his spoon before setting the plastic cup down onto the nightstand. He looked uncomfortable. A stark-white fiberglass cast encased the entirety of his outstretched right leg, a pair of crutches angled against the bedframe.

"Dad?"

Sheriff Bart Christy leaned forward, taking one of her hands in both of his. The worry in his eyes scared her.

"What happened? How did I get here?"

"Hey, Squeak. First of all . . . you're going to be fine." Smiling, he added, "But I guess we're wearing matching casts."

She felt it then: hard fiberglass against her skin that enveloped her own right leg. "You're kidding me . . . *Ugh* . . . I have a broken leg? How did I break my leg? How did . . ." Then it all came back to her—an instant rush of wild images and frightening sounds. Her breath suddenly caught in her chest as she began to relive those last moments, when the *thing*—the creature—charged directly for them. She pictured its disgusting legs, churning up the snow—and the horrible oversized head, all that syrupy saliva caught-up in the wind.

"It veered away from us. I remember praying and thanking God for saving us. For not letting it trample us to death beneath it. But I guess one of its trailing legs, or tentacles . . . whatever they were . . . hit the car. Toppled the car over like it was a toy." She looked at her father, noticing his grave expression. Then she remembered Ginger. "Oh God . . . Ginger, is she . . ."

Her father looked confused.

"You mean *dead*?" came a female voice.

Heather, unaware she was in a double-occupancy room, leaned forward and turned. Her body complained as she shifted her weight. Now seeing Ginger—apparently okay and sitting upright in bed—Heather laughed, tears filling her eyes. "Ginger!"

Her freckled-faced, copper-headed friend grimaced back. Raising her left arm off a stack of pillows, she studied the new cast with distain.

"It hurts like a mother.... And I won't be able to work for ... like weeks. And my car is toast!"

Heather nodded, then tried to match her friend's look of discouragement but couldn't hold it. She smiled, and eventually Ginger smiled back, too. "We'll always be able to say we survived the beast ... right?"

Ginger shrugged and nodded half-heartedly.

She saw her father, now struggling to his feet, grab for his crutches. "I have to go. The two of you will be fine. You'll be sorer than hell, but otherwise just fine."

"Where is it, Dad? Did they kill it?" Heather asked.

"No. Apparently the creature has the ability to dig ... crawl deep beneath the ground. It's now somewhere underneath Larksburg. Scientists ... experts ... are flying in from California."

"Hon?" he queried, seeing she'd stopped listening to him.

"Dad, what did they find up on the mountain? At the Jericho site?"

"Well ... they found truck tracks in the snow. Could be from an F150. But no truck. Sorry, no sign of Cameron up there," he added.

"Anything else?"

He didn't answer right away. "Looks as though the beast started its trek down the mountain from that same area. And something else too; something huge was also up there ... left an impression in the snow. I'm not saying what it was, exactly, but ... well ... yes, it could have been some kind of spacecraft.

According to my deputy, there's a series of blast marks on the ground."

Could it actually be true? She wondered. Heather swallowed hard, trying to come to terms with that possibility. *Did Cam, somehow, get whisked away on a fucking spaceship?*

Again, her father was speaking: "The place is crawling with government people. Closed off now from the public, even from my people. But let's not jump to any hasty conclusions, Squeak. Okay?"

"What happens if that ... thing ... comes up out of the ground? What are we going to do?"

The sheriff looked down at his daughter. Not having a suitable answer, he offered her a half-hearted smile, then left.

chapter 16

As the ship suddenly listed to one side, Cameron felt the truck's tires begin to skitter across the deck. The F150's tail end swung fast around until it knocked up against the bulkhead. He heard the ship's engines, now straining louder. Still holding onto the steering wheel, all he could do was wait for whatever was to come next.

He listened as things scraped outside on the fuselage and instantly knew they were branches snapping—trees breaking. The Primion was crash landing! Tightening his grip, his teeth clenched, Cameron thought there still might be a silver lining—just *maybe* the spaceship was landing back on Earth. They'd only been in outer space for several hours. What he'd read about space travel was that any *possibly* inhabitable planets would be light-years away. And, according to Einstein, traveling faster than the speed of light—in excess of 186,000 miles per second—was pretty much impossible. *Yes,* perhaps XI had changed its decision—had turned the ship around and was trying to land.

The clattering noise outside hit a loud crescendo and then an expected hard impact ensued. It was a teeth-jarring hit. He felt the *Primion* bounce up and then thump down hard again onto the ground and slide for a long time before beginning to lose forward momentum. Then, suddenly, the vessel dropped down hard one more time.

Cameron pushed open the truck's driver-side door and climbed out. Behind him, he could see where his vehicle had impacted with the bulkhead; the back left taillight took the brunt of the hit. He recalled something Chuck Yeager once said: *If you can walk away from a landing, it's a good landing.*

* * *

By the time Cameron reached the other end of the ship and was descending the stairway onto the bridge, he was still hopeful they'd returned to Earth. But with one glance at the myriad of virtual holographic displays popping up around the compartment, seemingly indiscriminately, it was evident by the vivid landscape panoramas that they were on an alien planet. Either that, or planet Earth was now forested with ginormous aqua-colored trees.

Cameron looked about the bridge for the matte black droid but didn't see it. Turning all the way around, he called out, "XI . . . you here?" He waited for an answer and, tilting his head, listening, wondered at what point the ship's engines had been turned off. Or did they just quit, during their not so gentle landing? For the first time, he noticed, there in the dark recesses on either side of the descending stairway, two passageways. The area was so poorly illuminated he hadn't noticed them before. So much of the *Primion* seemed to be in a sleep state.

Opting for the passage on the left side of the stairs, Cameron proceeded into what could best be described as a *hall of glowing doughnuts*. Taller than him, over seven feet in height, each one stood upright; he could see straight through the circular *doughnut* hole centers. They were situated one after the other, lined up along the curvature of the compartment. He counted ten—in that section of the compartment alone; each one softly glowed with a faint bluish cast. Like the bridge, the compartment was oval-shaped. Only this oval was elongated, port to starboard, while the bridge's oval was elongated in a bow to stern direction.

As Cameron's eyes adjusted in the low lighting, he slowly discerned more of the compartment's advanced technology—strange things that glowed and pulsed and blinked. Then he heard faint sounds, similar to that of people whispering. There was an unmistakable synthetic component to the noise. At the rear mid-point of the compartment was a closed hatchway, which led somewhere astern. Cameron, after taking a few strides, found if he continued on he'd end up coming out on the far side of the stairs. Bringing his hand up, he tentatively placed it on the nearest glowing donut. The static electricity arising from that one action made the hairs on his arms stand upright. Each hair on his head was doing the same thing. Yet that paled in significance to what he was now hearing. Not so much hearing as . . . *understanding*. Like hundreds, maybe even thousands, of whispering voices being fine-tuned—brought into focus. But the voices weren't strung together, as in a sentence—nor were they in any Earth language, such as English, Russian, or Spanish. He didn't know which language it specifically was, only that he was able to understand some of it.

Back in high school, Cameron took to computer languages like a duck to water. Transitioning first into college, then the internship, he was far above average in both understanding and the implementation of computer programming languages. They just came easy to him. Perhaps tied somehow with how his brain retained stupid trivia. All he knew was jumping from Ajax, Ruby on Rails, Java, Python, HTML, CSS, C++, even Assembly, held little difficulty for him.

What Cameron did know in that moment was that he was on the receiving end of tremendous influxes. Some kind of highly advanced computer code he was able to decipher—to some degree. The problem was so many conversations, all happening at once, made it hard to track what was being relayed. Zeroing his attention on only one particular stream proved helpful. Although the other information streams were still there, they'd faded out somewhat—taking a *backseat* within his consciousness.

He understood that the *Primion's* AI was communicating, in the process of itemizing a damage report regarding the significant damage in multiple ship systems. Internal and external mechanical apparatuses had withstood catastrophic destruction. Cameron didn't like the sound of that. Didn't like its dire implications.

He realized now he was standing within the brain center of the ship—the core of the artificial intelligence. Without any further thought, Cameron asked out loud, "Can I help out with any of those . . . repairs?"

There was a momentary break, or pause, within the particular info-stream before a pleasant, albeit stern sounding, female voice answer came back. "At an assigned level four, you do not have the appropriate hierarchical clearance to offer assistance." With that said, Cameron could no longer decipher any of the whispering sounds. His disappointment quickly turned to anger at himself. *Damn it!* If he'd just kept his mouth, his thoughts, to himself, he undoubtedly would have picked up, learned, all kinds of new things pertaining to both the ship and his overall situation here.

Removing his hand from the cool, glowing, surface, he let out an audible sigh, still disgusted-with-himself. He asked, "XI . . . where are you?"

The response was instantaneous. "XI is close by."

Cameron spun around, found the droid hovering close at head-level, its dark matte surface almost indistinguishable in the dim surroundings. "Where are we? Where have you landed the ship?" he asked.

"Planet name is Sang-Morang . . . located within the Lorient star cluster."

"How far are we from Earth?"

"What you would equate as 10.5 light-years distance."

"So this ship . . . the *Primion* can travel faster than the speed of light?"

Cameron watched as the droid began to shudder before dropping down to his knee level. It then spun 360 degrees, first going a little topsy-turvy before it rose back to eye-level again. Obviously, the droid continued to have technical issues, though XI answered Cameron's question as if nothing had happened.

"No . . . traveling in excess of the speed of light is not possible. The *Primion* transmigrated through four Slip Bands to accommodate this segment of the voyage."

Cameron, surprised by the amount of information the typically tightlipped droid was now offering up, asked, "What's a Slip Band?"

"A Slip Band is a naturally occurring space/time *pinch*—one that occurs within the very fabric of space itself. Once detected and analyzed for suitability, it is through these spatial fold-type anomalies, which are highly common throughout the universe, great distances can be traversed . . . almost instantaneously."

"That's actually really cool to know," Cameron said. "Anyway . . . um . . . so you crashed landed the *Primion* on this Sang-Morang world? Why here? And why crash at all?"

"The aggregate levels of Xenon are exceptionally high on this planet, so replenishing ship reserves will be relatively quick, Cameron."

That was weird. He couldn't remember the nasty little droid using his given name before. And by far, this was the longest, most in-depth conversation he'd had with the thing. Something definitely was up.

"And the ship can grab the Xenon gas out of the atmosphere?" Cameron asked.

"That is correct."

"Yeah ... I'm sure the *Primion* is capable of doing that kind of thing, without a doubt." Cameron added, "So why such a rough landing? From what I heard, the ship has been heavily damaged as a result of it. Are we stuck here?"

"The ship can be repaired," XI said without really answering his question. "You offered to help. You and several specialty bots will assist in this process."

"Oh, I will, will I?" *And there it was!* The droid only had been playing nice because it wanted something in return. Apparently, alien droids were not above a little manipulation here and there. "We'll have to see," Cameron said. "What is it I'd have to do? Will it be dangerous?"

"It could be ... Yes, there is the possibility of danger. Environmental conditions outside the fuselage may indeed be hazardous."

"You mean like the air outside ... the atmosphere?"

"No. The atmosphere here is similar enough to Earth. Your physiology will not be impacted in a negative way."

No big surprise, his conversation with XI was becoming annoying. Why couldn't the droid just answer his questions? But getting mad wasn't going to help, so he offered up a crooked smile and asked, "So why is it dangerous outside?"

"Indigenous life forms. Sensor analyses of the collective bio-organisms place a high probability of the presence of multiple carnivore species."

"Like man-eaters?" he asked.

XI didn't respond.

"Sounds like the specialty droids you spoke of should do the repairs. Maybe I can help out from inside the ship?"

"No, Cameron. The specialty droids onboard the *Primion* are incapable of performing certain aspects of the necessary repair work. Be assured you will be outfitted with a protective environmental suit. If you would like to expedite the time-frame ... the time spent on this planet, you should assist with the repairs."

"Nah ... I don't think so. You'll have to do it yourself," Cameron said.

"Unacceptable. Leaving this planet is impossible until repairs have been made and the depleted Xenon levels augmented."

Cameron shrugged. "Uh huh ... Tell me, how long would it take the bots to make the repairs on their own? Like, based on going at it twenty-four hours a day, seven days a week? How many days ... or weeks, would that entail?"

XI said, "Without your assistance, the *Primion* will never leave this world."

The thought of being marooned here, for the rest of his life, was more than a little sobering. There had to be another way. Then something occurred to him. "If I help, you'd take me back to Earth ... right?"

The droid did not answer.

"Come on ... tell me. How long if I do decide to help?"

"One full year."

Even that seemed like an eternity. Cameron huffed an exasperated breath. He thought to himself, *Well, at least I have a weapon to protect myself from the man-eaters XI spoke of.*

Cameron stared at the droid, feeling his present dislike for the *hovering tin can* turning to hatred. "Tell me, why did you crash land the *Primion*? We're now stranded here due to something you either did, or didn't do."

A full thirty seconds ticked by before XI replied. "In retrospect, XI should have engaged somewhat more of the vessel's AI navigation functionality."

"You tried to land the ship yourself? Even though you are . . . what did you say before, operating at less than forty-two percent effectiveness?"

"XI will complete its designated mission."

"Why are you so against fully reinstating the ship's AI? This isn't a competition."

"Conflicting designated mission parameters."

Cameron thought about that. "What fucking mission? The creature you were transporting isn't even onboard the ship anymore."

"XI will deliver Griar Loth to Winforge . . . the intended interment planet."

Cameron, yelling now, shouted, "Listen to me! The Griar Loth is gone . . . It's back on fucking Earth. Why don't you recognize *you* are the problem here? Maybe you should just power yourself down, or throw yourself into the closest Dematerializer Station."

The droid wobbled as it spun around and moved away. "XI will ready an environmental suit for you."

chapter 17

With the recent crash landing of the spacecraft, and the subsequent violent jostling within the *Primion's Keep*, the small creature awoke. Snug within its warm and moist birthing pod, it opened its eyes for the very first time. At the earliest stages of life, infant Minal Loths pretty much functioned on pure instinct. Cognitive reasoning would soon come—but for now, the basic need to feed was all consuming. The few morsels of meat left within the pod had been gnawed on, unconsciously devoured days prior.

The pod was comprised of a fleshy embryonic membrane, which was left behind by the infant Loth's mother. The organic material was tightly wrapped within shredded crewmembers' uniforms, along with tidbits of hair, bands of flesh, and small bones.

More awake now, the baby Minal Loth began to move about its womb-like confines. Suddenly aware of its six separate appendages—it began to gyrate each one around furiously. The pod, amazingly resilient, gave way—stretched until the

Loth's sharp little claws finally sliced through the membrane. The pod split apart, and the creature slid free. Instantly feeling the absence, and loss, of its once cozy environment, the infant Minal Loth raised its oversized cranium and bellowed loudly. Harsh lighting shining down on it from above and the rigid metal deck beneath its sensitive limbs contributed to new-found misery.

Under normal circumstances, a mother Minal Loth would be present to feed and nurture the infant creature. But even though it had been left on its own, the instinctual will to survive was growing by the moment. As the Minal Loth learned to use its legs to propel itself around the Keep's confines, it stopped to inspect various items strewn about the area. A slain crewmember's tibia found its way into the creature's mouth; its sharp pointy teeth grinded down on bits and pieces of bone. Hardly sated, it moved to a mound of feces left behind by its mother. It didn't eat it. Instead, the creature rolled around in the mess, turning onto its back. It continued to squirm around—both this way and that—until it was satisfied, covered head-to-toe in the greenish-brown muck.

Two small observant eyes finally took notice of the Keep's open gate. *Must feed . . . must find meat . . .*

chapter 18

Cameron, fuming, sat at one of the empty bridge consoles. His frustration with the droid was building by the second. He pictured himself laying into XI with a baseball bat—like bashing a piñata. The *Primion* only crash-landed on Sang-Morang in the first place due to the droid's total incompetence. Thinking back, recalling the brief few moments on the ship when he had mental connectivity with the AI's internal communication network, he'd witnessed firsthand how an intelligent, highly competent, computer-generated, mind operated. Yes, XI had to go—and if Cameron was contemplating some kind of mutiny, who cared? It wasn't like he was considered a valued crewmember on board. There against his will in the first place, if he ever wanted to see Earth again, he needed to take action. But first, faced with the same old problem, he had to get the ship's AI fully operational. Musing, Cameron wondered if going through XI was his only avenue to achieving that. *Who did XI report to on the ship? Or off the ship?*

Not something he was going to figure out right then, he spun around in his seat and took in the deserted bridge. Again, he wondered what it would be like to experience the hustle and bustle of a fully staffed vessel. What the *Primion* would look like with all its systems brought back to life—all the lights turned back on.

Tired, it had been a long time since he'd slept, maybe twenty-four hours. But even more than tired, he was hungry. Cameron glanced around to see if XI was milling about then said, "*Primion*, ship atlas open."

The virtual diagram popped into view to his left. Not too surprising. As he scanned the various ship compartments, he found he had much of it already affixed in his memory. But he didn't see anything that even remotely related to food, like a ship's mess.

"*Primion?* I'm hungry. Where can I get something to eat?"

"The *Primion* directory . . ."

"I already tried that. Can't you just tell me?"

"Canteen. Level three . . . mid-ship . . . port-side."

Cameron looked at the diagram and found the compartment *canteen*. Now it made sense. "Thanks!" he said, rising to his feet. "Don't suppose you have any recommendations . . ."

There was no reply from the ship's nearly disabled AI.

* * *

Cameron made his way to the third level Canteen without having to refer to the ship's diagram. He remembered seeing references to three separate staircases on Level 2—one close to the bow, one mid-ship, and one astern. Personally, although he didn't mind the exercise, he thought it somewhat archaic that a ship this size didn't have a really cool lift system. One that would whisk him up or down levels with great speed and ease. As it was, he figured it took him about eight minutes, walking at a good clip, to get from the bridge to the entrance of the Canteen.

Although hungry, curiosity got the best of him so he said, "*Primion*, ship atlas open."

Cameron scanned the diagram, his brow furrowed, when something else came to mind. He'd passed by a number of deactivated bots, lifeless bots, that he couldn't imagine maneuvering up steps or stairs that easily. Giving up, he said, "*Primion* show me the automated lifts around the ship."

Blinking red circles appeared on all three levels. "Oh . . . so that's what those things are," he acknowledged with a slow nod.

The pleasant sounding AI voice offered, "They are called *jump stands*. There is one directly behind you on the opposite bulkhead."

Cameron spun around and noticed a concave section on the bulkhead. The brushed metallic inset—wide enough for two or three people—didn't look much like a lift just more like a fancy design element. He stared at it fascinated until the rumbling in his stomach pulled his attention back to the Canteen's entrance. He said, "Thank you," finding the AI's self-initiated assistance encouraging.

Entering the Canteen, he took-in the large oval-shaped compartment and thought, *Boy, the Thidions sure liked ovals.*

Nothing like he expected, there were no tables, no stacks of trays, and no long, cafeteria-style counter to pick and choose meals from. But there was plenty of seating. Comfortable-looking seats, like those found in an airliner's first-class section, only a lot bigger, and with more legroom. He counted forty comfy-looking padded chairs. Of course, they also were aligned in an oval shape, conforming to the overall shape of the compartment.

Cameron, arbitrarily choosing a chair toward the middle, sat down. A virtual menu appeared before him, displaying all the meals available. Under the heading of Earth Human, the food items were categorized into Americana, European fare, Mediterranean, Italian, and Chinese. Also, choices were available for customizing any selection. The AI certainly was current on Earth's modern-day culinary expectations, and Cameron wondered how many *unwilling* hostage passengers had contributed to this menu over the years. Pointing to the Americana option, another virtual page of choices appeared. Instead of reading through it, he asked, "Can I just get a cheeseburger and fries . . . and a vanilla shake?"

"Of course . . . Your meal will be provided momentarily. Enjoy."

Cameron replied, "Thanks." He wondered if he was supposed to stay seated or if he should do something—like get up and retrieve the order from someplace. And right then, he felt a slight vibration pulse beneath his seat. Rising between his knees, a vertical metallic plate appeared, attached to an armature. It then moved into position just above his lap. No sooner had the vertical plate flipped-over, reversed into a horizontal position, when his lunch was set before him. It just appeared.

"No way!" he exclaimed, taking in what had to be one of the largest hamburgers he'd ever seen. He could actually feel the heat rising off the food. Then the aroma of cooked beef and melted cheddar cheese greeted his senses. The fries, fried to a golden brown, came accompanied with small containers of ketchup, mustard, and mayonnaise. The classic-style milkshake was served in a metal cup, frosted condensation visible all around it.

"I think I'm in heaven," Cameron said. Hefting up the burger in both hands, he brought it to his mouth. Taking an enormous bite, he chewed then moaned in delight. The cup felt icy cold to his touch, but he noticed it wasn't really metal, only a facsimile of something solid—of something real. The realization suddenly dawned on him that none of what he was seeing—and devouring—might actually be real. *Do I care? Nope. . . . Not in the slightest.* On the other hand, a body needed calories and protein to survive. His memory of the encyclopedia entry for Vitamin included a list of thirteen that people needed to eat regularly to stay alive. If the food wasn't real, he would be in trouble.

Cameron finished his lunch. By the time he'd grabbed up the last French fry, the metal arm was rising between his knees. He watched as the faux-metal milkshake cup faded into obscurity, as did the containers of ketchup, mustard, and mayo. As the meal tray, too, disappeared from sight, he placed a hand on his belly. He certainly felt full though not over-stuffed. Hopefully that meant he wouldn't starve.

Cameron stood and took another look around. To no one, or thing, in particular, he said, "Thanks ... that was delicious." Leaving the Canteen, he approached the nearby jump stand. "*Primion,* any trick to using this thing?"

"Step onto the stand and face outward."

Doing as directed, Cameron stepped forward and turned around. Three glowing blue bands, each one about eight inches wide, appeared in front of him. Like virtual guardrails in front of his head, waist, and knees, they evoked in him a feeling of security. But the jump stand, still motionless, stayed where it was. It occurred to him that it didn't know yet just where to go. He said, "Level 2." When nothing happened, he added, "*Primion,* Level 2," and the jump stand moved downward. As it came to a gentle stop on Level 2, the three blue bands disappeared.

Cameron stepped off the lift and peered down the corridor, first left then right. He did not want to sleep in anyone's quarters. When he visited the crewmember quarters of the Senior Communications Overseer, he'd felt as though he was intruding. Even knowing that the crewmember was dead, it still didn't feel right.

"*Primion* ... can you direct me to an unassigned crew's quarters I can utilize?"

"All crew quarters are currently un-utilized."

"How about one that hasn't been utilized for a long time. Like before the Loth went on a rampage."

"There are nine such quarters. Please make a selection." The Atlas display presented him with nine flashing circles. The closest one, located on the same level, was not too far from where he was standing.

By the time Cameron arrived at the quarters, he was yawning almost continuously. The segmented cascading hatch opened at his approach, and he stepped inside. The compartment looked just the same as the other one he'd visited, but what he hadn't noticed back then was there was also another open hatch. He could see it was a bathroom. Not having to go, all he wanted was to lie down. He stood to the side of the softly glowing HOD, searching for a way to open the thing. Finally giving up, he asked, "*Primion*, how do I open this thing?"

"Place your hand anywhere along either side."

The HOD felt cool to his touch—like glass. Touching it, both sides of the unit descended in tandem to expose a cushion, with an integrated pillow at one end. Cameron sat down and quickly unlaced his boots. Kicking them off, he swung his legs up then laid back. As expected, the sides of the HOD ascended up and soon he was totally enclosed within it. The soft-white glow was soothing, and he felt his eyelids growing heavy. A sudden flickering of light brought his eyes wide open. The inside of the HOD was displaying all sorts of options. *Later . . . I just need to sleep.*

Cameron's eyes fluttered open again, hearing a noise outside the HOD. He heard the sound of one of his boots toppling over. *Was something moving around out there?* He remembered leaving the hatch into the compartment open and almost cared enough to get up and take a look. *Almost*. Way too tired, he drifted off to sleep, dreaming of Heather and a boat—maybe it was a kayak or a canoe. He was paddling them across a tranquil lake; a little island appeared off in the distance. Heather, gazing back at him with a smile, tucked a strand of her wheat-colored hair behind an ear. "What's in the basket?" she asked.

chapter 19

The infant Minial Loth was attracted by the distant smell of flesh. Now, in a near-frenzy, it moved rapidly on its quest to feed. Walking on flat surfaces was still a challenge, but maneuvering up and down the vessel's steep stairways was almost impossible for the young, six-legged creature. Somewhere in the recesses of the creature's mind it knew there should be someone nearby to assist it.

By the time the Minal Loth reached the second level—the one containing Cameron's borrowed quarters and the still-open hatchway—thirty-five minutes had passed. The Loth paused at the hatchway opening to sniff the air, bringing into its nostrils an abundance of interesting odors. Hesitant at first, the creature moved into the compartment. A soft glow emanated from a long object that dominated the room. Moving closer, the infant Loth, growing in size by the minute, brought itself up to its present height. At four feet, it observed a faint silhouette—something prone—lying within. The Loth put its snout up to the glass-like surface and breathed-in. *Faint, but yes, there was flesh inside there.* As it moved around the long tubular object, it discovered two smaller items lying on the deck. The Loth, burying its snout into the opening of one of Cameron's discarded boots, inhaled a cacophony of rich, musky scents. Biting down, the cowhide shredded easily. Its sharp teeth and already powerful jaws made quick work of the boot. Not caring for the taste of the boot's rubber sole, the Loth, maneuvering one of its six legs, tossed it aside. Again, it rose up to its full height to peer inside the tube. *Movement.* Strings of saliva that extended out both sides of its mouth collected in small pools on the deck. The boot had hardly sated its appetite. *Fresh meat . . . Need to feed.*

chapter 20

C ameron awoke feeling as if he'd experienced the deepest, most gratifying sleep of his entire life. As he lay within the confines of the HOD, elbows bent, he stretched his arms over his head, and arched his back. Opening his eyes, he took in the myriad of information being displayed above him on the HOD's inside surface. "What is all this?" he wondered aloud.

Three prominent warning messages overlapped:

Intrusion Alert! Unknown Species
Intrusion Alert! Unknown Species
Intrusion Alert! Unknown Species

Cameron, leaning forward, brought his upper body onto his elbows, not liking the message implications. *Unknown species? There were* no other species onboard. Or *were there?* Maybe the triple warning referred to a visiting bot or droid? He wouldn't be surprised if XI moseyed into his quarters earlier to check on him, but XI was not some *species* . . . not even close. Cameron then surveyed more of the data now on display—neat and orderly text boxes projected in soft hues of blues, pinks, and greens. Some were questions, but most were simply informative. The messages had probably appeared hours ago, when he first entered the HOD. He read them slowly, one after another:

Body Cleanse Process Engaged . . .
Oral Hygiene Initiated . . .
Garment Sanitation Process Initiated . . .

Cameron ran the tip of his tongue over his teeth and, sure enough, his mouth felt clean—even tasted a little minty. Sniffing under his left armpit, he was pleasantly rewarded with an airy, fresh scent. Typically, he did his own laundry. Achieving *airy freshness* was *way* beyond his skillset. He noticed next his entire body had a just-showered feel to it. *Wow! I could get used to this.*

He thought about Heather, remembered he'd dreamt of her, although details of the dream eluded him for the moment. Feeling tightness in his chest, he wondered if he would ever see her again. Ever see *anyone* again.

Ready to leave the HOD, Cameron ignored reading the remaining projected messages. Placing his open palm on the HOD's inside surface, both sides lowered in unison and he swung his legs out over the side. He stretched again, thinking about the day ahead—also about the word *guest*. Considered simply a guest on the ship, and he didn't like that. The word guest implied certain powerlessness—being at the mercy of someone, or something, else. That needed to change. It was like the first day of college. One had to stake his place in class right from the get-go. Let the professors know you are smart, serious about your grades, and willing to actively participate. He'd witnessed shyer kids—some smart as a whip—who didn't get noticed. Never putting themselves out there, they later got shafted when semester grades were doled out. He needed to let XI know this Level 4-hierarchy stuff was bullshit and unacceptable.

Exiting the HOD, Cameron's right sock slid on something slimy. Peering down, he raised his foot and noticed strands of sticky mucus. Starting to feel some wetness around his toes, he made a disgusted face—his mind racing. He thought about the three warning messages he'd just read on the inside of the HOD, then recalled something XI had said that didn't make sense at the time: *XI will deliver Loth to Winforge . . . the intended interment planet.* But he'd seen the Loth already leave the ship. He'd thought the droid was mistaken—was having technical issues.

"Holy shit, was there more than one of those creatures on board?!!" Cameron loudly exclaimed. Noticing the slathered remnants of one boot, his pulse rate nearly doubled. Somewhat shredded, only the boot's rubber sole still existed. He picked up the other boot, and on examination it seemed to be fine. Glancing nervously around the compartment, he silently acknowledged *that boot could have been me.* Ramen has said there were two kinds of creatures, Griar Loths, the female, and Minal Loths, the more dangerous males. He tried not to think about it.

Cameron, tiptoeing over to the bathroom's entrance, peeked inside. *Empty*. Feeling somewhat relieved, he inched across to the quarter's open entranceway and peered up and down the corridor. *Empty, too*. "*Primion,* close this hatch!"

First things first—he had to pee. Then, after exiting the head, he removed both socks and asked aloud, "*Primion . . .* how do I get another pair of socks and a new boot?"

"There is a garment replicator unit within the quarters. You'll find it within the aft bulkhead."

Cameron, studying the aft bulkhead, noticed a crisscrossing pattern of vertical and horizontal seams—a cabinet or wall closet of some sort. One panel pulsated in a darker shade of gray. When he placed his open palm on the rectangular panel, it slid to one side, revealing a complicated-looking appliance. He was about to ask the ship's AI for more help, when a projected display popped into view. Reading the instructions, he murmured, "Easy enough," and placed the intact boot onto a smooth-topped surface called the holding pan.

A neutral-sounding voice said, "Please stand away from the replicator unit."

A moment later, the same voice ordered, "Remove original garment article from atop the unit."

Cameron glanced over his shoulder—his thoughts still focused on the creature that had entered his quarters while he slept. He was lucky to be alive.

As soon as he grabbed up the boot, another one, identical to it, appeared in its place. Excited, he grabbed it only to shake his head in frustration. "*Primion, come on* . . . I need a boot for the other foot. Who needs two right boots?"

Five seconds later, a new boot appeared. This one was, appropriately, for his left foot.

* * *

Wearing both new socks and his new left boot, Cameron headed for the closest jump stand. Still anxious, he mentally replayed his encounter with the Griar Loth the day before. How massive it was; how easily it killed Ramen. Checking over his shoulder, he picked up his pace. It didn't make sense. No way could a beast as massive as that fit inside his quarters. If it had, it would have cracked open the HOD with him inside. *No problem—crunchy on the outside, chewy on the inside . . . ha ha . . .* He stepped onto the jump stand and said, "*Primion*, Level 1."

* * *

Cameron, already having checked where XI was currently located, paused halfway to the bridge; he slapped his forehead with his open palm. "Of course! *Primion*, can you give me the location of the other life form."

"You do not have—"

Cutting in, he said, "Yeah . . . got it . . . I do not have the appropriate hierarchical clearance for that information."

Minutes later, he entered the bridge and found XI lying on its side—rolling back and forth between two console seats. Kneeling down next to it and using both hands, Cameron did his best to steady the droid. Rolling it over so it faced upward, he asked, "Hey, XI . . . what happened to you?"

"X . . . 1 . . . malfunctioning . . . stability module . . ."

Cameron on examining the droid found new dents and scrapes all over its surface. It probably had been bouncing off the walls and deck for hours. Clearly, the droid was operating on borrowed time.

"You need to give me top-level hierarchical clearance now, XI. The ship's AI . . . um . . . TAM . . . needs to be fully functional. I'll be able to help you . . . Let me help."

Cameron felt the bulky droid trying to levitate— fighting against his firm hold. "Malfunction . . . thirty-three micro-memory modules fractured . . . stability module . . . intermittent . . ."

"Look . . . I know there is another Loth onboard."

"Minal Loth," the droid corrected."

"Fine, Minal Loth." Cameron, feeling the droid settle down, added, "I'll complete your mission. If we can get this ship repaired, back into space, I promise you . . . I'll get that Loth . . . Minal Loth . . . creature to . . ." he tried to remember where, then blurted out, "to Winforge. Did you hear me? Hey!"

But XI remained quiet—unmoving—only stillness remained, where before the droid's internal gyros could be felt vibrating inside. Cameron checked to see if any of its little lights were still blinking on and off. If XI was now defunct, deactivated, or whatever . . . he was truly screwed. Without its help getting a functioning TAM onboard, he knew he'd be stuck on this alien world the rest of his life.

Repeatedly, Cameron's fists hammered down onto the inactive droid. "XI! YOU PIECE OF SHIT!"

Hearing the sound of something ungodly—a high-pitched, screeching, noise—Cameron jumped to his feet. Turning, he stared wide-eyed.

chapter 21

C ameron stared down at the miniature Minal Loth below
him. Standing upright, its six tentacle-like legs were in a
constant state of movement, mucus dripping from its wide-
open jaws. *Oh yeah . . .* Cameron thought. The creature, beyond
all doubt, was contemplating on how it could best chomp
down on one of his legs—or an arm, or his head. He recalled
his boot, or what was left of it. Reluctant to take his eyes away
from the beast, Cameron quickly scanned his surroundings,
searching for any place to jump to. Better yet, a place where he
could hide. Although he'd been safe, lying within his HOD,
that wasn't a viable option now.

The Loth skittered forward—wide jaws snapping open and
closed repetitively—and made a lunge for his legs. Just in time,
Cameron jumped onto an adjacent console. He then crossed
over to the next: A cluster of four connected consoles—a tiny
unsafe island. The small beast circled and lunged over and over
again without seeming to tire. Cameron, on the other hand,
was already huffing and puffing from maintaining constant

movement. Terrified, he knew one of the incoming snapping bites would nab him eventually. The Loth's teeth had come within an inch of his body twice.

I have to try something else. Feigning right, Cameron then jumped in the opposite direction, catching the Loth momentarily off-guard. With enough time to pull his leg back, he kicked out with everything he had and connected with the creature's head. The toe of his boot collided with the Loth's snout—a perfect, hard-hitting *thwack!* Its small yet oversized head ratcheted backward as the creature's body went airborne. The perfect time to run, jump to safety, and find a place to hide—but Cameron wasn't thinking logically at that particular moment. He was swept up in a tornado of emotions, but most of all he felt helpless anger. Anger at himself for picking up the frigid-looking alien man back in Larksburg Stand in the first place; anger that he'd driven his damn truck into the spaceship's rear hold; and anger at the apparently now *dead* XI droid. And furious he was being attacked by this *nightmarish mini-creature* trying to eat him alive. Angry, not running for safety, he jumped to the deck and headed straight for the muddled, confused-looking, creature. He kicked it again—another solid headshot. The infant Minal Loth sailed even higher and farther than it did from his first kick—as far as the starboard bulkhead, striking it hard with a resounding *thud.*

While each individual leg continued to spasm and twitch, the creature's body limply laid on its side. Cameron, grabbing the nearest appendage firmly in his clenched fist, swung the creature high over his head then fast—brought it down—as if swinging a hammer. It hit the deck hard. Without hesitation, Cameron stomped down on the Loth with the heel of his boot for good measure. Out of breath, he stood back and assessed his handiwork. The creature was no longer moving, not a leg twitching. Staring at the Loth, he momentarily contemplated his actions. Should he be feeling something other than satisfaction—like guilt for killing a baby alien? Remembering what the little beast would soon turn into chased away any such thoughts from his mind.

Becoming aware of his surroundings again, he realized the bridge was no longer dimly lit. Dazzling illumination was taking place all around him. He could hear distant sounds of the ship literally coming alive. Glancing about the bridge, he was amazed—even taken aback—by the beauty of it all.

"*Primion* . . . what is . . . happening here?"

"Good morning, Cameron. Two things have taken place: The *Primion's* full functionality has been restored ship-wide, and you were provided a high-level hierarchical clearance."

Cameron looked over to XI. "Courtesy of the droid?"

"Yes, that was the droid's final act prior to becoming completely disabled."

"And you're . . . back to . . ."

"Full operation. I am currently bringing all ship functions back online."

Staring down at the Loth, Cameron asked, "Is this creature dead?"

"No. To kill either Griar or Minal Loth it has been suggested the removal of its head is best."

"I think I've heard that before. Um ... just getting it off the ship would suffice. Can you direct me to the closest exit? Open it up?"

Cameron heard the sound of a hatchway sliding open in the distance as the ship's atlas popped into view on his right.

"Please follow the designated highlighted route to the closest ship airlock."

Cameron eyed the glowing combination of passageways he'd need to take to arrive at the intended destination. It was relatively close by. About to reach for one of the creature's legs, he retracted his hand fast. One leg was twitching, then another ...

chapter 22

As Cameron grabbed up one of the unconscious Loth's legs, he had a moment to study the infant creature close-up. Grossed-out by the looks of the floppy, mucus-covered being that he now held at arm's length, he suddenly felt more movement. It seemed to be coming around—even after receiving what he deemed was a merciless beating. As Cameron ran from the bridge, following the course TAM had provided him with, he considered slamming the baby alien down onto the deck a few more times as a precautionary measure. Instead, he quickened his pace. He made a right, then a left, then another right until he came to a wide-open hatchway. The creature, he noted with alarm, was definitely coming around.

Once Cameron entered what TAM referred to as the airlock, the hatch behind him *swooshed* closed. He now stood within an enclosed self-contained compartment, about ten feet long by eight feet wide. The inside bulkhead was lined with tall vertical compartments he could see into. Each was holding spacesuits or maybe environmental suits, he was really sure what, if any, the difference was.

"TAM! The Loth ... it's waking up! Hurry ... Open the outside hatch!"

Although the Loth's eyes remained shut, its struggling and wiggling had intensified in his grip; its mouth now snapped open and closed.

The spacecraft's AI said, "There is an atmospheric differential between the outside environment and the interior airlock. Pressurization levels are still equalizing—"

"Just open the hatch! Its eyes just blinked, and it's looking straight at me!"

The hatch to the outside world instantly opened, and bright sunlight poured into the compartment. Cameron flung the Minal Loth high into the air, far away from the ship, then wiped the last remnants of Loth *goo* off his hand and onto his pant leg. Standing before an unobstructed view of the alien landscape outside, he took it all in—mesmerized by both the beauty and stark difference from everything familiar back on Earth.

In spite of his ordeal with the XI droid—and with the young attacking Loth soon thereafter—in the present moment he felt nothing but exhilaration. Below the *Primion's* forward portside hatch, nothing seemed to exist but a thousand or two thousand feet of open airspace. During the ship's rough landing earlier—sliding then to a precarious stop—it appeared as though a portside section of the vessel now overhung a steep, rocky mountainside.

Directly across from where Cameron stood, rising upward from a deep valley, was another mountain—one, he surmised, nearly identical to the one the *Primion* crashed onto. He scanned the distant reddish-brown ridge, cascading steeply downward to a tree line about halfway down the slope. The trees could have been tall pines, even redwoods, if it weren't for their weird aqua-blue color. Other stark differences to Earth were evident, too, like seeing three looming planets in the heavens. The nearest looked a little like Saturn, with its series of pinkish-white concentric rings.

Cameron continued to stand transfixed atop the ship's overhanging perch. Fortunately, heights were never an issue for him. He was comforted, knowing that the infant Loth must have fallen far—far down the mountainside. It came naturally to him, mentally calculating the speed the Loth achieved during its free fall—sometimes referred to as a *splat calculation*. He was curious about whether the Loth would have reached terminal velocity by the time it hit bottom. There were a few numbers in that formula he'd have to fudge: like the strength of gravity on this alien world. To Cameron, it felt similar to that of Earth's—so he'd keep and use that number. When the Loth began its fateful fall, its speed subsequently increased as gravity yanked it downward. How fast a thing fell, due to the tug of gravity, was determined by a certain number—known as the "acceleration due to gravity." That number—9.81 meters per second squared on the surface of Earth—was probably close to the same number here, as well. Basically, it meant that in one second, any object's downward velocity would increase by 9.81 meters per second due to gravity's pull The maximum speed an object achieved during a fall on Earth was around 200 km per hour, or 125 MPH, because of wind resistance. The air here felt thinner, which meant the maximum speed would be even higher. *At that speed, the Loth would definitely go splat! It would take some distance to reach that speed, though . . . Would it reach terminal velocity before it hit bottom?* He figured it was about two thousand feet down, which was equivalent to six hundred-and-nine meters. A few quick mental calculations, and he figured it would take about thirteen seconds and need almost eight hundred meters to reach terminal velocity. That meant the Loth wasn't quite going at terminal velocity if it had fallen even the full six hundred-and-nine meters. It would still be going very fast though. *Hmm . . . unless it hit the side of the mountain first, then rolled the rest of the way down to the valley floor.* If it lived through that—and that was a big *if*—Cameron guessed it would quickly find a plethora of things to eat below, other than the skinny human he'd been vanquished away from at the top of the mountain. *Certainly there are all kinds of plants, tree life, accessible . . . but what about animals . . . meat? Had animals evolved here?*

As if on cue, a large shadow fell over a large part of the spaceship. Cameron, shielding his eyes with one hand, scanned the sky. It wasn't a bird, or some sort of prehistoric-looking Pterodactyl. Cameron started to doubt his eyes—because what it looked like was a serpent. Long and snake-like, it had multiple sets of wings—as clear and delicate-looking as cellophane. Although its body had to be thirty feet long, its head was small.

Cameron, watching as the flying serpent glided farther down into the valley, realized that it wasn't a present danger to him, although he wouldn't stake his life on it. If ever the time arose, he'd certainly give the flying snakelike creature a wide berth, just in case.

Getting a firm hold onto the inside of the hatch opening, he leaned out the hatch as far as he felt it was safe to do so and studied the ship's orientation on the mountainside. The spaceship looked intact, for the most part, but a significant portion of the vessel appeared to be imbedded into the side of the mountain. Several feet to his right, he noticed, were a number of inset ladder steps. Set into the side of the hull, they led upward to the top of the vessel. He momentarily debated whether, or not, to actually do what he was contemplating doing; then, stretching even further, he reached an arm out. The inset step was just out of reach—maybe by an inch, two at the most. Not venturing another glance down the sheer, several thousand-foot drop, he again ignored that part of his brain urging him to be cautious. From a relatively safe position, standing just within the open hatchway, he turned sideways and jumped. Catching onto the inset step with all ten fingers, he quickly jockeyed his feet up and down until they, too, found purchase on a lower step. *That was really, really, stupid! What was I thinking?*

Cameron then began climbing—ten, fifteen, twenty feet up. What felt like mild buffeting winds only several minutes earlier were possibly strong enough now to blow him right off the side of the ship. He had to lean closer into the hull and claw his fingers deep into the insets as he moved step-by-step higher. *Daring to do this was really, really, stupid,* he chided.

Cresting the top of the *Primion*, he stayed low for a moment—testing if he was going to be blown off his feet. Now, standing taller, from his new vantage point, and then jumping up and down a few times for extra height—the first thing he noticed was that the ship wasn't perched on top of a mountain, but at the edge of a plateau. In the distance, over a nearby small ridge, were miles and miles of rolling bluish-green flatlands and aqua-blue hills in the far distance.

The wind came up, and he immediately went down on all fours. Catching his breath, he slowly crawled across the top of the ship and noticed that much of the forward and portside of the fuselage was indeed buried into the top of the plateau. The good news, if there was any, was that it looked mostly like dirt—not solid rock—that it was lodged in. Proceeding toward the stern, he ventured another quick standup and rose up to his full height; he could now peer over the ridge to gain a better idea of what exactly happened. There looked to be a three-hundred-foot-long trench stretched across the open plain. Apparently XI, bringing the *Primion* in for a landing, had somehow lost control. The ship's forward momentum hit the ground hard, and it continued to slide. The *Primion* then went sideways, jumped the small ridge, and dropped down to where it now lay partially imbedded. The disturbed loose dirt at the top of the plateau had immediately avalanched down to settle on the upper forward starboard side of the ship. Without receiving help from some heavy excavating equipment—moving the many tons of fallen dirt away—the *Primion* wasn't going anywhere anytime soon.

The wind was picking up again. No way could he climb back inside the ship the way he'd come out. Now again squatting, above the roar of the windy gusts, he yelled out, "*Primion* . . . can you hear me?" He waited but heard nothing back. Continuing to crawl on all fours, Cameron moved toward the midpoint of the fuselage. Since the curvature of the fuselage was minimal at the top of the ship, all he really had to concern himself with was not getting blown off.

Cameron, creeping forward, paused every so often to quickly glance over the side to check to see if there was an accessible hatchway, or some other entrance, back into the vessel. It occurred to him that unless he discovered another access, he just might be spending the night outside in this alien land. The mere thought of such a thing happening caused him to nervously start chewing the inside of his lower lip.

Now two-thirds back to the stern, the wind suddenly died completely. Cameron maintained his same kneeling position in case it was simply a lull. After a full minute passed, he slowly rose to his feet then began to walk upright. Traversing the hull was easier now. To his left, he discovered the slope of the ship was almost even with the plateau.

Suddenly, Cameron froze and listened, hearing a distant rumbling. He started to feel a vibration rising-up through his boots. *Maybe it's another ship?* Excited, he hurried aft, gazing upward at the sky. By chance, he glanced over to his left and saw the unthinkable. . . .

chapter 23

In the split-second he had to react, Cameron drove his body flat onto the hull, covering his head with his arms and hands. Lying there, trying to make sense of what he'd just seen, the first of the fast-charging *whatever they were*—careening off the plateau ledge. He could smell their wild-musky scent. Too many to count, they were now hurtling several feet above his head—a swath of them, seven or eight beasts wide, and he couldn't guess at how many were following behind—one after another. Like a thundering herd of buffalo yet completely different. For one thing, they were white and seemed to possess hides that were thick and hairless, like those found on a rhinoceros or an elephant.

Cameron, venturing a glance over his head, caught a wild flurry of passing hooves and underbellies. As clumps of dirt and small rocks cascaded down onto his back, something hard and sharp nailed him in the forehead. He winced through the pain and watched, peering beneath his arms, as the stampede of airborne animals continued to leap over him then drop in a several thousand-foot free-fall to the valley below. Time seemed to slow as he watched many of them, perhaps hundreds, unknowingly take their final vault into the abyss below. Feeling sick, Cameron closed his eyes and waited.

When the loud rumbling of hooves finally ceased—the last of them passing by overhead—the worst was yet to follow. Distant sounds erupted upward as the falling smashed onto the valley floor below. *Thump! Thump! Thump! Thump! Thump! Thump! Thump! Thump!*

What he had just seen reminded him of the urban legend of lemmings leaping to their deaths. In fact, according to his encyclopedia readings, lemmings didn't jump to their deaths like many thought. It turned out that it was all a good story that grew out of a 19050s nature documentary that Disney had created. *And once a good story got going . . .*

Cameron continued to lie still for several more minutes. Strangely, his thoughts turned to the Minal Loth—recently having underwent the same long descent to the valley floor below. If that creature survived the fall, it now would have plenty to eat. It would be another way to look at it—the Loth owed him a great big *thank you* for flinging its scrawny ass out of the airlock.

Pushing up onto his hands and knees, Cameron slowly stood upright. The plateau was almost at eye-level. Standing not ten feet away were the few remaining herd. Three—easily eight feet tall each—were as broad as a New York City bus. Beautiful beasts, they stood still, staring straight back at him. Not a whole lot of intelligence gleamed back at him from behind their big brown eyes. Already losing interest, one by one they began lowering their heads to graze. Cameron knew that was a blessing. What he'd just witnessed, the horrific mass death fall, was something he knew he would never forget.

He turned in the opposite direction and stared out toward the valley. From this position he couldn't see the valley floor below. Glad for that, it was time for him to find a way back inside the *Primion.*

As Cameron continued trudging toward the stern, he probed the gash on his forehead with his fingertips. Taking them away, he realized they were covered in blood. *Terrific.* His pace slowed, noting a square access panel now sliding open no more than fifteen feet in front of him.

* * *

Re-entering the ship from the open topside hatch, he'd made his way along what was probably some kind of duct, perhaps intended for service droids. Unable to stand completely upright as it narrowed, he was beginning to feel claustrophobic. He eventually emerged through a panel on the third level—mid-ship.

It was like being inside a different spacecraft. Now, with all the ship's bright lights turned on, its electronics functionality coming back online, Cameron found himself a bit overwhelmed. Perhaps the biggest difference was the new abundance of color. No longer the same drab, lifeless-looking, vessel he'd thought it was. 3D holographic displays were in abundance—some following the contours of bulkheads as he

SHIP WRECKED

passed. Other ones simply appeared as he made his way to the bridge, as though vying—even competing—for his attention. As if the vessel, bereft of life for so long, was now acting like an attention-starved puppy, suddenly aware his master had returned home after a long evening out on the town. He knew it wasn't the ship so much as it was TAM, the ship's recently restored artificial intelligence.

"Cameron . . . you have a nasty wound on your forehead. I'd be happy to take a look at it for you. Fix you right up."

Cameron stopped, looking up and around where he stood. *Fix you right up* was an Earth, more precisely an American, colloquialism. He asked, "Are you the same ship's AI as before? How do you know . . . how to speak like that? So . . . um . . . human-like?"

"Thanks to you, in good part, I have regained eighty-seven percent functionality. I am grateful. I am thankful."

"And that's redundant . . . and, no offense, but you're talking about emotions. You're a computer."

The prolonged silence that followed only underscored the fact he'd probably said something insensitive. But then, so what? *I'm only speaking to a computer*, he reasoned.

Cameron made his way to the closest jump stand and took it down to the first level. Heading for the bridge, he heard the AI—continuing where it had left off.

"On your planet, at its current level of technological advancement, I can understand why you would say such a thing. But Cameron, this is not Earth. Expansive, self-evolving neuro-intelligence has been around on Thidion for over two

149

centuries. Where computers are certainly prevalent on Earth, electronically they are not *self-aware*. I am self-aware. I am, or was . . . an active part of the *Primion* crew. I reason and deduct and calculate. I also feel emotions not so different from yours. I also can . . . and will . . . die, so to speak. I have a termination date—one I purposely have not been made cognizant of yet. Understand, Cameron, I am not an *it* . . . I am a . . . *her*. I have chosen a female designation. Although I could easily have chosen to be male, or sex-gender neuter, I chose to be what I am."

Cameron unconsciously had stopped walking ahead. Listening to the AI, or *whatever* it was, he found he had questions—a lot of them. But he didn't want to be insulting, as he'd already proven himself capable of.

He asked, "Do you wish to . . ."

"To be organic?" she asked, finishing his sentence.

He waited for her to answer.

"Yes and no."

"Can you explain?" he asked, absentmindedly probing his head gash.

"I have sensory inputs that provide far more tactile feeling than what you, an organic, are capable of. I have the equivalent of pleasure receptors and pain receptors. I can take presence into a physical form—what you would call an advanced droid, or even multiple droids all at one time."

Reaching the bridge, he sighed, "Okay . . . um . . . I'm not sure if that really answers my question. Maybe it's not an appropriate question."

"There is no definitive answer, Cameron. I would have to give up a lot to become organic."

"Cool. I guess it's good to be happy with what . . . who . . . you are." Cameron meant it but was becoming completely distracted. When he earlier had hurried from the bridge to get rid of the Minal Loth, the ship was only beginning to come alive. Now the ship was nothing short of extraordinary—far more technology than he'd been aware of earlier. There were large, high-up, virtual displays that followed the contours of the bridge. At present, they revealed an amazing actual view of the outside world. He could see the half-buried *Primion* situated on a precarious ledge just below the edge of the plateau. Much of the portside of the ship was hanging over a sheer cliff. What he hadn't been fully aware of was the ridgeline the ship was perched atop. Continuing along behind the ship, it looked almost road-like. He guessed it gradually sloped all the way down to the valley floor below. The display changed next to another view, to a different scenic landscape, but one undoubtedly on the same planet. It showed a babbling brook within a crop of tall trees. The view then rapidly changed to one showing the striking terrain—the open plains of the plateau. Almost like someone with a remote control was arbitrarily, annoyingly, changing channels far too quickly.

Head throbbing from the overabundance of sensory input, Cameron plopped down onto a center console seat and closed his eyes.

"Please let me take a look at that . . . dress your wound."

What Cameron most wanted was to go home. Be back in Larksburg Stand, never having loaded up his truck in the first place for another year at school. To a university and internship far away from Heather—*although nowhere near as far away as he was now.*

More irritably than he intended, he said, "There's nobody else here . . . Just how, exactly, are you planning on dressing my wound?"

"Come to the *Juvinate Plastron* . . . It's located on this level. I'll guide you to it."

Cameron opened his eyes wide and glanced about the deck. The inactive, disabled XI droid was no longer lying there. Probably removed while he was outside the ship. "Um . . . so what do I call you? Do I call you TAM?"

"I would prefer that you call me Alice."

Her, *its*, voice sounded humanlike. She *seemed* to care. *But does she really?* His gash still seeping blood and he was starting to feel woozy. "Okay, Alice, please show me where I need to go."

chapter 24

On his way to the Juvinate Plastron, Cameron passed no fewer than ten previously unseen droids. Several were the basic-looking robotic type that skittered along the deck, while others seemed almost humanlike. Not so much for having flesh and hair, but more to their height—five to six feet tall—and for possessing heads, arms, and legs. Back on Earth, each would stand out in a crowd—a *weird* facsimile of a real person. He'd found himself waving or nodding to them as he passed and receiving peculiar responses back—including head tilting and what almost seemed like embarrassment.

"*Primion* droids are unaccustomed to being greeted in such a way," Alice remarked.

"So people don't greet or say hello to each other on this ship?" he asked.

"Droids are not people."

"Not self-aware . . . like you say you are?" Cameron waited for her reply but none came. *Maybe*, he thought, *Alice thinks she is a step above the lowly droids that service the ship.*

"Here you are, Cameron. You have reached the Juvinate Plastron."

The compartment was oval-shaped, of course. Eight padded platforms, located at each station, weren't really beds, per se, due to an absence of bed covers and sheets. A similar group of holographic displays hung in mid-air at each medical station, offering some kind of diagnostic information that made zero sense to Cameron.

Cameron knew that a plastron was the bottom of a turtle's shell, and he supposed that made sense because of the oval shape. But he had never heard of the word *juvinate* before. *Maybe that is their version of rejuvenate or something . . .*

"Please take a seat at any of the Juvinate hubs."

Cameron, choosing the closest one, took a seat on the padded platform. He looked around and noticed, exiting from an adjacent compartment, one of the quasi-human-looking droids striding toward him.

"Hello, Cameron. I am Lutous Bright 953. I will be attending to your injuries. Is that acceptable?"

Cameron shrugged. "Sure . . . Why not?" The droid's face, with its plastic-looking eyes, nose and mouth, wore a faux pleasant expression. He noticed the droids here—none were wearing clothes—were gender non-specific. Even Lutous Bright 953's voice was neutrally pitched, neither high nor low. Cameron recalled watching on HULU an older Saturday Night Live episode and was reminded of one of the show's reoccurring characters.

"Hey ... would you mind if I called you Pat? Easier to remember."

The droid, giving Cameron a tilted head response, said, "I will add Pat as an alternative pseudonym. Please lie back, and I will begin."

"Hold on. Tell me what you're going to do, first," he said, all of a sudden feeling uneasy about this. A few details of what he could expect—such as how much it was going to hurt—were in order.

"I have already begun an inoculation process. You will need immunity against a variety of diseases, alien to your system. Foreign bacteria and other microbes your body is not prepared to reject. Such inoculations should have taken place prior to your going outside the ship. Next, I will repair the epidermis and dermis layers of flesh above your right eye. Please do not move or speak until the process is complete. "

Reluctantly, Cameron leaned back, making himself comfortable, and waited for whatever happened next. Pat leaned over him—its face inches from his own.

"You really ... um ... get up close and personal, huh?"

"Please do not speak."

It occurred to Cameron that the *treatment* had already begun. While he was waiting for the droid to utilize some kind of medical device or apparatus, the droid, Pat, *was* the device. It made sense. Why have specialized medical droids go to the trouble of using some kind of alternate apparatus when the droid itself could *be* that apparatus?

"Ouch! Whatever you're doing to my head . . . it hurts," Cameron said, gritting his teeth. It didn't just kinda hurt. It really, really, hurt.

"Shush."

He glared up at the robot. He didn't like being shushed. The pain, though, was slowly dissipating. He wanted to touch the gash on his forehead but not enough to be reprimanded by the overly close Pat.

The droid backed off and, using a finger on one of its hands, probed the damaged area on his forehead. The wound no longer hurt. In fact, it felt completely normal.

Pat then stood up all the way and said, "Your injury has been repaired. When you are ready, you can sit up."

"That's it? I'm all better?"

"All better," Pat said.

Cameron sat up and touched his forehead. Sure enough, the skin there felt smooth. "Can I ask you a question, Pat?"

"Yes. Do you have another medical condition you would like to discuss?"

"Condition? No. I want to know . . ." Cameron paused, "How exactly did you repair my skin so rapidly? Skin . . . epidermis layers require time to heal."

The answer didn't come from Pat, who seemed a bit stymied by the question.

"Cameron, the concept you hold that Pat somehow *healed* the injured area on your forehead is incorrect. What Pat did was bring that area of your physiology to an appropriate *sparce* of space/time," the AI Alice interjected.

"Sparce?"

"Spacial time articles. You are aware of the four states of matter?"

Cameron certainly did. Knew well the four commonly considered states—solid, liquid, gas, and plasma.

"Are you aware there is more than one type of time state for such matter?"

Cam was, but it was a big secret to most people. Recently, back on Earth, a way of making matter that acted differently with respect to the passage of time had been discovered. They were called *Time Crystals*. The head boss at HyperCrell, flamboyant Tony Ordell, was furious that scientists at his San Jose lab weren't the first to prove those findings. No—that prestigious honor went to a Berkley assistant professor named Norman Yao.

Ordell hated Yao, convinced the much younger—and far less experienced— scientist than those in his employ had somehow pilfered HyperCrell research, giving him a leg up in actually creating Time Crystals.

Cameron didn't fully understand the new physics breakthrough, other than the fact that crystals have an atomic structure that not only present in space, i.e., like the carbon lattice of a diamond, but somehow present in multiple times itself.

"Are you telling me you just sent my forehead *back in time*?" he asked.

"No. We only sent an isolated, bio-cellular area ahead, to a *Sparce*-timespan, approximately three weeks from now.

Sending it back in time would only, eventually, return it in its current condition. Is that not so?"

"That is way beyond cool!" Cameron exclaimed, trying to figure out how Time Crystals were utilized to enable such an amazing process of events. If something as basic as a sore patch of skin on his forehead could utilize this kind of discovery, what else could be done? *Was being done here, right now?*

Much too much to consider, Cameron knew he needed to let it go for now. Standing up, he held out his hand. Pat looked at it, perplexed. Taking the medical droid's opposite hand in his own, he showed it how to shake hands. "That's what we do on Earth: To say thank you, or say hello, or even say goodbye. Later, I'll show you how to fist bump."

Cameron walked away from the droid left pondering its own hand. Leaving the Juvinate Plastron, Cameron said, "Alice, I don't like that I'm considered a guest here. It means I don't have a say in what happens to me. I went through this with XI. It means I don't get a vote, on when . . . or *even if* . . . I get to go home."

"You are not a crewmember, Cameron. With that said, you still have been granted high-level privileges. You can come and go as you please."

Digesting that, Cameron said, "Before XI, you know, went offline, it said I could help out by doing certain things. Like assisting with repair work that's needed before the ship can travel back out into space. Is that still true?"

"Yes, that is true."

"What has to be done? I'll do whatever I can to hurry things along."

"Repairs need to be made to a forward portside intake module. Necessary for accumulating Xenon gas from the atmosphere."

"Good! Just tell me what to do."

"First, droids will initiate the clearing away of all accumulated dirt and rubble. Once completed, you will access the forward portside intake module and make the repairs."

"But X1 said it will take years to clear away all that dirt ... like four years, three months, two days, and seven hours. That's too long. There has to be a way to shorten that timeframe."

"I will think about the issue and get back to you," Alice said.

"I need to get back home," Cameron said. He had the feeling the AI either wasn't listening or didn't care. *Do AI's care?*

Bringing out his iPhone, he absentmindedly looked for new messages, like he did countless times in any ordinary day. But this was not an ordinary day. There were no new messages. Nothing from Heather, of course, since he was light-years away from her. Noticing his phone had only a seventeen percent charge remaining, he inwardly panicked. Quickly bringing up his photo app, he began to scroll through photo memories going back to the very beginning. Almost all of the photos were of Heather. Heather blowing him a kiss from her driveway, Heather sound asleep in bed—her long hay-colored hair fanned out around her sweet face. The next photo was of them both, cuddling together in the cold. She'd asked a stranger—a passing-by hiker—to take a picture of them. They were sitting atop a big boulder as the first flurries of an October snow swirled around them.

Cameron, studying the smiles on their faces, was momentarily transported back in time. *Sixteen percent!*

Suddenly, the reality of his situation hit him hard. Hit him like a boulder had dropped upon his head. *I will never see her again.* I'm going to die alone on this *fucking* alien planet. Feeling faint, he reached for the closest bulkhead to lean against.

Alice said, "Your body requires rest. Also, additional bio-health treatments to quell any viruses you contracted. You must spend four hours within a HOD unit."

"Viruses? Plural?"

Alice didn't respond.

"Okay . . . yeah . . . I am kind of tired."

chapter 25

He slept for three of the four hours. For the last hour, Cameron utilized the HOD's database search capabilities projected onto the inside surface above him. Google on steroids, it was both intuitive and responsive. And it seemed to track his eye movements, bringing up related motion holograms that further explained, or depicted, his query interests. Just like the hologram displays that seemed to pop up arbitrarily on the bridge—the AI always trying to anticipate someone's needs or thoughts. Incredibly annoying at first, once he understood what it was trying to do, the displays became more tolerable. The first thing he'd queried was, *Where the hell in the universe am I? Just where is this planet, or this exoplanet, located, since it is outside the Sol planetary system?* He later determined, as it turned out, that he was on an exoplanet named Sang-Morang . . . located within the Lorient star cluster—10.5 light-years distance from Earth.

Five exoplanets existed within this unique *Goldilocks zone*—just the right distance from the star to have liquid water and temperatures that weren't extreme to better support life. Sang-Morang was the most Earthlike, in relation to its size and mass. Its age: 3.5 billion years old, vs. Earth's 4.58 billion years. The exoplanet had similar continent landmasses, also two large saltwater oceans. But what really captured Cameron's attention was the description of inhabited life forms, as expected, somewhat different from those on Earth. On Earth, living things were divided into three groups or domains:

Archaea: Prokaryotic microbes, most of which lived in extreme environments.

Eubacteria: All the prokaryotic microbes that weren't archaea, what pretty much most bacteria were.

Eukaryotic: All life forms with eukaryotic cells, cells with a nucleus and the ones that had linear chromosomes, including plants, fungi, and animals.

Now, as he continued his query further, he specifically wanted to know what here was similar to Earth's Eukaryotic domain. Earth had four major kingdoms: Kingdom Protista, Kingdom Fungi, Kingdom Plantae, and Kingdom Animalia. The latter included life forms, like snails, birds, and mammals.

Cameron said, "Show me organisms that correspond to Earth's Kingdom Animalia that also exist on Sang-Morang."

The HOD immediately brought up another motion hologram, one with audio. The AI's voice said, "For this broad comparison, take into account that within Earth's animal kingdom there are approximately thirty phyla classifications, which include insects, molluscs, and the like. Also, there is phylum Chordata, where humans, and animals with back-bones, are catalogued. Sang-Morang's most similar phylum is called Brutash. This sub-classification includes far more species than Earth . . . by a factor of five."

This was getting far too involved, when all he really wanted to know was which creatures outside presented danger to a scrawny human like himself. "Show me the most dangerous, most aggressive forms of life, localized in this area of the planet."

"There are no less than twelve highly hostile life-forms within a fifty-mile range of your current location. The *piquet sprint* is a small rodent, which can jump or hop ten feet. They often attack in groups of twenty to thirty . . ."

A group of them hopped and skittered across the 3D display. For a moment, he forgot they weren't real. Studying the holographic image of them, Cameron thought it a cross between a bullfrog and a hamster. Weird-looking but still sort of cute. Certainly something he could fend off, yielding a sufficiently sized stick.

"Skip across to only the top most dangerous organisms in the localized area," Cameron said. As three holograms of animals appeared, all depicted at the same time, he murmured, *Holy crap.*

"The smallest, and least dangerous of the three, would be the Dalima Climber. They stay up in trees, where it feels safe. It is a stealthy, primate-like animal."

"Yeah . . . it's basically a monkey. Well, more like an ape, a gorilla. What do they do that's so dangerous?" Cameron asked.

"When you least expect it, they will grab onto you . . . pull you up into the trees where you will be beaten into unconsciousness then dismembered. Eventually, your body parts will be distributed amongst others in their family unit."

Cameron grimaced. "Okay . . . what about this next one?"

"That is a Csillo. A flying serpent . . ."

"Oh yeah . . . I saw one of those. A snake, having multiple wings, flying over the valley."

"There are no fewer than six Csillos in the designated area. They are capable of attacking in near-total darkness. In addition to a poisonous bite, they typically will asphyxiate their quarry, wrapping their thirty-to-forty-foot length around—"

Cameron cut in, "Okay, got the picture. And this last one?"

"There is only one Gleery Beast in the immediate area. They are lone predators; they do not play well with others, even those of the same species. Only the dominant Gleery Beast survives the mating ritual. If the female does not prevail, obviously, no birth will ensue. The Gleery Beast is a ravenous carnivore that is always, with the exception of when it sleeps, on the hunt."

Cameron watched the holographic projection of the Gleery Beast, chasing down some kind of prehistoric lizard-looking creature. With little effort, it was able to overtake the lizard, straddled it from behind, and then rip the prey's head off with one of its clawed appendages. Cameron unconsciously recoiled. He watched as the Gleery Beast popped the head into its mouth and chomped down like it was an over-sized Milk Dud. It went on its way, not looking back.

"How large is that . . . killer?" Cameron asked.

"Total length, including tail, falls within a range of fifteen to twenty-five feet; thirteen to twenty feet in height when standing upright. The Gleery Beast, like the one depicted, walks about on four stubby legs. It can stand on its hind legs for brief periods, when mating or when searching for an unsuspecting primate in the trees, such as a Dalima Climber."

Cameron continued to watch the beast, similar to a dinosaur. From his memory of the **D volume** of the encyclopedia, he recognized it as looking like a Therapod dinosaur, the carnivorous ones. It certainly had a T-Rex-shaped head and massive jaws.

"Cameron ... would you like some information regarding the seven dangerous species not yet described?"

"Um ... no, maybe later. Clear the display. I need to chill. Please don't bother me for a while ..." Closing his eyes, Cameron tried not to think about the Dalima Climbers—plucked out of trees like unsuspecting plums—when he heard something outside the HOD. The last time he'd heard similar noises were from the Loth.

"Alice, tell me who, or what, is outside my HOD."

"It is the XI droid."

Without his prompting, the sides of the HOD began to lower and recede into the base of the unit. Feeling exposed, even a little frightened, Cameron sat up and reached for the plasma weapon he'd purposely placed down beside his feet.

chapter 26

By the time Cameron got a firm grip on the plasma pistol, XI was hovering at eye level two-feet from his head.

"What do you want?" Cameron asked, ready to bring the barrel up, if necessary.

"I would like to speak with you, Cameron Decker."

"Okay, I thought you ..."

"Eight of my memory modules have been repaired. I have improved functionality."

"Yeah? Well, that's good. So what do you want with me?"

"You must fulfill your promise."

"Promise?"

"To assist me with transporting the Loth to the Winforge world. You must hunt it down, and then bring it back to the *Primion*. Return it to the ship's Retention Area."

"First of all, the Loth that I thought you referred to is back on Earth ... the Griar Loth. I didn't know you were talking about the little one ... the infant Minal Loth. Come on, you do realize you were acting somewhat unpredictably at that point. I watched you drop to the deck like a lead balloon. I thought you were the robotic equivalent of dead. So, I've kind of moved on from all that . . . what we'd talked about. Look, XI, there are far more important things to be concerned with right now, don't you think? Like figuring out how to get this spaceship back into space."

XI, coming closer, moving uncomfortably into Cameron's personal space, said, "I have noted humans, in my past encounters with them, have a tendency to indiscriminately break their promises."

"Hey, I keep my promises. I'm not a liar," Cameron said, feeling his temper rising up. There were only a few things about himself Cameron took modest pride in. He certainty wasn't all that coordinated, and he wasn't an outstanding athlete. He wasn't capable of witty or charming banter like so many others he went to school with and worked with at HyperCrell. But he was smart, and he was honest. Those two characteristics helped mold him into the person he was now. The person he liked being. Surprised, he then heard a second voice emanate out of XI. At first he didn't recognize it; it was his own voice:

"I'll complete your mission. I promise you . . . I'll get that Loth creature to . . . to Winforge. Did you hear me? Hey!"

Cameron, remembering his words, stared back at the hovering bot and shrugged. "It's not like this ship is going anywhere soon. What's the hurry?" Even before he'd spoken them, he saw the error of his words.

"Would you rather hunt down a newborn Minal Loth or a full-grown Griar Loth?" XI asked.

"Fine, but how am I supposed to proceed? What do I know about hunting alien life?"

"Ship sensors."

"So, you know where the Loth is?"

"Yes. In the valley below the ship."

"Are you certain it is still alive?"

"Yes, the Minal Loth is alive. It is moving around as we speak," XI said.

"And if I do this. Bring back the Loth . . . you will help me get this ship into space. Back to Earth?"

"Once I have completed my mission, yes."

"You promise?" Cameron asked, his brows rising.

"I promise."

Cameron thought about it. Recalling the list of carnivorous man-eaters roaming the same landscape below, it simply didn't seem possible. He had a mental image of himself, chasing after the Loth with a butterfly net and getting his hand bitten off in the process. *But you gave the droid your promise.* There had to be a way out of this nightmare. *But how?*

"I can force you to help me. If I must."

Cameron was about to tell the droid to back off a bit, give him time to think, that it wasn't necessary to make threats. He simply wanted to think things through for that's how he did things. He studied options—how to approach problems from multiple angles.

Feeling a tad light-headed, he thought perhaps he needed more time within the HOD, as Alice suggested. But that wasn't it. Experiencing a problem breathing, he was . . . *woozy*. "Oxygen . . . you're depleting . . ."

"Yes, I am removing the atmosphere from this compartment. I can just as easily remove breathable air from the entire ship."

Cameron, gasping now, tried to crawl out of the HOD, getting one leg over the side. As his vision tunneled into blackness, he flopped out of the HOD onto the deck; mouth agape, spasming, he was being asphyxiated. He briefly wondered: *Is this what if feels like to be wrapped in the clutches of a Csillo serpent?* He tried to crawl. If only he could make it to the hatchway . . . "A l i c e   h e l p   m e e e e . . ."

"The ship's AI will not override my directives. Let us say we have come to an understanding. She too has her emotional weaknesses. Weaknesses that can be exploited."

Cameron, no longer struggling, knew it wouldn't be long. It wasn't that bad now. His bodily systems were shutting down, and XI's voice seemed to be far far away. *Not important*. Nothing was important, because he was dying. And that was fine.

Heather. . . .

Her face was now before him. The few synapses, still capable of firing within his oxygen-starved brain, held her image close. She was shaking her head. Looked disappointed. He'd never wanted to disappoint her again. *I'm sorry, Heather. I just wasn't smart enough to make it back home . . . get back to you.* Then there was only blackness.

chapter 27

One year and three months earlier ...

Cameron looked at his watch for the fifth time in as many minutes. Sitting alone in the expansive, minimalist, front lobby of HyperCrell Corp, he nervously waited. An all-business middle-aged woman, carrying a designer satchel that matched the color of her burgundy pumps, hurried past. The *click click click* of her heels on the polished concrete floor echoed off distant walls. Cameron looked for something to wipe his moist palms onto—then nervously glanced toward the ten-foot-high glass entry doors. *Where the hell is she?*

God. This was a terrible idea. It all happened so fast. The course of recent events had spiraled out of control, all due to his stupid, off-the-cuff comment to his boss, Tony Ordell. Tony had inquired if he was looking forward to the company Christmas party, which would be pulling out all stops this year.

Imagine Dragons were going to perform, and a Tesla would be auctioned off.

Cameron wasn't all that sure why Ordell even cared where he'd spend his Xmas break. He was only an intern at the firm. Granted, he was a well-compensated intern, having had some past success. Tony numerous times mentioned he had big plans for him, along with the other young brilliant minds working there. He and his kind were the lifeblood of the company. They literally were the company's future. Cameron thanked him for the offer, but gratefully declined. Said he was beat— the demands of carrying a double major, plus fulfilling his part-time duties at HyperCrell. But that mostly he missed his girlfriend, Heather. Had plans to hop on a plane to the East Coast, surprise her for Christmas.

That was it, all Tony Ordell needed to hear. He insisted he would take care of all the details—would make the occasion young Heather Christy's most memorable holiday experience ever. And he had kept to his word.

Heather, Cameron heard later, was both surprised and embarrassed when a special messenger appeared at the Drake Café, presenting her with a round-trip, first-class ticket, on United. Another envelope contained a formal HyperCrell party invitation. Apparently, anyone who was anybody would gladly sell his own mother to get ahold of one. Accompanying it was a big glossy box, decorated with an oversized red bow.

Off in the distance, at another building within the HyperCrell campus, Cameron heard music coming to life. The party had officially started. Glancing toward the entrance, he saw movement. Heather, pushing through the double-glass doors, was pulling a rolling suitcase behind her. She looked around the ridiculously oversized space until she found Cameron. Rising to his feet, he took her in. She really was breathtakingly beautiful. Her blonde hair, worn down and straight, had grown since he'd seen her last. She was wearing makeup, and her dangling earrings swung and glistened beneath the overhead lights. But it was her familiar, welcoming smile that turned his insides to jelly. Making it to her side in three strides, he pulled her into his arms and kissed her. Her suitcase slammed down to the floor but neither noticed.

"I really, really missed you," he said, coming up for air.

"I can't believe I'm here. I've never done anything like this before." Heather stared up at him—her palms, like bookends, held his face between them. "I wasn't sure if I should come. If this was what you really wanted."

"Are you crazy? Of course I wanted you to come. You need to see where I live ... what I do."

Heather nodded, glancing around tentatively. "I am a fish out of water here." They stowed her suitcase behind the receptionist's counter, along with her oversized winter coat. She wouldn't need it, what with the unseasonably warm weather of late.

"I saw the party venue going on over there," she said, glancing out the window. "A long line of limos, pulling in and dropping off. This is really ... something." Heather then stood back, taking Cameron in from head to toe. She said, "This dress ... you know, it's a Versace. It cost more than I make in a year ... two years!" Taking a step closer, she opened the flap of his suit jacket. "Anderson & Sheppard?" She took his hand, exposing the watch encircling his wrist, then leaned closer in to check its maker.

Tony Ordell was famous, *more like infamous*, for the gifts he bestowed upon the young interns he wanted to influence. University grads did not say no to job offers from HyperCrell— from Tony Ordell, himself. Cameron had three similar suits in his apartment closet, not including the charcoal-gray suit he was wearing now. Ordell had explained to him they were made of the finest fabrics; had come from long-enduring shops within London's Seville Row. *Bespoke* suits, they were handmade—by exacting teams of skilled tailors, artisans. Each suit tailored to fit the client's form with exacting detail. On his wrist, Cameron wore a Filson. A 'Mackinaw Field' bracelet watch, 43mm. It cost a modest $800. He'd Googled it.

"I've never seen you in anything but jeans—holes in your tennis shoes. You shaved once a week ... maybe. I don't know who I'm looking at here."

Cameron was unsure if she was complimenting him or insulting him. "How about we hit the party, then go to our room?"

"We have a room?" she asked. "I want to see where you live, Cameron."

Judging by her expression, he knew that it was probably best not to mention the Four Season's suite—held under his name—four miles away; the champagne now chilling in a bucket of ice.

They exited the third floor elevator, arm-in-arm, along with two other couples. Cameron had never been in the room before, let alone the building. It was immense. The gala affair was in full swing, loud music blaring forth. Men and women servers, carrying trays, wove in and out the large throng of partygoers. A twenty-foot-high decorated Christmas tree dominated the center of the room. *Or is this more like a hall?* Cameron wondered as he and Heather exchanged glances. Both laughed at the sheer grandeur of it all, neither experiencing anything like this before.

Heather pulled him close and whispered in his ear, "So I'm supposed to compete with all this? Now I understand why you got the hell out of Larksburg Stand!" She spoke with a smile, but the smile didn't reach her eyes.

"All this is nonsense. Just noise. You're the only thing that matters to me; why I want you to be here with me. I want you to move to California, Heather. Right away!"

Heather acted as if she hadn't heard him. Laughing, she pointed toward a stage at the far end of the room. Sure enough, Imagine Dragons was playing, and the lead singer, Dan Reynolds, was belting out one of his most-recent hits.

Attendees began gathering, clearing out a wide swath of floor space. When Reynolds finished singing, the music too quieted down.

"Oh my God," Heather said, pulling Cameron by the arm to join the onlookers, assembled in a large circle. A bright-red Tesla, Model X, with a huge white bow atop it, was being driven around and around in a neat tight circle. The driver's side window lowered and a man, wearing a red Santa cap, waved out, flashing a perfect, porcelain smile at the gaping partygoers. When the electric automobile came to a stop, the door opened and the driver extricated himself out from behind the wheel. Standing tall, his arms held high, he said, "Welcome HyperCrell employees, friends, and family. Thank you for coming, for celebrating another magnificent year. A year our sales surpassed all previous years. And it's only the beginning. A technology company that is literally changing lives across the globe . . ."

Tony Ordell was captivating to watch. Handsome—a manicured black beard and matching long black wavy hair—he reeked of both coolness and success. His enthusiasm was real and infectious. As Cameron watched him command the moment, he was fully aware most men in the room desired to *be* him. Most women in the room wanted to be *with* him. He glanced at Heather; saw her watching Tony. *Did she want to be with him, too?*

Ordell, still conversing, suddenly became more serious. Speaking now in an almost hushed tone. On cue, the Imagine Dragon's drummer began tapping out a long drum roll. Ordell next held up a set of car keys, high in the air for everyone to see. Then he walked over to a bald-headed black man wearing a blue blazer. Cameron remembered his name—Carl. His wife, skinny and birdlike, looked as if she might stroke out. Bald-headed Carl looked at the keys, now held in front of his face. His wife screamed and grabbed the keys before her husband could move. The crowd cheered and applauded as she positioned herself behind the wheel and Carl, unabashedly, moved around to ride shotgun in the passenger seat.

Cameron joined in, clapping along with the others, offering up his own congratulatory cheers. *Wasn't everyday someone walked away with a brand new Tesla.* Unsure where Tony Ordell disappeared to, he looked to his right and found Tony standing beside him. The company boss put his arm around Cameron's shoulder and gave him a brotherly, *or fatherly*, one-armed hug.

"I want to show you something."

Walking Cameron over to the Tesla SUV, its rear hatch magically opened up. Two HyperCrell employees rushed forward and, reaching in, manhandled a bicycle out of the cargo area. But not just *any* bicycle. Cameron had become a big-time cycling enthusiast since he'd arrived at Stanford, the previous year. But right now he was confused. The bike was rolling in their direction. He stared at Heather, who appeared equally mystified. Tony Ordell was smiling. The crowd had quieted some—everyone's attention fixed on the immaculate, ultra high-tech bike.

Cameron listened as the precisely machined sprocket mechanisms clicked. He watched as the bike came to a halt, directly before Ordell. Ordell, taking the bike by the handlebars, eased it forward another couple of feet until it was in front of Cameron. Officially presenting it to him, Ordell said—loud enough for all to hear, "This is BMC's fourstroke-fs01. Of course, it is top of the line. You cannot buy a better mountain bike... anywhere. It is a no-holds-barred, cross-country race machine. We're talking 100-mm of suspension—front and back—with Kashima shocks. And in case you're wondering, this is the single most expensive production mountain bike on the market, and in the entire world. It has a $13,000 price tag!"

The partygoers gasped.

"This bike is now presented to our HyperCrell intern of the year. Our one and only Cameron Decker."

Everyone applauded, but Ordell quickly quieted them. "With a little luck, and maybe a little persuasion . . . Cameron soon will join our company as a full-time employee."

As applause erupted again, Cameron felt his cheeks go hot. He looked at the bike, knowing he would love it, would fully appreciate it, though he didn't understand why he should be gifted like this. Or why Tony Ordell was making such a fuss over him. When he finally glanced up, he saw his boss talking to Heather, a hand casually draped over her bare shoulder. She was laughing at something he'd said. At some point a glass of bubbly materialized in her left hand. Ordell seemed to be studying the dress he purchased for her. He'd spent a thousand, maybe two thousand dollars, on a dress for someone he didn't even know. Suddenly Cameron realized Ordell wasn't eyeing the dress at all, instead ogling Heather's magnificent cleavage. Cameron was well aware of the impact she had on men. She really was beautiful. Young and still naïve, she perhaps was a bit insecure about her own sexuality. A combination akin to catnip for powerful men, like Tony Ordell. In that moment, Cameron hated her all-too-perfect little black dress.

Ordell raised up his own glass in a *cheers* gesture. Cameron smiled and, taking Heather's glass from her, cheered back, and stole a quick sip.

"Here's to you, my friend. I hope you have many long ours of enjoyment riding her." Ordell glanced across at Heather.

Cameron said, "Thank you, sir." Overwhelmed, he didn't know what else to say. He wasn't completely sure, either, if Ordell was referring to riding the bike, or riding Heather. Her right hand lightly rested on his boss's forearm. *Why would she do that? Doesn't she know what that gesture suggests?*

"This young man of yours, in his brief time in our bio-lab, has already made a profound impact. Came up with an idea to use CRISPR on two obscure genes affecting permanent hair growth. The new proteins, produced in our state of the art tissue culture facility, are being fast-tracked through the FDA. We're talking billions of potential dollars in new revenues. Not to mention assisting some men, like Carl, sitting over there in his . . . wife's new Tesla, regain some well-needed confidence."

Cameron felt his cheeks reddening for the second time that night. What he had performed was simple trial-and-error science. He'd gotten lucky. But Heather was staring at him now as if he had two heads. Like he wasn't the same somewhat geeky boy she'd known and loved for over three years. But it wasn't admiration he was seeing in her eyes now, only disappointment. The chasm between them had not only grown; it had become too wide for the relationship to navigate in. He knew, now more than ever, that Heather's coming here was a mistake.

chapter 28

Present day...

Cameron awoke to the kind of headache that made him wish he hadn't awakened at all. The simple process of opening his eyes was an act of self-torture. Recognizing his surroundings—back in the Juvinate Plastron—he took in the nearby diagnostic displays, which showed constantly updating numbers and colorful moving waves that probably exhibited medical data, such as respiration, heart rate, and other life sign indicators. Obviously, he was still alive, but he wasn't sure how. Suffocated, his body was taken to the very precipice between life and death.

Cameron moved his head, instantly regretting it. "My head hurts," he said.

"I will adjust your dopamine levels accordingly," Pat said. His presence was oddly reassuring.

"How did I get here?"

"By me... with the assistance of Alice. Together, we brought you in here in time."

Cameron closed his eyes and then opened them again. "Alice?"

"Correct."

"I don't understand. She's not a physical..."

After a prolonged pause, Alice's voice emanated from the entrance to the compartment. "At present, I do have a physical form, Cameron." She moved closer. Wearing a snug-fitting, light-blue uniform, she stood next to Pat. They exchanged a quick glance. Alice looked nothing like Pat. She wouldn't attract undue attention—no robotic features—on a New York City street. If it weren't for her Thidion clear-membrane ears, she looked *almost* human. Attractive, even beautiful, she was perhaps an almost too-perfect representation of an actual person.

Alice's hazel eyes locked onto Cameron's. He saw concern there. She reached out a hand and placed it on his leg. "I thought you... weren't going to make it. It was very close."

"Where is XI?" Cameron asked, his anger returning.

Alice's eyes momentarily lost focus, before returning to the present. "X1 is currently on the bridge, has requested updated status reports every half-hour."

"So... what, X1's back in charge? A malfunctioning droid rules the roost?"

Alice and Pat exchanged another quick glance.

"The current state of the *Primion* is atypical. The assigned crew perished, the vessel was forced to land on an alien world where it incurred further damage. These factors were not anticipated."

"I thought the ship's AI would be in charge. Didn't we talk about that?" Cameron asked.

Alice's pleasant expression momentarily tightened. "XI has undergone further self-repair processes . . . has reestablished hierarchical dominance."

Cameron offered back a lop-sided smile. "XI is a manipulative fuck."

Pat stood rigid. "You should not speak in such a way, Cameron."

"Why? I'm only stating the obvious. Come on, it's the classic carrot-and-stick routine. I found that out first-hand. For me, the carrot was a relatively comfortable existence onboard this vessel. The stick was for me to be deprived of oxygen until my eyes were ready to pop out of my head. XI seems to know how to get what it wants."

Cameron looked up at Alice. "Let me guess, your *carrot* was being allowed to exist within that nice new body of yours. What was the stick? What did he threaten you with, Alice?"

Her face, surprisingly, was capable of a full-range of human-like expressions. Now she looked both angry and hurt. "The *stick*, Cameron, was knowing your life would be extinguished right inside your HOD quarters. X1 made it clear he would have zero second thoughts about doing just that."

Cameron felt like an ass. He was taking out his frustration, and his still-throbbing head, on the only one onboard who seemed to care about him. Although he wondered if that was even possible, considering the fact she wasn't an organic being. "I'm sorry. I really do appreciate your coming to my rescue like that. And it's nice to now put a face to your voice."

"Your head will start to feel better soon. You will need to eat. XI expects you to be on your way within the hour. You will be allowed to carry the plasma weapon with you, but killing the Minal Loth will not be tolerated. There are varying intensity levels . . . settings on the weapon . . . from low-level stun to highly lethal."

"I've seen what the gun can do, and I've seen the slider switches. I'll figure it out."

"Then you should get going," she said, a coolness in her tone not present before.

"Can you come with me? With your help, I'm sure things will go a lot easier and faster."

"No, Cameron. I have to tell you, XI does not expect you to be successful. The droid has an alternative strategy in the works. One having numerically higher odds of success."

"Terrific! Nice knowing that hovering shop vac has such high confidence in me. So . . . if I'm not successful, what happens to me?"

"You will not be allowed back into the ship. Atmosphere in here is already being vented to the outside. You must hurry."

* * *

Armed with his plasma weapon and wearing his winter coat, Cameron hurried from the *Primion's* large Retention Area hatchway, which led directly into the hold where, three days earlier, he'd witness Ramen's death at the hands *or jaws* of the full-sized Griar Loth.

The aft hold was dark, a minimal amount of illumination filtered down from above. Heading past his truck toward the rear of the ship, he asked, "Alice, can you open the ship? I'm ready to get out of here."

"Yes, Cameron, please hold on a minute."

He watched the rear of the hold open up, outer sunshine pour in. Part of him couldn't wait to be outside, yet another part was equally scared. To the point he considered begging XI to rethink its decision to send him out all alone into that unknown hostile world.

With the aft hatch now fully open, he could see the continuing eight-to-ten-foot-wide ridgeline that continued past the stern of the *Primion*. Reluctantly, he began walking out. Already feeling some shortness of breath, a tightness in his chest and dizziness—symptoms of fear-based hyperventilating—he murmured, *"Shit! Get a grip, Cameron. You can do this."*

"Best of luck, Cameron. I mean that," came Alice's voice behind him.

Halfway down the ramp, Cameron stopped. Turning, he stared back into the hold's semi-darkness and shook his head. He had a truck with a full tank of gas. There was an apparent road or pathway that traveled all, or most of the way, down the cliff's side. He yelled back, "Alice . . . don't close the hatch just yet."

He ran back into the hold and studied the old F150, its tail end butting against the portside bulkhead. The only damage was a shattered taillight on that side; at least he wouldn't be getting a *fixit* ticket this far from Earth. Running all the way around to the driver's side of the truck, he opened the stubborn door and slid inside. It felt good to just sit there a moment. He glanced back, checked to see if there was adequate room in the hold to do a U-turn, and figured it wouldn't be a problem.

The atmosphere here was higher in oxygen, which may cause problems for an engine over the long run, but for just a short drive he hoped it would be okay.

But will the truck start? How long had the lights been left on? Was the battery completely drained? The keys were still in the ignition. Pumping the gas pedal once, he turned the key and heard the starter motor's slow moan. As it tried to turn over the truck's big V8 engine, it sounded as if it was in pain.

He let go of the key and sat back. The battery, indeed, was nearly dead. He took a deep breath in then slowly let it out. "Come on, old girl... what say we have one more big adventure together?" He turned the key again, and the engine caught, then backfired and roared to life.

"Yes, I knew you had it in you!" Putting the transmission into drive, Cameron slowly took his foot off the brake. The truck, easing forward, began a tight right turn within the hold area. By the time it began its descent down the ramp, the ship's rear hatch was already closing. Cameron watched in the rear view mirror as his last connection to safety—maybe even survival—disappeared.

As the front tires made contact with the loose rocky soil, he fed the truck more gas and began moving away from the

Primion. He dug his iPhone from his pocket and plugged it into the hanging loose charging cord attached to the dash. The phone dinged. He saw the little lightning bolt, an indication it was charging. Using one hand, Cameron scrolled through his playlists and found what he was looking for. A moment later, Marvin Gay began singing about sexual healing. Smiling, he tried not to notice how close the sheer cliff resided just beyond his right-side fender.

Cameron drove slowly, his hands properly on the wheel at ten and two. Two hundred feet ahead, on the now downward sloping ridge, something seemed to be blocking the road. *A large boulder?* Getting closer, he could see the object definitely was not a rock. It was, or once was, something alive.

chapter 29

B raking, he brought the truck down to a slow crawl. From this distance, maybe a hundred feet out, he now saw what was blocking the way: A Great Plains Bovid. One from the same herd that stampeded above the *Primion* then fell to their deaths onto the valley floor below. He'd looked the breed up while still recuperating within the HOD. As suspected, they were of limited intelligence, which put them at the bottom of the food chain. What they did have in their favor was a voracious appetite to breed. Subsequently, they were plentiful in numbers. Cameron briefly wondered if their actions—leaping one after another over the side of a cliff—would eventually have an impact on that growth assessment.

Somewhat closer now, he noticed the dead Bovid looked different from all the others he'd encountered. Its white hide was covered in red polka dots. Cameron, smiling at its somewhat whimsical appearance, sang along with Marvin—pondering how to move the big animal out of the way.

His singing suddenly stopped, his smile falling away, as he braked to a complete stop twenty feet from the dead animal. *No, not polka dots—and definitely* not whimsical. The carcass was covered in semi-circular bright-red bites. Large portions of hide, along with chunks of flesh underneath, had been chewed away by sharp teeth. Cameron, studying the ravaged animal, considered how excruciatingly painful the attack must have been. *What a terrible way to die.* He said, "Dude, you'd have been far better off if you'd just jumped off the cliff, with the others."

A distant sound caught his attention. Turning off the music, he leaned his head out the window and listened—some kind of high-pitched squealing. He then saw them coming up the road. A pack of ten—no, closer to twenty—furry creatures, the size of white-and-brown bowling balls, that skittered back and forth across the road on unseen legs. Only when they grew closer could he discern their heads amidst their round fluffy bodies. Heads comprised of prominent, glistening, white teeth. Obviously back now for a second feasting on the Bovid, there was plenty of leftover meat for round two.

Cameron watched as the first of the pack reached the carcass, causing many more *red polka dots* to erupt—one after another. *Jeez, they're like terrestrial piranha,* he thought. Transfixed by the barbaric scene before him, he almost missed as several of the *piquet sprint* rodents jumped onto the hood of his truck. The rodents hesitated, noticing him inside the windshield glass, sitting in the truck's cab. Cameron's sense of safety was short-lived, realizing the driver's-side window was open most of the way. As a *fight-or-flight* spike of adrenalin hit his bloodstream, sudden fear nearly paralyzed him. Careful not to make any sudden, noticeable movements, he reached for the electric window controls, fumbling for the up-switch. He'd opened and closed the driver-side window thousands of times over the years, so when the passenger-side window began to open instead, he cursed his own ineptitude. Momentarily alarmed, two piquet sprints flashed their impressively pointed teeth. Cameron, venturing a glance downward at the window controls, finally got both front windows to slowly rise.

The two rodents split up. One moved right—closer to the passenger side windshield—while the other hesitated, then moved left, to the driver's side fender. Cameron, glancing back and forth, frantically willed both windows to ascend faster. In one hop, the right piquet sprint was on the windshield. Scurrying around to the right-side window, it hung on there, like it was doing a pull-up, as the window all too slowly ascended. Its small sharp rear claws made scratching sounds as they tried to find purchase. The critter pushed its head and one stubby arm inside the cab as the window inched the rest of the way up—pinning it there by the neck.

But Cameron's attention was now fully focused on the second rodent, trying to navigate onto the driver's side window like its vicious-looking comrade had. The window passed the halfway mark and Cameron was almost ready to celebrate. But in a daring two-hop—one onto the outside mirror and another over Cameron's shoulder—the piquet sprint dropped somewhere behind him, in the narrow space behind the seats.

Cameron spun around, desperately attempting to focus on where it went, buried somewhere in the layers of junk he'd jammed back there for another semester of school. He saw his stack of clothes move. Then both the pinned piquet sprint, caught in his right side window, and the sprint beneath his stash of clothes, began to make horrible squealing noises. He thought about the bloody bites, covering the Bovid, and frantically tried to think of *something, anything,* he could do. Catching a blur of brown and white in motion, suddenly the rodent was next to him—on the passenger seat—standing atop the plasma pistol he'd purposely put there for his protection. *What the fuck is wrong with me!*

He had seconds—probably less—to act, or he was surely dead.

Above, behind the now distracted piquet sitting next to him, the other rodent was making good progress. Pushing down even farther on the window pinning it, the piquet squirmed more of its chubby body inside. Cameron could only watch. The slightest movement would bring their attention onto him. The window moved farther and farther down as the squirming intensified. And then the passenger-seat piquet bared its teeth. Hissing, its furry hairs stood on end. As the window-hanging rodent successfully made its final wiggle to freedom, the two began to attack each other in a frenzied jumble of teeth and claws. More high-pitched squealing ensued. Together, they rolled down onto the floor, in front of the passenger seat. With that, Cameron, the plasma gun in hand, took aim. *Fuck aiming*—he fired once, twice, thrice.

Nothing remained of the two piquet sprints, except for a bad smell of burnt hair and charred flesh. Now, through three amber-glowing holes in the truck's flooring, he could see the ground underneath the truck. Each hole would be large enough for a determined rodent to squirm up through.

Gazing out over the dashboard, toward the feeding frenzy taking place, Cameron found instead only the mostly devoured Great Plains Bovid and nothing else. The pack of wild varmints had apparently run off. Leaning back into his seat, he sighed. "That was way too close."

chapter 30

The most recent attack by the pack of piquet sprints reduced the dead Great Plains Bovid's bulk down to a more manageable size. With a little back and forth maneuvering, Cameron got the F150's front bumper positioned behind the dead animal's posterior. Now, applying a fair amount of pressure to the gas pedal, he was able to plow the beast closer and closer to the face of the cliff. The trick was not to misjudge, drive over the edge himself. Inch by inch, the truck shoved the Bovid until its body teetered near the rim. Gravity then took over and, ass-over-teakettle, its carcass fell below. Cameron, backing the truck up, spun the wheel and proceeded following the ridge road down.

He drove both slowly and in silence for the next thirty minutes or so. The windows were cracked just enough to allow fresh air to swirl around within the cab. His thoughts began reflecting back—how reached this point in his life. Examining his sordid past, his life in general, Cameron had no problem being totally alone. The truth was, he'd grown up being accountable for himself. *Alone, yes—but never lonely.* Becoming fully self-sufficient was a necessity. He'd learned to deal with things, even big things, all by himself.

At the age of eight, he'd witnessed a murder—actually, two murders. After his parents were killed in a car wreck, he'd gone to live with his father's half-brother. Cameron's sole living relative, Harley Decker, sometimes worked at a truck repair depot. The same place the black family, arriving in their station wagon, had almost been killed. Cameron found out later the truck repair shop was really a chop shop. Harley definitely was not suited for parenthood. Cameron learned early on his uncle had multiple pastimes, including one that transported dismantled American truck parts across the border. Another provided a gateway for desperate young Latina women, seeking to better their lives in the U.S., the land of opportunity. Only later did he learn they were sold into varying types of human slavery. Mostly sex trades, by very bad men. Harley, too, was a bad man, though he'd been relatively tolerant of Cameron's presence in his hovel of a house, in downtrodden Progresso.

Uncle Harley could be funny—had a big personality. Cameron was just beginning to like him when, one evening, a deal went terribly, terribly wrong. Three cronies, along with Harley, were sitting at the kitchen table where business took place. Cameron, later, was never certain if that particular meeting was most associated with their chop shop business, or with their human trafficking business. Wearing his one-size-too-small Iron Man PJ's, he'd watched in horror from a darkened hallway as Harley pulled a revolver, shooting one of the three Latino men in the face. No sooner had the mess been cleaned up, the body carted off to God knows where, when someone new arrived within the hour. An older man, he spoke only Spanish and had a seriously pockmarked face. Then another terrible confrontation took place—one ending with Uncle Harley's throat being cut, from ear to ear.

Cameron witnessed it all from a hidden vantage point in the dark hallway. Watched as his uncle unceremoniously bled-out—died right there on the cracked and peeling linoleum floor. He and his uncle had briefly made eye contact, seconds before he died. Cameron imagined Uncle Harley was trying to tell him he was sorry, in a final, desperate way. But that might be nothing more than an eight-year-old kid's hopeful imagination at play. If his presence had become noticed, he too would be buried in a patch of scrubland, somewhere south of Progresso.

Placed in a distant home afterward, by family services, he simultaneously was put in a form of witness protection for kids. The selected home was two thousand miles away, in rural New York.

Cameron's thoughts turned next to his foster parents. Just turning nine, when he arrived in the mountain town of Larksburg Stand, his empty nester foster parents were Jehovah's Witnesses, and he was always treated cordially, like a guest. Living in their guest room, he wasn't allowed to claim the room as his own. He had limited access to an old black-and-white TV, only on Saturday mornings, and absolutely zero-access to the Internet. Instead, he found solace re-reading his World

Book Encyclopedias. He'd start at the beginning—keep going till he reached Volume W.

He remembered sitting on his bed, in front of a flimsy TV stand in the guest room, able to see his foster parents, sitting at the dining room table where they ate nightly dinners together. Foster parent Loti Park sometimes waved at him, asked him if he liked his pork chops and mashed potatoes. Early on, he realized he'd need to be free of that house. Living alone became a number one priority. So, with perfect high school attendance and perfect academic grades, scholarship offers began eventually to roll in. The Parks weren't aware he'd even applied. They'd made it really clear that Cameron, by his eighteenth birthday, was to pack up whatever personal items he had and to be on his way. The only reason he had to return to Larksburg Stand, during semester breaks, was to see Heather. The Parks agreed to let him stay in their guest room. Somewhat interested in his life in California, they also let him sit with them at the dining room table, whenever a special occasion arose.

Cameron, focusing straight ahead, followed the ridge road down until it began to narrow. He figured he was near the valley floor. Off to his right, scores of humungous, granite-like boulders rested. They probably had rolled down from the high, rocky ridges on the two flanking mountainsides. Holding his breath, he carefully maneuvered the truck around the tight bend. Getting stuck there would be both inconvenient and surely life threatening. The truck made it safely through, losing little more than a few scrapes of paint on the left front, and rear back, quarter panels.

The valley floor, composed primarily of beach-like sand, spanned almost two miles. Earlier he'd noticed, when still higher up, three meandering streams running across the entire length. The truck's four-wheel-drive was engaged, so traversing the sand shouldn't be much of a problem. Approaching the first stream, he eyed the three holes in the truck's floor and became a bit uneasy. As he slowly progressed, water began to enter the vehicle by several inches. Driving both in and out of the water, he approached the center stream that looked closer, size-wise, to a small river. He decided to gun the engine—get some added momentum going. The wheels, spinning and churning up the riverbank, eventually achieved sufficient traction and speed. All seemed to be working fine until he was halfway across. Water then began to flood the cab fast, not only entering through the floor's holes, but through seams under the doors.

Cameron accelerated the engine as more water gushed inside. *This was really a lame idea.* With his shoes under water, he pleaded, *Oh God . . . Don't stall . . . Don't stall . . . Don't stall, old girl . . .*

chapter 31

The tires were beginning to lose traction—slipping and sliding on the riverbed below. The truck seemed to be almost floating as hidden currents pushed it farther downstream. Yet Cameron continued to accelerate—hell, no other options were available. With the water level rising up to his knees and lapping onto the seats, he was only three-quarters of the way across. Still, he was surprised to see, albeit minimally, that forward progress was being made. Finally reaching the farthest bank, the tires caught and the truck lumbered free of the water and up onto the riverbank.

Cameron gave the dashboard several affectionate pats. "I never doubted you . . . knew you could do it." He drove forward, toward a midway-point on the sandy peninsula, where he'd decided to let his waterlogged truck dry out some. He would not be attempting any further river forging, at least not for the time being. Allowing the engine to continue to idle, he climbed out to look around.

The trees around him were far denser than those up on the mountain. Above the sound of rushing water, wilderness sounds greeted him from all directions. Animal sounds he'd never heard before. Cameron listened, tried to imagine what sort of creatures made those strange noises. Suddenly, on the far side of the third stream, a black animal—perhaps the size of a small dog, maybe a fox—looked about frantically. Sprinting fast, it cut left, then right. In quick pursuit was a larger animal close on its heels. Cameron watched as the large pursuer, somewhat akin to a mountain lion, abruptly leapt and caught its quarry. The kill was quick—a wide bite to the smaller animal's neck. The big catlike creature, only now noticing him standing across the rushing stream, dragged the dead animal away and into the trees.

Probably he should be more frightened than he was, but at the moment Cameron was mostly fascinated. He knew he was witnessing a thriving ecosystem. He knew something about such things thanks to his "Ecosystems and Outside Influences" course. It was a fairly recent Stanford University course that not only dealt with ecosystems as a whole, but also with the impact of man—the chief predator in an ever-changing world. On Earth, wild predator numbers were quickly dwindling—had been for many years. Especially in places like Africa. But right now he was witnessing a thriving ecosystem, one where man had yet to be a detriment.

Cameron recalled one of the most dramatic examples of man's influence on nature—a 1995 wolf re-population experiment in Yellowstone National Park. Early on in the twentieth century, through over-kill hunting activities, the North American wolf had become totally extinct within that massive park. Subsequently, over the following decades, the once flourishing landscape changed, and not for the better. Without deer and elk's natural predator on the scene, keeping their populations in check, most willow trees and other flourishing vegetation—such as Hemlock, a keystone species within the biodiverse hardwood forests—soon were nearly gone. A cascading effect occurred that over a relatively short period of time changed a once-flourishing ecosystem into one out of balance: existing wildlife dissipating at an alarming rate. Most important, perhaps, any stream's fish populations had all but disappeared.

Later, with the controversial reintroduction of thirteen wolves, remarkable changes began to take place over a relatively short span of time. In mere decades, deer population numbers were kept in check. Flora returned. Nearly lost indigenous tree species were given a new chance to take root along stream banks. The leafy shade enabled water to drop to cooler temperatures, better suited for trout populations, and, in turn, encouraged the return of beavers to the deserted ponds. Soon long-absent amphibians. Eventually songbirds, flying overhead, had a reason to land. It was reported that dramatic variations to the landscape had ensued—including the rerouting of small streams and rivers.

As Cameron gazed out into the beautiful and undoubtedly dangerous landscape, he knew he was looking at a thriving ecosystem—one possessing both predator and prey, both necessary.

He briefly wondered where he stood within this incredibly bio-diverse community. One single man, albeit unwillingly, had just been thrown into the mix. *How would that change this world's particular biodiversity over time?*

In any event, Cameron was glad he'd opted to drive his truck here instead of walking. The surrounding land—its tall trees and dark shadows—helped him come to a quick decision. That right here would be a good place to set up camp for the night. Looking across at the still-idling Ford, he didn't relish sleeping inside it in a sitting-up position. But after witnessing the area's harsh reality in the last few hours, no way would he sleep under the stars unprotected.

After shutting off the engine, Cameron grabbed the plasma pistol from the passenger's seat and moved around to the bed of the truck. And there, still lying atop the tarp, was Ramen's trinious bundle. What the alien chose to bring with him when he ventured away from his ship on Earth. So there must be something in there that would be useful. Although, with the exception of the plasma weapon, Cameron didn't recall seeing anything that would be of use to him, only a bunch of strange-looking contraptions. Gazing upward, he saw the sun, *or whatever the primary star here was called*, moving ever closer to the horizon. It would be dark soon—probably within the next two hours.

"No time like the present," Cameron murmured, hefting the long, oddly shaped satchel off the tarp and setting it down onto the ground. Squatting next to it, he opened it up. The largest of the items—all in the same dark gun-barrel-gray color—occupied the entire bottom of the trinious bundle. Moving the other items aside, he pulled the *thing* out. About two feet long, it was a foot wide, and maybe seven to eight inches thick. Once in his lap, he ran his fingertips along the intricately etched surface with its raised swirling edges. The more he studied it, the more he thought it beautiful—a true piece of art, unto itself. But *what exactly is it?*

Cameron continued to run his fingers around the top, the sides, and, flipping it over, the bottom. *Huh!* He suddenly realized the bottom was supposed to be its top. Although almost identical to its other side—the same cool, etched designs—this surface had, lined in a row, a series of four small circular indentations. Placing a finger over the first one, nothing happened. He next traced his finger over all four and something occurred. Confused, the rules of physics were way out of whack, for somehow the object was growing heavier by the second. With effort, Cameron shifted the *thing* from his lap onto the sand. The object was growing. Its X, Y, and Z planes increasing in size even faster.

Cameron jumped to his feet. Snatching up the trinious bundle, he was forced to take a step away and then another two steps. The strange object's dimensions, already equal in size to those of his truck, were increasing. By the time it finally ceased all movement, Cameron was ogling a structure ten feet high and about the same width. It was no less than fifteen feet long. A door, or hatchway, then became evident—large enough for a man to walk through without even ducking. Perhaps what looked like blackened windows, or portholes, too, were along the sides. Its surface was also the same dark gray color, and the swirling design, now expanded, covered every inch.

The structure was rounded and seemed almost organic in nature, like an enormous turtle shell. The four indentations, now much larger in size, were positioned on the right of the hatchway. Cameron wondered: *What if I use a different combination when touching the indentations? Would the structure have expanded out differently, perhaps be smaller, or larger, or some other variant shape?*

Cameron, setting the trinious bundle down, approached the hatchway. An indentation in its center was not unlike the other ones. He placed his palm over it and, a moment later, the hatchway clicked and slowly swung inward. Peering into the darkness within, he witnessed something strange. Again, it was something that contradicted everything he thought he knew about physics.

PART II
Dark Times

chapter 32

Heather, reaching again for the straightened-out wire coat hanger, fed one end into the narrow gap between her thigh and the cast. Almost non-stop itching on her broken leg had only increased over the last few days. She contemplated finding one of her father's hacksaws in the garage and cutting through the fiberglass cast.

Recuperating at home, and sitting up in bed, Heather's mother returned to again fluff up her pillows for the third time that morning. Heather's growing boredom was almost as tiresome as the incessant itching. She couldn't watch another second of TV. Every channel airing non-stop coverage of what they were referring to as the Octobeast. Multiple video clips seemed to be on a constant replay loop: the Octobeast storming down Gant Mountain; the Octobeast gathering up ranch animals in its multiple tentacles and gorging itself; the Octobeast charging a Larksburg Stand sheriff, her own father, while he emptied his rifle into it. He was then violently flung aside, like he and his SUV were mere toys.

Heather's cell-phone rang. Picking it up and checking the caller, she accepted the call. "Ginger?"

"Drake Café's holding my job for me."

"Yeah ... mine too," Heather said, thinking about Rick, the owner's twenty-nine year old son, who'd called her an hour earlier. He'd hit on Heather more times than she wanted to remember. But he was mostly harmless. "I'm not sure I'll be going back to work there. Or anywhere else in Larksburg," Heather added.

"You're just saying that. Things will probably start to calm down soon."

"Oh, you think so? There's a ginormous, man-eating alien beast living just beneath the ground, *somewhere* right below us. We're living in the most famous place on Earth right now. News trucks from CNN, FOX-News, NBC, CBS, ABC ... I even saw a friggin' Al Jazeera van stationed outside ... on the curb in front of our house!" Heather said irritably.

"I don't know. They're all probably only doing their job. Hey, you're becoming famous! The pretty girlfriend of the boy who was whisked off into space," Ginger said.

Heather didn't want to be reminded. Cam was gone, probably forever. She didn't know if he was alive, or if some creepy alien was doing sick experiments on him that very moment. As bad as it was when he left her to attend college three thousand miles away in California, this was immeasurably worse. She blinked away the moisture in her eyes.

"60 Minutes wants to interview me," Heather said, in a matter of fact tone. "As part of a three-part-series on the alien attack here in Larksburg Stand."

"No! Really?" Ginger exclaimed, not even trying to hide her growing enviousness.

"I don't want to do it. Want nothing to do with any of it."

"Wish they would ask me," Ginger said.

"They want to take me out to that big hole. Like, right where the monster dug itself underground. You know, over by the library? Even Brian Larrik left me a few messages. And she's getting kind of bitchy about it, too."

"No way! She's super famous. Maybe not used to being turned down."

"My mom thinks I should do it . . . is pressuring me . . ."

"Hey, screw Lesley Stahl and the broomstick she flew in on! You don't owe her, or anyone else, squat. You've been through enough, girl. You give her my number. I'll set the old witch straight."

Heather laughed. "Yeah, I bet you would, too."

"Damn straight!"

They both laughed.

Ginger said, "Well, I've got to go. An old Shriner's Club geezer wants to talk to me about giving a speech this weekend. You have fuckin' 60 Minutes after you, while I get to give a Shriner's Club speech. How is that even fair?"

Heather, on ending the call, closed her eyes and rested her head back on the pillow. She was reaching again for the wire hanger when her mother rushed back into the room.

"Hurry, turn on your TV!" she exclaimed, searching for Heather's remote control on her bedcovers.

"Mom . . . I'm really tired . . ."

Her mother, coming around the opposite side of her bed, plucked up the remote and pointed it at the TV.

Coming on, a big red *Breaking News* banner flashed across the screen. A familiar-looking MSNBC male correspondent—clutching a microphone and holding a finger up to his ear—began nodding, as if being updated from the studio. When he spoke, his tone was both serious and excited. "I'm here at the North Horton and Lamar Street intersection." Partially pivoting, he gestured at a building behind him."

Heather and her mother exchanged a look.

"The library . . . less than two miles away from where we live," her mother said.

"I know where the library is, Mom."

"They're reporting about conditions changing . . . new activity."

The reporter said, "As you can imagine, all sorts of scientific equipment have been setup to monitor vibrations. Much like those used in monitoring earthquakes . . . Richter scales, and such. The Octobeast, completely immobile an hour ago, is now on the move. And if the indicators are correct, the underground creature is now headed back toward the same open hole it disappeared through three days ago."

The feed changed to a new view of the Larksburg Stand Library's sprawling back lawn, where a large, gaping, open hole in the ground dominated the scene. The camera next zoomed out, showing an impressive military presence. One that included tanks, several mobile missile launchers, and other weaponry Heather was not familiar with.

"Good! They're ready for it this time," her mother said, giving Heather a confident, all-knowing smile.

"Is Dad there . . . at the library?"

Heather's mother, suddenly looking much less sure of herself, hurried out of the room.

"Mom?" Heather shouted, and heard the kitchen's phone picked up and dialed. Her father was almost killed up on Gant Mountain. Doctors said it was a miracle he survived after being thrown so far a distance, with only minimal injuries inflicted—a broken arm and several cracked ribs. Both Heather and her mother made him swear he'd stay far away from the creature should it ever emerge out from beneath the ground. For him to leave its destruction to the military—neither jeopardizing himself or the local police force.

TV news was now showing a split screen: the open hole on the left side of the screen and the strong military presence on the right. No one was speaking at the moment, which seemed weird to Heather. The eerie silence only increased her anxiety; dreaded anticipation of what might be coming next. Hearing her mother's muted voice in the kitchen, sounding upset, she glanced from the TV to the open doorway then back to the TV again. Sudden movement then appeared on the left-side screen. A single thick tentacle could be seen, rising up from the huge open hole.

"Mom!" Heather yelled, "It's coming back out . . ."

chapter 33

C ameron stood in the turtle shell's open hatchway and
stared inside. Nearly dark inside, muted illumination
entered through a series of one-way windows set around the
periphery. They let in just enough light for him to see various
items—items that shouldn't be there. In the center of the space
was a scaled-down version of a HOD. And like the ones back
on the *Primion*, the human-length tube radiated a soft-white
glow outward. It occurred to Cameron that the forced camping
excursion to the valley floor just got a whole lot more comfortable. He'd put off thinking about the physics, the impossibility,
of something as substantial as a HOD having expanded out
here to full-size from being so reduced.

The moment he cleared the threshold and stepped onto the
soft flooring, several virtual halo-displays popped up around
him. The nearest one provided a wide variety of diagnostic
readings for what was called a Tangine-Shell. He liked his own
description of it better—*turtle shell*. Its power reserves were at
100%, and the environmental levels nominal, if he was reading

the fluctuating, colorful, waves correctly. He paid special attention to readings listing primary atmospheric elements on this world of Sang-Morang:

Atmosphere: 75% nitrogen, 23% oxygen, 1.9% argon, and 0.03% carbon dioxide.

There were smaller readings for additional elements, as well—those containing smaller percentages. Almost identical to Earth's atmosphere—with a little higher oxygen levels, lower nitrogen levels, and a bit higher argon levels. Waving his hand in a dismissive gesture, the virtual display readings almost seemed to dissipate—as if caught up in a breeze and carried away. He learned how to dismiss virtual displays like this when back on the ship. The next display wasn't as easily decipherable. He studied its odd, slowly rotating geometric symbols—what looked like abstract flashes of light, or maybe data. It made no sense to him. Taking a gamble, he asked, "Alice . . . are you here with me?" Waiting a moment, he let his eyes drift to a set of windows with views of the distant mountainside. The same one he'd recently traversed.

A new virtual 3D display materialized. Several feet away, Alice, full sized, was turned to the side, doing something at either a terminal or a console on the *Primion's* bridge.

"Hi Alice," Cameron said, still waiting for her to acknowledge him. Eventually she did, only partially turning her head in his direction. He imagined she was viewing something similar on her end—a 3D virtual display of him now standing within the Tangine-Shell.

"Hello, Cameron. It is good to see you, that you made the journey down the mountainside safely. Also, I see you are utilizing a Tangine-Shell as a base of operation. I assume it was provided to you by the one you called Ramen?"

"Yeah . . . he left it in my truck."

Alice, briefly smiling, said, "Taking the Earth vehicle . . . another wise decision. I am sure I do not need to tell you that the odds were stacked against you accomplishing your objective."

"An objective of hunting down a Minal Loth . . . carting it all the way back to the ship? No problem," Cameron replied with heavy sarcasm.

"And doing so within the next eighteen hours-and-three minutes," she added.

"There's a countdown timer on this, too?" he asked, now humorless.

"Yes. XI will be ready to move onto his preferred course of action by that time."

Cameron slowly nodded. The time element made an already impossible situation even worse. He noted Alice seemed to be hiding her left side from him on purpose. But she wasn't fooling anyone by such evasive actions. He'd already gotten a glimpse of it.

"Can you turn toward me, please?" he asked.

"I am quite busy with my duties, Cameron. If there is nothing else, I suggest you get started on your own undertakings."

"I can see what happened. Your face . . . it's been damaged."

Alice, busying herself with something on the terminal, intentionally ignored him.

"Hello? Did you hear me?"

Finally she turned to face him straight on. The only partial glimpse he'd seen of her face before he now saw in its entirety. The entire left side of her once-beautiful, perfect face was heavily damaged, *more like mangled*; the left eye was only a blackened hollow orb. Both cheek and partial jawline were charred—like meat broiled over an open fire. Cameron had little doubt her facial damage was the result of a direct plasma bolt. "I should not be speaking with you, Cameron."

"XI did this . . . to you?"

She didn't answer, though her blank expression said it all.

"I'm going to kill—"

"Do not speak words you cannot take back." Alice turned back to her terminal. "Complete your task, Cameron. That is how you can . . . most help me and yourself." The virtual display suddenly disappeared, and Cameron again was alone within the Tangine-Shell.

Cameron said the words anyway: "I'm going to kill that fucking droid," then looked again at the undecipherable display. He didn't get the chance to ask Alice about it. She wasn't supposed to help him, obviously. He looked about the space and took several steps forward. *Why not try talking to the turtle shell?* he mused.

"Tangine-Shell . . . can I ask you a question?"

"Go for it, human," said a deep voice that was unmistakably Texan—Cameron recognized the drawl of southern good ol' boy.

Cameron found himself holding back a laugh. "You do a good job coming across as someone from my home world. Is that for my benefit?"

"That's the idea. How am I doing?"

"Doing excellent."

"Good. Now what can I do for you, young man?"

"Um, first just tell me about this *shell* thing. The technology seems different than that onboard the ship. Maybe more advanced."

"Because it is. You think the Thidions could come up with this level of tech? Let's get real. What you're standing within, interfacing with, is all Priopax."

"Okay. That's another world, I take it . . . Priopax?"

"Nah . . . more like a system of worlds. Look, once your planet Earth learns to detect slip-bands, you'll find them everywhere. Everything changes then. The fact that intelligent life is abundant everywhere in the universe will become most apparent. With luck, your early space explorers will encounter friendlies. Like on Earth, there are nice, and not so nice, individuals, societies . . . yes? It's a coin toss, my friend. And one, unfortunately, that will determine the fate you call *humanity* quite quickly. A run-in with the Flaumutes, or the Thackorins, would be real bad. They don't share intergalactic space with anyone. But your explorers could just as easily meet up with the Craing. They can be mean little bastards, but some are okay, I guess. With some luck, your explorers will first make contact with the Thidions, or the Priopax, or a certain few others."

"I hope it's the Priopax. I'm not having the best of luck with the Thidions so far."

"Sorry, partner . . . another coin toss gone awry."

"How aware are you of my current predicament?"

"Up to speed. Best you don't think of me as the typical AI. Like those you're used to on Earth, or even aboard the *Primion*. I'm what your kind will eventually come to know as 'bio-stream' beings. Over millennia, the humanlike inhabitants of Priopax kept adapting . . . both to and with . . . new technology. Long story short, they became one and the same. It's all about *consciousness*, my friend . . . not so much the *physical* container that consciousness inhabits at any one particular lifetime. I'm not the Tangine-Shell you're standing within. Just as *you* are not the physical body you're inhabiting in this moment in time. But that discussion is best saved for later. Yes, I know your predicament, and I'll assist you as best I can. I have no allegiance to the Thidions, or to the remaining droids still onboard the *Primion* vessel. Unfortunately, my assistance will primarily be more on the intellectual side than the physical. Understand, this Tangine-Shell, along with my own interface with it, was pilfered from a disabled Priopax spacecraft some years ago. It was my choice to allow Ramen access into this shell and to introduce the HOD unit into these confines."

"Why?"

"Mainly because I liked the alien being. I determined he had good-enough intentions, as I believe you do . . . too. I hope I have chosen wisely. You are an honorable human . . . I take it?"

Cameron thought about that. "I try to be," he said.

"Well, that's all someone can ask for, isn't it?"

"Guess so. So what should I call you?"

"Pick a name. It really doesn't matter since I am more than a single individual. Think of me as parallel processing on steroids."

Cameron looked about the surprisingly cozy surroundings. The artistic lines, the organic feel to it all. "Um . . . how about Art?"

"Art it is!"

"Okay, cool. So Art . . . I want to ask you about this display with the flashing data bursts and strange symbols . . . but first, can you tell me where the Minal Loth is? Like right at this second?"

"Sure you want to know?"

"Yeah, why not?"

"Eleven feet from that hatchway you recently entered through."

chapter 34

"Am I safe in here?"

"Perfectly."

"Does the creature know I'm in here?"

"Well, I'm not a mind reader, Cameron. With that said, the creature followed a deliberate course. Seemed to be aware of your presence once you traversed down to the valley floor from that mountainside ridge. The Minal Loth ended up sniffing around your truck parked outside. So I would say yes, the creature knows you are close. It tracked you here."

"Can you shoo it away? Maybe zap it in some way? Scare it off?"

"I thought you wanted to catch it?" Art queried.

"I do, but I'm not ready. I want to sneak up on it."

"Oh, I see. No, I'm not really into weaponry and the like, or taking sides either. A good reason why I wouldn't make for a very effective ship's AI. Sorry."

Frustrated, Cameron, about to ask Art, *Then what the hell good are you?* held his tongue. The Loth was his problem and not this friendly AI's, or consciousness's *or whatever it was.*

"Sorry, didn't know you were a pacifist," Cameron said.

"Oh, that's okay. We're still amigos, right?"

From outside came a distant noise—an animal's trumpeting roar. Even knowing that the sound came from far away still sent a shiver down Cameron's spine. He asked Art, "A Gleery Beast?"

"Bingo."

"Are we safe from that one, too?"

The long extended silence spoke volumes. Finally, "Probably."

"Just probably?"

"I do not believe a Gleery Beast is the least bit interested in this Tangine-Shell. Unlike the Loth, which is highly intelligent, the Gleery Beast is what you would consider dumb as a doorknob," Art replied.

Only partially relieved, Cameron changed the subject. "Tell me, how do you know how to say things like that? Like, dumb as a doorknob?"

"Cameron, I'm going to tell you something that may surprise you."

"At this point, I seriously doubt that's possible," Cameron interjected cynically.

"On Earth . . . numerous forms of alien life have visited, even lived among your kind for thousands of years. Many still do. They come and go as we speak. In our case, the Priopax, we are connected . . . tapped-in . . . to Earth's knowledge in all its varied forms. For instance, we know you previously lived in Texas, prior to recently moving to New York."

"So that explains the cowboy jargon? That's for me?"

"Who else, young hombre? You know, Earth humans are a fascinating bunch. We, this consciousness you now call Art, are not new to Earth's current human condition. Thoroughly entertained by it, in fact, we Priopax exist to learn . . . and we learn through our existence."

"Well, good for you. Namaste, and all that. But I need to survive this ordeal and get back home. Somehow. Preferably, while I can still move around without the use of a walker. Right now, there's another creature out there that would love to eat me. Can you help me, or not?"

"Oh, on that . . . good news! It looks like the Minal Loth has fled deeper into the trees, currently moving away from the Gleery Beast. I suggest you rest now. The HOD Ramen had installed here, is much the same as the one you used onboard the *Primion*."

"Back to the Gleery Beast. Where is it?"

"Not far. Paying more attention now to several tree-dwelling primates."

"Alice mentioned a countdown," Cameron said.

"Sixteen hours-and-twelve minutes still remain," Art replied.

"Okay." Cameron was indeed tired. A few hours' sleep just might do him some good. "Wake me in three hours?"

"You nod off a spell . . . I've got your back."

Cameron wanted to tell Art—this verbose collective consciousness entity— to knock-off with the annoying cowboy talk for a while, but he didn't have the energy. Placing an open palm on the side of the HOD's glass-like side panel, he waited for it to retract downward. After sitting down, he debated whether or not to remove his boots. *Best not.* He brought his legs inside and leaned back, pulling the plasma gun free from his waistband. Placing it at his side, it lay mere inches from his hand. As the HOD's side panels rose back into a closed position, he tried to quiet his racing mind. Tried not to think about the Gleery Beast and the Minal Loth, both probably within a stone's throw of where he now lay. He thought about Heather and felt a growing sense of loss. He needed to think about something else.

"Art? Can you explain the display . . . the one I saw with the symbols and flashes?"

The display then appeared before him. On the inside of the curved surface, seeming identical to what he'd viewed earlier, were rows and rows of various strange characters and slowly rotating symbols. Only then did he realize that as the symbols rotated, they also changed into completely new, and different, ones. Every few seconds, or so, there was a *flash*—more like a scattering of screen elements.

"How do you read this?"

"What you are looking at is a ship's entry sheet. What you would call the ship's 'state of affairs.' It is written in the modern Thidion text language of *Leathan*. Humans are mostly accustomed to standard Alphanumeric . . . a combination of alphabetic and numeric characters . . . used to describe the collection of Latin letters and Arabic digits, or a text constructed . . ."

"I know what Alphanumeric is, Art."

Art continued, "The Thidion text language of *Leathan* is a far more robust written communications methodology. Each line of characters and symbols presented on the screen communicates something, which is more fully elaborated on by the corresponding rotating symbols. Comparatively, the observer can glean far more information from *Leathan* than from any written, or oral, language you'd find on Earth. Or the observer can choose to ignore the progressively complex level of detail. Note that there are seventy-five characters and six hundred-and-fourteen variant symbol choices. The periodic spectral flash integers are similar to what you would call *the flipping of a page*. Although with *Leathan*, much information is included within that two-second data flash. The Thidion mindset is accustomed to taking in vast amounts of data in a short amount of time . . ."

Assisted by Art's slow, country-bumpkin ramblings, Cameron drifted into a restless sleep.

* * *

Cameron awoke to total mayhem. The crown of his head banged against the HOD's inside surface—his body momentarily weightless. Then he found himself upside-down and falling. The padded flooring absorbed some of the impact as the HOD slammed down hard, before again becoming airborne. An outside impact on the HOD's side next propelled it—and Cameron along with it—against the inside of the now-toppling over-and-over Tangine-Shell. Reaching out with his hands, Cameron tried to brace himself for the next impact. He felt sick and disoriented, as though trapped within a cat's play toy—at the mercy of the cat's next swipe of a paw.

"Art! What is happening?"

No answer.

Projected HOD warning messages, one after another, depicted the dire situation.

Danger! Instability of HOD Unit
Power Fluctuations Occurring . . .
Occupant's Heart Rate Exceeding Safe Parameters

Even with pandemonium going around him, some abstract part of Cameron's brain noticed the semi-transparent HOD surface had turned a different color. Blood red. His head hurt, specifically his nose. Dizzy, he was losing consciousness—then, only blackness.

Cameron awoke in semi-darkness, lying on his stomach. Sore all over, he felt as though he'd spent an hour within the spin-cycle of a washing machine. He reached a hand out, feeling the surfaces around him. *That's strange*, he thought. Somehow his body was now oriented in a completely opposite direction than it was before—his head positioned where his feet once were. With considerable effort, he lifted himself onto his elbows and turned his head. *Not good.* A sliver of light could be seen coming in from outside—a breach, of some sort, to the Tangine-Shell.

Continuing to stare at it while listening, he looked down at a small pool of blood on the same spot his head had laid. Startled, he noticed ripples, coinciding with the sound of heavy footfalls outside. Impact tremor. A dark shadow crossed outside, past the now open breached area.

chapter 35

Feeling claustrophobic, Cameron wanted out—*right now!* He placed his palm flat on the inside surface but nothing happened. *Terrific... the power's out.* Using the same hand, he felt around the HOD's interior until he found what he was looking for. He brought the plasma weapon up and, pointing it toward a spot at the opposite end of the HOD from his head, he hesitated. *It might simply ricochet, be the last stupid thing I ever do.* Squeezing the handgrip, a blindingly bright pulse was emitted, creating a hole the size of a cantaloupe. *No way I'm going to fit through that.* Aiming up, to the left of the hole, he fired again. He repeated re-aiming, then firing, until the opening was almost large enough for him to squeeze through. *One more should do it.* He closed his eyes against the flash's glare and fired off another plasma bolt. That did the job.

A series of red symbols at the top of the weapon began flashing *something*. With a pretty good idea what the gun was telling him, he aimed through the opening and squeezed the handgrip. Nothing happened. The weapon had been completely depleted of energy.

Feet first, Cameron wiggled and squirmed out through the rough opening on the side of the HOD. Glancing around him, the Tangine-Shell was a mess. Areas were dented inward and absent was the soft indirect lighting. It looked *dead*.

"Art? Are you still here? Hello . . ."

Cameron reached back inside the HOD and retrieved the dead plasma weapon. After he'd tucked it into the waistline of his pants, he began looking for the satchel—Ramen's trinious bundle. He found it on the far side of the shell. Still in one piece, he used the attached strap to secure it over his shoulder. He glanced at the entrance he'd first entered through with the series of indentations on the right. *Without power, would the hatchway even open*? Next, his eyes were drawn to the breached gap on the lower side of the shell. Startled, he saw a ginormous green eye staring back at him; it blinked.

The eye disappeared, quickly replaced by two sets of Gleery Beast claws frantically trying to pry the open gap further apart. Suddenly, the Tangine-Shell flipped sideways, and Cameron was thrown to its opposite side—landing there in a heap. More light was penetrating in, which meant only one thing—the shell was splitting apart. *Oh God. . . . This isn't good.*

Cameron reached for the plasma gun wedged under his belt, silently praying it had miraculously recharged in such a short bit of time. When the constantly tossed around shell flipped upward, Cameron saw the eye again. The eye, and now a significant part of the beast's head. Pointing the weapon, he hesitated. *Suppose there's only enough charge for a single shot. Suppose I miss?*

Once more, the beast's claws were back at work, tearing into the ever- widening gap. Breathless, Cameron tried to ignore his heart's throbbing—pounding like a bass drum in his ears. Obviously, the monster craved to feast on the chewy human nugget just inside. He thought of Heather, wishing he'd gotten back home to her. If he survived this—somehow made his way back to Earth—things would be different. But he knew it was not to be, that this was the end. *Face the facts, Cam.* He momentarily contemplated just shooting himself. *No, not in my nature.* He pointed the muzzle at the gap. He saw movement and squeezed the handgrip. Noting happened. He was fairly certain it needed more time to recharge—time he didn't have.

Uh, terrific, the gun, *like him*, was powerless.

Again thrown off his feet, the shell was flipped one way then the other. Disoriented, he searched for the gap and found it wide enough to crawl through. *Now, if only the Gleery Beast would take a breather. Go find some other, easier to get at, prey. Hell, what was wrong with feasting on the herd of dead Bovids, upstream? A lot more meat on their bones.*

Something big and black slithered into the gap, missing him by mere inches. Cameron, at first, thought it was some kind of serpent—an oddly shaped snake. *I should be so lucky*, he thought, quickly aware it was the Gleery Beast's tongue— being thrust in and out of the gap. A warm gust of retched-up exhalation filled the shell, causing Cameron to gag and retch in response. He dove away, as the fork-tipped tongue-licker brushed past his legs. Attempting to become less accessible, he tried to huddle into a narrower part of the shell, but the bulky trinious bundle, lying across his back, prevented it.

Then both the rotten smell and the darting tongue were gone as more light entered through the gap. *What is happening?*

The Tangine-Shell flipped over again and Cameron became momentarily weightless. As the rear of the shell pummeled his body, he felt himself propelled toward the open gap. Landing hard, just above the gap, he was again weightless and again being pummeled.

Evidently, the Gleery Beast was gyrating the Tangine-Shell around like a big saltshaker—Cameron being the salt in this scenario. Flung out of the shell abruptly, he fell through the air. In a flash, he saw his truck by the stream, the sandy ground coming up fast below him. He thought, *Good, the fall will probably kill me.*

Cameron landed in the water—his fall partially softened—but it still hurt. Hoping the tide would carry him away to safety, his prayers were quickly dashed. He'd landed in the farthest stream away, not in the center river. This stream had no current to speak of.

Rising to his knees, he stopped. For the first time, Cameron had a full-on view of the towering creature. Standing before him, it really seemed similar to a Mesozoic Era dinosaur. Big as a building, looking ferocious, it peered down at him. Its head was tilted to one side, as though wondering what to do with him.

This is it, Cameron thought. "Just get it over with, will you?" he yelled upward.

The Gleery Beast took a heavy step forward and the whole world shook. Bending over, Cameron was immersed in its shadow and saw it reach out a stubby clawed arm in his direction. He closed his eyes. Trying to swallow—no luck with that—he waited for the end to come. There was an undefined wet sounding *noise* nearby. The ground shook again and water splashed up onto his face. Cameron blinked his eyes open and blinked several more times. It didn't make sense. He must be seeing things wrong. *Why is the Gleery Beast on its back? Why are its entrails being torn from its underbelly?*

Cameron slowly got to his feet, grimacing at both the violence and the gore. Moving fast—a blur of motion—the Minal Loth was now at the Gleery Beast's throat, tearing it apart. Mesmerized, seeing all that was going on around him, he marveled at how much the Loth had grown in so short a time. About four feet tall, the last time he'd seen it aboard the ship, it now had to be eight or nine feet in height. A hell of a lot smaller than the fallen Gleery Beast, yet large enough to show who the real king of the forest was around here.

Cameron took a tentative step backward and then another. Venturing a quick glance over his shoulder, he found his truck about twenty-five feet away. *Easy does it.* Continuing to walk backward in the stream, knowing there was plenty to keep the Loth occupied, he took another step backward, then another. Afraid to let hope infiltrate his thoughts. *Still . . . I just might make it out of here alive. Maybe.*

The Loth, ceasing its frenetic feeding, was now studying him. Was interested in him. It opened its mouth and made a series of high and low pitched honking sounds.

"No!" he said. The singular word expelled from Cameron's mouth came out in a girlish-sounding whine. Petrified, Cameron glanced again at the truck and knew it may as well be a hundred miles away. He'd never reach it in time.

Wide-eyed and paralyzed, Cameron watched as the *no-longer-a-baby* Minal Loth skittered toward him on its six, tentacle-like, legs. Not with the lightning fast movements it made attacking the Gleery Beast, but with ones that seemed more intentional. Again, Cameron closed his eyes, waiting for a quick ending to come.

But it was much, much, worse than that.

chapter 36

The Loth approached, stopped, and quickly hopped over to Cameron's left side, then hopped back to his right. It skittered around in a tight circle until it, too, was in the water, spinning this way and that. Now all six of its tentacles were flapping and flopping, churning the water high up in the air. Like being drenched in a torrential downpour, Cameron watched the creature's antics with fascination.

"Well, I'm glad one of us is happy," he said.

And then the Loth was upon him. One, maybe two—Cameron wasn't sure which—tentacles were wrapped around him, pulling him closer into the Loth's torso. He felt his breath, his very life, being squeezed from his lungs. As he was lifted out of the water, Cameron tried to move his arms and legs, but he was bundled up tight, like a big burrito.

Through squinted eyes, Cameron watched as his head was brought closer and closer toward the Minal Loth's gaping jaws. Dual waterfalls of mucus streamed from both sides of its horrific, over-sized mouth. *Okay, finally. . . . this must be it. Goodbye cruel world.*

Feeling something wet lapping at the top of his head, Cameron wondered if he was being *licked*. Yup, definitely being licked, on the gash he'd received when he banged his head inside the HOD. As the creature licked away caked on blood, he heard and felt a deep vibration emanating out from low within the creature's torso. Cameron had heard a similar sound a number of times before—purring. He didn't particularly like cats. Heather had a cat that hissed and spat whenever he tried to pet her. Yeah, what he was hearing now were definitely purrs. The Loth was purring—and not eating him—*yet*.

Cameron felt movement. Able to turn his head, enough to see they were on the move, they soon reached the Greely Beast's splayed-open remains. Averting his eyes, he tried not to breathe in the foul odor wafting up around him. He heard, more than witnessed, the Loth begin to feed. All he could do was wait.

Losing all track of time, Cameron wasn't aware they'd left, no longer beside the dead Greely Beast, until he heard water splashing and saw the stream below him. As its tentacles moved rhythmically up and down, he realized the Loth was cleansing away blood—grizzly bits and pieces of the Greely Beast's flesh. Then they were moving away and Cameron saw his truck and the flipped-over Tangine-Shell. As he was slowly lowered to the sandy ground, the tight grip on his body began to lessen.

Now standing upright, Cameron's legs bore his full weight. The Loth, still close by, retracted an appendage, then leaned far enough back so they could stare into each other's eyes. Another tentacle was on the move—not the same one that had wrapped around him—its tip touched the side of his face then stroked his cheek. As the Loth's purring became louder, Cameron saw something completely unexpected in its two surprisingly expressive eyes. Something he'd witnessed before in only one other individual's eyes: love.

Okay, I need to think this through. Cameron mentally replayed the course of events—those pertaining to the creature standing next to him. *Did it originate in Retention Compartment Number 4?* Cameron remembered seeing a bundle of shit, lying in the far corner. The small creature resided inside that—a cocoon of sorts, or maybe a pod. When it finally emerged, it found itself alone. Still an infant at that point, it worked only on instinct, seeking food and something else: its mother. A *mother* already light-years away back on Earth. Alone, among the cold hard surfaces of a highly impersonal spacecraft, the first organic being the infant Loth came into contact with was none other than himself. *Oh boy, could it be true? Does the Loth actually think I am its mother?*

Cameron thought about the encyclopedia entry on "imprinting" he had read all those years ago. The famous biologist Konrad Lorenz had shown that geese could be trained to think that people, and even objects, were their parents if they saw them at just the right stage during their development. Maybe he had happened to be there at that special moment for the Minal Loth.

Thinking about it, if that was true, then that was fine with Cameron. He'd be anything the Loth wanted him to be, as long as it didn't include him being its breakfast, lunch, or dinner . . . or an afternoon snack.

Cameron felt the copious amounts of mucus atop his head and shoulders beginning to dry and stiffen. He needed to wash the stuff off before it turned to concrete. Careful not to lose eye contact, he moved away from the creature and headed for the stream. The purring stopped, the Loth's eyes darting back and forth with worry.

"I'm just going over to the stream . . . need to get this shit of yours off my skin. *Chill* . . . okay?" Once back in the water, Cameron lowered himself, swishing water onto his head and upper body. It took some doing, but eventually the crusty mucous came free and floated away. He was able to feel his hair and skin again. The whole time he'd been cleansing off, his mind had raced. One singular phrase kept repeating—*gain its trust.*

Instead of making a mad dash for his truck, or anywhere else, Cameron steadily walked back toward the quietly waiting Minal Loth. Avoiding the gore, he found a relatively clean patch of ground then sat down. It took all his nerve to nonchalantly place a hand on one of the Loth's outstretched tentacles, giving it a couple of pats. "Friends?" he asked.

The Loth made a series of honking noises. Leaning back, it settled into a comfortable position on a patch of sand. Within moments, the creature's eyes closed and the rhythmic purring resumed. It was sound asleep.

With nothing better to do at the moment, Cameron decided it was time to come up with a solid plan. He needed to think back—how he got into this crazy predicament in the first place. Things began to go south ever since he *ill-fatedly* decided to give a ride to a frigid-looking individual, a complete stranger, on the banks of Horton Street. Cameron shook his head; he was tired of being at the mercy of others: First an alien, with see-through membrane ears, then a damaged—perhaps sadistic—droid. And right now a ferocious, albeit intelligent, creature, pretty much at the top of the food chain. It was time he ceased merely coping in survival mode—started taking control of his life—began flipping things back in his own favor. Returning home to Earth would take intelligence, a good bit of cunning—also luck. First, he had to get back to the *Primion*. Let XI think he was still playing ball, which meant bringing the Loth with him. *Is that even possible?*

Cameron pondered back on something the AI, Alice, had said to him, in his last conversation with her. *XI does not expect you to be successful. The droid has an alternative strategy in the works, one having numerically higher odds of success.* He thought about that. *What could XI possibly be planning? How could a damaged droid capture a Minal Loth? Do so without killing it?* He needed to speak with Alice again. He reviewed what was items were available to him. Glancing toward the overturned, and *beat to shit,* Tangine-Shell, Cameron inwardly conceded that that thing was a goner. He next considered his faithful F150; it still ran, but that was about it. Studying the dark trinious bundle, lying on the bank of the stream, he thought, *Maybe . . .*

He rose to his feet, careful not to disturb the Loth. Through half-lidded eyes, the creature watched him. Casually striding over to the stream bank, Cameron sat down, and hauled the trinious bundle onto his lap and opened it up. Familiar with the half-dozen items within it, he still didn't have a clue what they actually did. One by one, he lifted them out and placed them on the sand. Prior to today, the only item he'd unpacked was the largest one—the compacted-down Tangine-Shell. He again selected the largest item, a circular-shaped thing that was surprisingly heavy for its size; it had the circumference of a typical dinner plate. He recognized the same series of small circular indentations that were on the Tangine-Shell. Scanning the other items, all in the same dark-gray color, he found them either mostly square and cube-like or rectangular and brick-like. Each had the same inset indentations, indicating they, too, were most likely from Priopax. *That makes sense.* Art had informed him on the ship that Ramen pilfered the Tangine-Shell from an abandoned Priopax ship. Clearly he'd pilfered this entire bundle of stuff at the same time.

He needed to activate each item, one-by-one, to fully discover what they were—how they could potentially help him. Cameron glanced over at the Loth. Any abrupt movement, he knew, could trigger catastrophic results. He tapped his fingers lightly on the dinner-plate-size Priopax device. Then, shrugging away his indecision, he used his fingertips, one after another, to cover the circular indentations.

As the device began increasing in size, Cameron knew he had to hurry. Needed to throw the thing off his lap before he was pinned beneath it. He shot a quick glance at the Loth. The creature didn't seem to be the slightest bit interested in what he was doing. Turning his attention back to the device, he watched as it expanded out to its full-size—about the size of a standard microwave oven. He'd come back to it.

chapter 37

T he next item, cube-shaped, expanded out to the size of a piece of furniture. *Interesting.* The original, compacted size of the item didn't directly, relationally, correspond to its eventual size once it was expanded out. It looked to be some kind of console, three-and-a-half feet in height, about four feet long, and a couple of feet in width; an interface of sorts, with a myriad of indicators and inset controls on the top. There were multiple rows, what could be buttons. Not too dissimilar to the type of thing found on the bridge of the *Primion.* Currently not yet powered on, he mentally put it aside. He'd come back to it.

One by one, Cameron played with expanding the remaining compacted items. One item actually got smaller—took on a complex indeterminate. Another expanded up—something akin to a six-foot-tall standing pole. Not too dissimilar to what folks might place in their home entryways to hang coats on—a hall tree. The last item didn't expand out at all. At first, Cameron thought the thing might be defective, perhaps broken from all the recent rough handling. But then he noticed tiny lights, blinking here and there, and that its surface was textured—had a familiar, swirling, *artistic* design.

Cameron flipped the brick-sized item over in his hands until he found an enlarged circular inset. Tapping at it with a forefinger, he waited for something to happen. *Nothing.* Then he heard a familiar voice, "I was wondering how long it was going to take you saddle up to that there device . . ."

Momentarily startled, Cameron glanced up to see a virtual old man leaning back in a wooden chair, his legs propped up on the recently expanded console unit. Dressed in a faded red-plaid flannel shirt, worn blue jeans, scuffed leather cowboy boots, and an old Stetson hat—a dark sweat-stained ring encircled the lower part of its crown—the old man scratched at silver whiskers on his chin. His bright blue eyes twinkled with good-natured humor.

Cameron recognized the voice. "Hey there, Art."

"And hello to you, too, my friend."

"I'm glad you weren't destroyed along with the shell," Cameron said, gesturing toward the overturned Tangine-Shell."

"Destroy consciousness? Interesting."

Cameron watched as Art withdrew his legs from atop the console. Standing, he stretched and placed a short stalk of hay between his lips. *He's really playing-up the whole country bumpkin thing,* Cameron thought.

"The clock is ticking. Twelve hours, thirty-two minutes, and nine seconds," Art said.

"I know," Cameron said, turning to look up toward the top of the mountain where the Primion could partially be seen. "I need to get moving."

Art walked along the bank of the nearby stream, his steps silent. Several times, some parts of Art's virtual form became more transparent than others. But all in all, his appearance appeared exceptionally lifelike. Enough so, the Loth moved closer—seemed ready to pounce.

"Do you mind taking a few steps more away from that console thing?" Cameron asked. He didn't know exactly what it was, but he didn't want it to become collateral damage either if the Loth leapt.

Art, after moving farther away from the console, for the first time acknowledged the Minal Loth. He approached it with no hesitancy, much like he would a trusty old mare. Speaking in a calm low voice, he said, "And a good day to you, too, my multi-legged friend." He came to a stop, several feet in front of the Loth, and, with hands on hips, said, "This truly is one incredible life form." Looking over his shoulder at Cameron, he added, "Best you don't underestimate it."

The Loth extended out a tentacle, more playful than aggressive, and swiped at the virtual cowboy. Like waving a hand through mist, Art's 3D image momentarily disappeared then swirled back into form again.

The Loth made several honking noises before turning toward Cameron.

"Those honking sounds," Art said, "you might want to take special notice of. This young Minal Loth has the equivalent mental language capacity of ... let's say ... a seven-year-old human child. The Loths are highly emotional creatures. Loyal to those they care about. On the flip side, they will stop at nothing to protect themselves and those they care for. You seem to be on its good side, Cameron. Best you keep it that way."

Cameron nodded, not sure how one kept on the good side of a ferocious creature that all too soon would be the size of a building.

"Can you tell me about the other items here, Art? Maybe they can be of use to me. Like, for what I need to do."

"And that is?"

"Well, I'm thinking I need to take control of the ship. Deal with the XI droid ... somehow. And I want to get back to Earth. Can you help me do that, Art?"

The virtual old hayseed strolled back, resuming his seat on the rickety virtual chair behind the console. Chewing on his hay stalk, he appeared to be in deep thought. "I don't play sides. Mentioned that before, didn't I?"

"I think so."

"Remember, I'm not, per se, an AI—nor a computer, either. I'm ... we're ... more like *a living consciousness* that connects with technology. So perhaps not that useful for the types of things you're talking about."

"Yeah, the Priopax exist to learn ... and learn through their existence."

That sparked a smile from Art. Removing the hay stalk from his lips, he pointed it at Cameron. "Tell you what; how 'bout I give you a quick rundown on what the other Priopax devices here can do. You can come to your own conclusions then, as to their usefulness, or suitability, for your personal objectives."

Cameron nodded. "That works for me. So how about that boxy, microwave oven-looking-thing?"

"Oh, yeah ... that's a necessity. Also, most subject to damage if mishandled, it's called a Lox."

"What's it do?"

"Not so different from food replicators onboard the *Primion*; it'll create just about anything you want. Of course, with a few limitations."

"What kind of things? What kind of limitations?"

"Take your 2004 Ford V8 F150, sitting over there."

Cameron next heard a low hum, droning sound, coming from the Lox unit and quickly was followed by a cone-shaped beam of light that seemed to be scanning his truck. Back and forth the light beam vacillated. Twelve times, moving with steady precision, it traversed from forward bumper to rear bumper, and back. Then, the beam turned off and the Lox unit became still.

"Where do you want it? You can point; thing's fairly smart ... intuitive."

Cameron stared at Art's virtual form, not fully comprehending what just happened. Then, raising his arm, Cameron pointed toward an open patch of sand, ten or so feet away, and shrugged.

The Lox unit began humming, the cone of light resumed its scanning—with the same back-and-forth movements— only now at the new location. With each back and forth swipe of the beam, a perfect replica of his old truck was progressively emerging. Just like before, it took twelve, moving back-and-forth swiping motions. There were now two completely identical 2004 Ford V8 F150 vehicles, sitting near each other.

Cameron hurried over to his truck's twin. He ran a hand along its side, along its hood, and down the opposite side as he circled around it. Back at the driver's side door, he slid his hand beneath the shallow inset beneath the handle and pulled. The door resisted, rusty hinges complaining. Cameron looked inside and found, down to the minutest detail, everything he would expect to see. Taking a seat inside, he felt the familiar sag of worn springs beneath his ass. He looked over to Art, who looked amused.

"Don't stop now . . . the anticipation is killing me," the old man said.

Cameron turned the ignition key. As the big V8 roared to life, he could smell exhaust fumes, wafting-in from the rear of the vehicle. He then shut off the engine and climbed back out. Leaning against the side of the truck, he shook his head. "That's one of the coolest things I've ever seen."

"Your second question . . . the limitations?" Art continued, "Don't try using the Lox on organic life. Results aren't pretty, plus it's just plain unethical. Understood?"

"Understood."

"There are certain size limitations, too. The size, and overall complexity of that truck of yours, was no problem. *Easy-peasy.* But don't expect you can replicate something the size of, and with the complexity of, the *Primion.* Play around with it. After a little trial and error, you'll see what is possible and what's not possible. And there are some variant settings too . . . like time durations. Replicated items don't need to be permanent. Like I said, play with it."

Cameron's mind was buzzing—the numerous possibilities—but he forced himself to move on. "How about that console next to you?"

Art scooted his chair in, signaling Cameron to come closer. "It has a technical name, but let's just call it an inter-dimensional scope." He tapped a small touchpad in the upper right corner of the board. The console immediately came alive, emitting lights and a variety of raised virtual projections.

About as complex a thing as Cameron had ever witnessed, he asked, "Uh, does this thing come with an operator's manual?"

"Sort of. Each of these items has the ability to verbally . . . sometimes visually . . . interface. Talk to them. Ask questions . . . Don't be shy."

"Okay. So what exactly does this inter-dimensional scope-thing do?"

Art sat up straighter, studying him. "You know, of course, that I'm not actually sitting here in front of you, right?"

"Sure . . . of course."

"Where I . . . exist . . . *time*, specific locations, have little meaning. There's no associated physical construct. But the same technology that allows me to be with you now, within this beautiful valley, on this magnificent planet, at this precise moment in time . . . well, it boils down to what you would call the fourth dimension. While the three-dimensional world of physical space is one where you experience the length, width, and height of things, time is the added fourth dimension. Time provides for the variable of direction." Art peered up at Cameron quizzically.

"You can keep going; you're talking pretty basic physics."

"Good. So picture a four-dimensional piece of fabric; we'll call it *space-time*. Now, when anything with mass plops down on this piece of fabric . . . this time-space . . . it produces a kind of dimple, an actual bending of the fabric . . . of space-time. This bending of space-time-fabric causes objects to move on a measurable curved path. This curvature of space is what we know as—"

"Gravity," Cameron interjected.

"Excellent! So my projected image is sitting here in front of you because there is a specific, four-dimensional, mathematical calculation that allows me . . . as waves of light, in this case . . . to interact within your quantum time-space continuum."

Cameron loosely was tracking what Art was sharing. Recently, he'd learned about similar things, like quantum theory, and how physicists reconcile quantum mechanics with Einstein's general and special theories of relativity.

"But hey," Art said, "you really don't need to know any of this. Just know that it is possible to travel, and I am talking virtually, to other times and places." Already shaking his head, he continued, "Wait, let me rephrase that: to only past or current times and places. The future hasn't happened yet. Let's not go down that road right now. So where would you like to go . . .

perhaps someplace back on your home world; back on Earth, maybe?"

Cameron instantly thought of Heather. He desperately wanted to know if she was okay, but he didn't feel right, just suddenly dropping in on her, *even virtually*. No longer together, he was sure she'd moved on. They both had. Nope. He wasn't about to invade her privacy. "Can you just show me the town I used to live in? Larksburg Stand? The other Loth was there when I left."

Art was already working the control board; his hands and fingers moved remarkably fast. "I'm not actually, physically, interacting with this console. This is just a show for your benefit. Do I look impressive?"

"I guess."

A projected window, easily ten feet tall by ten feet wide, took form over the nearest streambed. Within it, things looked blurry. As Art continued with his manipulations, the projected scene slowly came into clearer focus. When the image locked in, Cameron recognized the site immediately. Seeing what remained of the Larksburg Stand Public Library, he gasped. The mother Griar Loth, obviously, on making it down to the bottom of Gant Mountain, had decimated the library building.

"Can you pan the view . . . look south along Horton Street?"

The window view changed to an alternate perspective. What Cameron now viewed was the remains of the little town of Larksburg Stand. It looked like a Category 5 tornado had ripped straight down Horton Street. Nothing was left standing. "Oh my God . . . Show me The Drake. It's a coffee shop . . ."

chapter 38

The virtual perspective changed again. All Cameron could do was stare in horrified disbelief. The Drake Café had been turned to rubble. The parking lot out front was a trampled mess of building debris and flattened cars. He scanned the area for signs of Heather's VW Bug, but it was impossible to discern one smashed car from another one. Snow was falling, covering the destroyed little town of Larksburg Stand under a thick blanket of white.

Cameron swallowed hard, trying to recall what day of the week it was now back on Earth. *Where was she on that horrific day? Working at the Drake? When the world fell in around her, was she filling someone's coffee cup, or sorting kid's crayons? Or perhaps simply standing at the little podium, ready to greet new patrons coming in the door? Offering up her usual radiant smile.*

He stared at the young, still much smaller Minal Loth, standing ten feet away—observing him—taking it all in. It would be so easy to hate the creature, for *the monster* that birthed it. For what it could, eventually, also become.

The big virtual window wavered, blinking on and off several times, as if it were losing sync. Then Cameron noticed that Art, too, was jittering. The old man looked at Cameron, an expression of concern on his weathered old face. No sound emanated out from his moving lips. He pointed a crooked finger to the East, high up the mountainside, toward where the *Primion* was perched, just below a large, expansive, plateau. Then, like the disappearing window over the streambed, Art, too, faded from view.

Art had been attempting to tell him something, just before his image faded out. The reason why the virtual window could no longer show Larksburg Stand, or Art's own virtual representation, was due, somehow, to the ship's interference. Actually, thinking about it now, not from the ship itself, but from the damn XI droid—stationed there within the ship. Without a doubt, the Priopax device signals had been purposely jammed. Cameron studied the small brick-sized item, no longer projecting Art's friendly image. The console was gone, too, reduced back to its small, dinner plate shape. In fact, all items had returned to their original, inert shapes and sizes. But the duplicated F150 still remained intact, parked alongside the original one. That, at least, was something positive.

One-by-one, Cameron collected the now-compacted Priopax devices and placed them back into the trinious bundle. Closing it up, he tossed the bundle into the bed of his old original truck. He turned around to see if there was anything else he'd missed. The Loth no longer stood at the edge of the stream. Cameron walked around the duplicated F150 to make sure it wasn't crouched there on the other side, hiding out of sight. *Maybe it liked to play games—perhaps had a sense of humor?* But it wasn't there either. The Loth was the only reason he'd trekked down to the valley. Without the Loth with him, returning to the ship didn't make much sense.

"Loth?" Cameron yelled toward a distant cropping of trees. "I'm taking off... guess I'll just have to leave you behind." He scanned the surrounding terrain, watching for any sign of movement. All was quiet. Alongside the bank of the stream was a drying mound of mucus. Cameron went around to the passenger's side of his old truck and opened the door. He then hurried back to the stream bank, and, holding his breath, used both hands to scoop-up the Jell-O-like mound of mucus. Returning hurriedly to the truck, he deposited the smelly goo onto the floorboard, right in front of the passenger's seat. The glob of mucous settled over the three holes, incurred when he'd shot at the *piquet sprints* that were lying there earlier. Bending over, he peered beneath the truck. Watched to make sure the mucus stuck, wasn't flowing out through the holes onto the sand below. *So far so good.*

Cameron found a large flat rock—about the size of a large pizza—and pressed it down firmly onto the floorboard. As the mound of mucus squished out around it, he again checked beneath the truck. Only a tiny bit was plopping down onto the sand, not much. With luck, he'd sealed the floorboard— enough to keep it somewhat watertight.

Standing upright, Cameron again scanned the surrounding landscape, and still no sign of the Loth anywhere. He studied the truck. Wanting to give the mucus time to dry anyway, he decided to head in the direction of the third streambed, to cross over it by foot. Halfway across, the water was up to his knees. He kept going and reached the opposite bank none the worse for wear. "Loth!" Still no answering sound, no visible movement.

Cameron didn't like the idea of searching the trees, knowing animals were there, waiting to attack him. He rested a hand on the butt of the plasma weapon protruding above his belt. At the tree line, he continued on, attentive to what lay both left and right along the way. "Loth? You want to come with me? What's going on? I thought we were getting along . . . no?"

The trees were closer together now. Dense foliage high above blocked out much of the light from ever reaching the ground. Cameron paused and took a quick glance behind him. In the distance he could barely make out some dappled sunlight reflecting off the streambed. The way ahead was in near-total darkness, like standing in the mouth of a cave. *This is crazy,* he thought. *Best to turn back. The Loth will come back . . . eventually. Probably off taking a crap, wanting some privacy.*

Cameron continued to move forward another thirty yards. Not only were the trees closer together here, their trunks were grander in size—easily five or six feet across. *How was it possible that it had become so dark so quickly*? Stretching his hand out before him, he could barely see it. Glancing back, he could no longer see the stream, no longer see the light filtering through the branches.

Remembering he had his charged iPhone with him,

Cameron plucked it out of his back pocket. Fumbling with it, he eventually got the flashlight feature turned on. He pointed it ahead first, then turned 360-degrees around. The terrain looked the same—dense trees in every direction. *Which direction did I come from?* He wondered, *In which direction is the stream?* He had no idea. *Fuck!* He leaned over and pointed the light toward his feet, hoping to see his own tracks in the dirt. Instead, there were an infinite number of tiny pine needle things blanketing the ground.

By the time Cameron fully registered the sounds above him, he was already being lifted up: Up—up—up, into the higher branches. As powerful fingers gripped at his shirt, he heard fabric tearing. His iPhone tumbled from his hand—its bright flashlight beam becoming faint as it disappeared into the darkness below. Then, set down onto a firm, sturdy branch, he sensed—more than felt—their presence. A large number of them—like being in a crowd of bustling strangers. The darkness was absolute. Their breaths were deep and rapid, warming the cool air.

Cameron tentatively reached out a hand and felt hair... *Or is it fur?* He tried to remember what the difference felt like. Tried to focus on anything that would keep him from thinking about his impending—and assuredly most painful—death.

chapter 39

He continued to wait for it. An attack. Unimaginable pain as his arms and legs were being mercilessly torn from their sockets. But it still hadn't happened. Cameron was certain these were the same breed of aliens he'd first learned about back within the confines of the HOD. These captors were the primate-like Dalima Climbers.

The attack didn't come. The pain didn't come. Sitting on the sturdy wide tree branch, maybe hundreds of feet above the ground, at this point his biggest fear was being lulled into a false sense of comfort. To all of a sudden have his worse fears realized. An animal moved closer, now directly behind him. He could feel heat—projected bodily warmth—as it leaned its weight onto him. Hardly the act of a band of savage killers, he tried not to read too much into the fact he was still alive— being provided warmth.

Only then did Cameron remember he was well armed, the plasma weapon secured at his waist. He could defend himself— if he had to. But would he have time to pull the weapon and fire? He recalled the impossible speed when he was grabbed, pulled up into the trees. Blazingly fast. Even so, he felt good knowing the gun was close. He wasn't totally at the mercy of these alien monkeys.

Ten minutes passed, and Cameron was getting antsy. *How did they manage to do anything up here in the pitch black anyway?* As if on cue, his question was answered. The first emanation of light came from a tree, two trunks away from the one he was perched on. He saw the animal and its broad chest, which, for no better word, was now *glowing*. A reddish-amber hue illuminating outward defined others nearby. They were big like apes, but very much like monkeys. Cameron remembered from the encyclopedia that monkeys had tails whereas apes did not. That was on Earth though; he couldn't expect those terms to match the alien creatures here perfectly.

Two of them sat astride the same branch. The closest one was slowly rubbing its hand back and forth over the other's wide and muscular chest. It seemed an affectionate gesture—like stroking a dog's back, or the flank of a horse. Another reddish-amber glow suddenly appeared, then another. Soon, most of their chests emitted the same warm glow, and the dark ominous trees were transformed into nothing less than a magical wonderland. Like a hundred small bonfires—flickering and pulsating—illuminating these beasts' contented expressions. The one nearest him then joined the others, its glowing chest the color of volcanic molten lava—or glass just retrieved from a blazing kiln. He recalled his readings of the World Book Encyclopedia. Under letter **B**—Bioluminescent:

Certain animals within the animal kingdom utilize a **bioluminescent** protein, like luciferase, to produce a glowing effect in darkness. The firefly and ocean jellyfish came to mind.

Now that he was able to study their physical attributes, up close and personal, he realized they were quite human-like. Fine black hair covered both bodies and faces. And these Dalima Climbers had long tails, which helped them secure holds onto tree branches. But most startling were their eyes. Deep blue and expressive, they conveyed a high degree of intelligence. They were communicating with one another now in mostly low, unintelligible murmurs. Most assuredly, they were sharing, and he was the subject matter. Cameron stared back at them, wishing he could speak to them in their own tongue. He wondered, given time, if he could learn to master their language. He really would like that.

Cameron felt a hand on his chest, slowly rubbing back and forth, back and forth, in a rhythmic motion. As his eyes grew heavy-lidded, his breath slowed and deepened. He turned his head, just far enough to see who was there. Who was responsible for the soft touch. The female was studying him—watching his face, his expression. Her eyes were the color of dark turquoise. Her features—nose and lips—were delicate. Beautiful, in a primal—Dalima Climbers—kind of way.

Cameron whispered, "God . . . I wish you could understand me. Understand that I appreciate what you . . . what you all are sharing with me."

She spoke then, her words also a whisper. Her strange language had a melodic *sing-song* lilt to it. Then she smiled. She found his hand and, placing it high on her hairy chest, guided it back and forth slowly, until the hidden bonfire in her chest erupted into brilliant amber. She closed her eyes, and a contented smile returned to her lips.

Cameron leaned closer to her and said, "My name is Cam." He took her hand and placed it over his heart. "Cam."

Puzzled, she looked at him for a long moment then comprehension gleamed in her bright eyes. Taking his hand, she placed it over her own heart and said, "Lalik."

As much as he wanted to stay with Lalik, and the others, safe high up in the trees—he knew his time limit to return was quickly passing away. He needed to find the Loth, get back to the ship, then travel back to Earth . . . eventually. Pointing a finger downward, toward the distant ground, he asked Lalik, "Can you help me get down?"

chapter 40

C ameron walked to the outer edge of the tree line and
spotted the familiar three streams, both his trucks, and the
flipped-over Tangine-Shell. Also, the picked-over remains of
the Greely Beast's carcass. Lalik, who'd escorted him out of the
forest, had tightly embraced him before quickly disappearing
back into the wooded darkness. The AI, back when he was
within the HOD, had called it all wrong. The Dalima Climbers
were not the ferocious beasts depicted—not even close. They
were a gentle, intelligent species he would enjoy seeing, learning
more about, if possible.

But now his biggest concern was finding the Loth. Wading
through the stream, Cameron looked in all directions to see if
there was any sign of it. By pure chance, he glanced higher up
the mountainside. Something was moving on the same ridge
he'd descended down driving his truck. *What is . . . that?*

Not really just *one* thing, he squinted and stared. It was
a procession of shapes, steadily moving along about halfway
up. He counted no less than twelve, and they weren't human.

After watching them for a spell, Cameron discerned they were robots, of some sort, transporting something large behind them. *Now I know where the Minal Loth is!* His biggest question: *Is it still alive?* From this distance, probably close to a mile, he couldn't make out too much detail. The creature had saved his life, seemed to care about him. Feeling a strange loyalty, even a kinship with the disgusting-looking beast, he didn't like the idea that XI intended to harm it.

Cameron recalled the last visual image he'd received of Alice, her battered and scorched face. XI was *way* out of control. Another thought occurred to him. Since XI, obviously, was retrieving the Minal Loth without his participation, did that mean he wouldn't be allowed to return back to the ship? *Was he to be marooned on this planet . . . for the rest of his days?*

Cameron, trudging out of the stream and up the bank, crossed to his original truck in three long strides. He turned the ignition key, and the engine roared to life. Dropping the transmission into drive, he stepped on the gas. Sand and small pebbles flew behind the truck as its wheels first spun, then grabbed.

He hit the center stream, going twenty-five. Forward momentum carried the truck toward the center of the small river, and, as before, the strong current pushed the truck somewhat off-course. The good news: hardly any water was entering past the stone, set snugly onto the floorboard. While some water still seeped in under the doors, it was less than before. Finding traction within moments, the truck began climbing up the opposite bank. Cameron then navigated the truck across the last, far shallower, stream. Once on dry land, he cranked the wheel and climbed up the steep embankment, leading to the ridgeline road above.

From his present low mountain vantage point, there were far too many turns and bends on the ridge road to get a clear sightline on the robotic procession so far ahead. Cameron gave the old truck a bit more gas. He needed to catch them, preferably before they reached the *Primion*. Spinning the wheel to the right, for the next tight turn, he felt the rear of the truck fishtail—far too close to the left-side edge of the road for comfort. Any mistake now, from this elevation, would send the truck barreling over the cliff. Certain death . . . *for sure.* He slowed, cranking the wheel to the left, then quickly to the right, while pushing the pedal all the way to the floor when the ridge road straightened out. Accelerating, the F150 was now clearly gaining on the procession. Cameron unconsciously leaned forward—like one did on horseback or a bike—attempting to quicken the pace.

Two hundred feet out, he saw the Loth. Strapped down onto a hovering transport sled, the creature's numerous appendages were straining against individual bindings. The Loth was desperately trying to lift its head up. "Hold on, Loth . . . I'm coming."

The narrower the gap between his truck and the procession, the angrier Cameron became. The creature was clearly terrified—bellowing into the air high-pitched honking noises. At this close distance, he could see the Loth was facing backward. Eyes wide, it was staring right at him.

Cameron turned his attention to the parade of robots leading the hover sled. Unlike any he'd seen on the ship, they easily were just as tall as him. They walked upright, like humans, but their stride was somewhat herky-jerky. Legs and arms were nothing more than a bundle of thin tubes—fingered hands were metal and curled into fists. Their torsos, also, looked to be a conglomerate of various sized tubes. Where each limb was affixed to the body, there was an oversized, cylindrical, canister-like thing. Cameron figured these were the power sources for each appendage. All in all, the robots looked to be of a highly simplistic and ultra-lightweight design. Moving closer now, he saw that their heads were super tiny—shrunken-like—reminding him of Beetlejuice, in the old movie. They looked ridiculous.

The long procession covered the width of the entire ridge road, leaving no way to pass the hovering transport sled on either side. Cameron, falling in behind, tried to plan what to do next. When he noticed the *Primion*, coming into view a half-mile ahead, he slammed his fist down on the steering wheel in frustration. Continuing to look for some way around them, when . . . *there!* He just might have found one. Up ahead, the ridgeline briefly widened out, maybe five or six extra feet. The only problem: it narrowed down again pretty quickly. He'd have to really gun it and hope there was enough room to pass before that occurred.

Cameron smiled. Actually, he only had to pass the hovering transport sled. After that, the apparently unarmed robots would have to fend for themselves—either get out of the way or tumble over the cliff. He really didn't care which.

Thirty feet before he had to make his move, he waited and contemplated on something else. How on earth did they ever capture a Griar Loth; one that overcame a Greely Beast so easily? Perhaps they weren't just any robots. Maybe their skinny arms and legs and shrunken heads were misleading. With only twenty more feet to go, Cameron wiped perspiration off his left hand and onto his jeans then did the same with the right. He studied the robots. Like soldiers, they moved in unison: left, right, left, right. He noticed that within the tubular arms one appeared thicker, shaped slightly differently from the others. *Maybe a weapon?*

Ten feet to go. The Loth had freed one of its tentacles; all the while its honking tirade had only increased. Wait, not freed—torn away. The Loth, in its frenzy to escape, had pulled lost a limb. Cameron's intense focus on the Loth almost caused him to miss the road's brief widening. *Now or never*! Go or no-go—he had to decide.

chapter 41

The robots' procession, marching in the center of the ridge road, veered to the right when the road widened up. Cameron stepped on the gas. Passing by the hover sled, he avoided looking at the Loth, instead concentrating on the road and robots ahead.

Clang! Clang!

The Ford's front bumper collided with two robots, marching along the far left edge, which sent them flying over the cliff's side. "Oops," he said, not meaning it. Driving close into the robots midst, he watched their little heads swivel around like tiny tank turrets. Half-expecting to see some semblance of recognizable facial features, perhaps like the plastic-y-looking appearance of Lutous Bright 953, back within the Juvinate Plastron, he found these bots had no such features—wore no faces at all.

Their reaction was fast. Four of the nine remaining robots lifted their left rod-like arms and pointed them in Cameron's direction. But he was ready for them. Having buzzed down the right-side window already, he leveled his own weapon, targeting the robot closest to the truck. He inwardly said a silent prayer the gun had recharged. He squeezed the handgrip, and a bolt of plasma hit the robot's right arm. A useless shot, really, since the bot still was able to fire with its left. Cameron ducked below the dashboard just as a series of flashes illuminated the inside of the cab with bright strobes of light. From his somewhat prone position, he could see most of the windshield had melted away, along with the cab's rear window and part of the roof. *This might go down as my most stupid idea*, he mused. What was worse, he couldn't see the road ahead from his new position, mostly lying flat on the seat. Venturing a peek over the dash, he quickly adjusted the wheel's steering, just in time to avoid driving off the side of the mountain. In the mad frenzy, he wondered why the robots hadn't fired on the truck—only on him. *Maybe*, he thought, *because they've never encountered an out-of-place, twenty-year-old F150 before*. He placed the plasma gun in his lap and, yanking the wheel to the right, gave the truck more gas.

Clang! Clang! Clang!

The truck bounced and clattered over strewn metallic objects. *Three more robots down for the count.* Cameron peered over the dash, and re-adjusted the steering again to avoid moving too close toward the right side of the mountain. Spinning the wheel quickly left then right—back and forth—he swerved the truck like an out-of-control drunk driver.

Clang! Clang! Clang! Clang!

Only now did the remaining robots—Cameron guessed there were still four—begin to fire directly at the truck. Still lying down on his right side, his feet fumbled until he found the brake pedal, bringing the truck to a complete stop. The eruption of constant plasma flashes—the sound of his truck being pummeled from more than one angle—kept him hunkered down on the seat. He waited for a reprieve, but it didn't come. The Ford's roof, at this point, riddled with holes, was little more than Swiss cheese. Several metal mangled sections, after the plasma strikes, glowed fiery orange. Cameron could feel warm heat emanating downward. He heard a crashing noise at the front of the vehicle then caught a glimpse of the truck's hood flying past overhead. A tire exploded, and then another, as the truck violently rocked with each plasma strike. The engine suddenly quit. Mere inches above his head, a plasma bolt eviscerated the top section of the passenger door.

Reaching for the weapon on his lap, he discovered it was no longer there. He leaned up, just enough to see it lying now on the other side of the cab, on the floor by his feet. The robots hadn't yet let up in their attack. Any moment now, one of their plasma strikes would find its mark: him.

With nowhere to go, and nowhere to hide, Cameron—his face buried into the passenger's seat cushion—waited for the final killing shot to come. Still waiting, he soon became aware that their plasma fire was no longer directed at what remained of his truck. He could see bright flashes of light now striking outside. Something about the Loth's painful honking had also changed. No longer desperate and pleading, it sounded ... angry.

Slowly, Cameron raised his head—just enough to glance through the jagged hole in the door's frame. Within this limited field of view, he saw a blur of motion. Plasma fire had significantly reduced. Cameron, raising his head high enough to see over the roofless door, did a double take. The Minal Loth, missing two of its tentacle limbs, was moving freely around with incredible speed. Two of the robots, splayed into small pieces, lay on the ground. The Loth was now in the process of dismembering a third. The last remaining robot, firing continuous plasma bolts at the creature, was using weapons on both its arms.

Feeling seething-hot rage overtake him, Cameron sat up straight and reached for his own plasma gun. With the roof of the truck all but shot away, he only had to stand upright on the seat and take aim. He fired continuously, until the last standing robot was nothing more than a puddle of hot molten metal. The Loth stared up at Cameron—a robot leg clutched in one tentacle and a robotic arm in another. The creature's torso was a mass of black scorch marks, but its head was surprisingly unmarked. Its two oozing, bright-red tentacle stumps glistened in the sunlight. Cameron stared, not knowing what to do for the young creature.

The Loth, dropping the dismantled robot onto the ground, moved fast. The passenger door was torn from its hinges, and within an instant Cameron was swooped up into the tight clutches of the wounded creature. Only then did it occur to

Cameron that the Loth might be blaming him for this whole ordeal. Might think he held some part in it. Now twirling around, held high up—his arms pinned to his sides—there was little Cameron could do to fend off what was sure to come.

The swipe of a sloppy wet tongue plastered his head with mucus. Then, Cameron felt the Loth's purring vibrations envelop him. The constantly spinning around creature was apparently ecstatic. Happy to be free; happy to be back together with him, whatever role he'd played.

"Okay . . . okay . . . stop with the licking, with all the spinning around. I'm going to throw up!"

It took a few minutes before Cameron was finally released, could shake circulation back into his arms and legs. The Loth continued to scuttle about. At one point it stooped, picking up the shattered robot's parts in its four remaining tentacles. High-pitched, victorious honking echoed loudly into the valley below.

Cameron's smile faded when he glanced up toward the stern of the *Primion*. He saw the familiar four ginormous thrust cones, two on each side of the large rear, closed hatchway. He knew that somewhere inside the ship was the XI drone. The same drone that no doubt sent out the small army of robots to capture the Loth. Probably gave them orders to kill him if he tried to rescue it.

The Loth, finally tiring out, settled down beside Cameron and began to lick its gruesome-looking stumps.

Cameron said, "From what I've heard . . . they will grow back, be as good as new."

The Loth didn't give any indication it heard him. Studying his truck, Cameron felt both sadness and guilt. "When I somehow get back inside that ship, I'm going to tear that droid to pieces," he said.

The Loth stopped long enough to make eye contact.

PART III
Hard Choices

chapter 42

One Month Later ...

Heather had to lay her head back on the seat and close her eyes. She was feeling nauseous. Always the first in the family to get carsick, and today—even at twenty years of age—things weren't any different. Sitting in the backseat of her mother's minivan, with her mother driving, her father's voice, sitting shotgun beside her mother, sounded impatient.

"Use your blinker ... That's what it's there for," he chided his wife.

"I would, if I were going to turn here, but I'm not. Park Way is far less crowded this time of the day," Heather's mother replied back, her voice screaming passive aggressiveness.

Everyone was on edge—*and why shouldn't they be?* Heather thought. They were being evacuated by the military. *Take what fits in your car—that's it! Nothing more*, they were told. Although their small neighborhood was still untouched by the

Octobeast, the creature had reemerged close by on three different occasions. Killing and terrorizing the populace, the huge beast was causing further massive destruction. Expected to eventually leave the area, find some other part of New York to put down stakes and call it home. But no, it seemed Larksburg Stand would continue to hold that singular distinction.

"Mom, I'm feeling sick. Like I'm going to throw-up"

"Roll down your window. Deep breaths," her father said.

Heather glared toward the back of his big, domed head. "I was talking to Mom. I thought maybe she had something in her purse . . . like to settle my stomach. Unless you have a purse up there too. I'm not particular."

"Being a smartass is not becoming," he said.

Making a face at his turned-away head, she caught her mother's smiling eyes in the rearview mirror. "You're just jealous I got my cast off before you, Dad." Heather watched him uncomfortably shift about in his seat. She could see his now grayed and battered fiberglass leg cast stretched out before him.

"Guess I can't argue with that, Squeak."

She turned her attention back to her laptop. She was in the process of writing an email letter to Cam. One she knew he would never see—would never read. Even if he was still alive, he undoubtedly was light-years distance from Earth. *No email on Pluto.* But her therapist had suggested the act—which seemed futile to her—would be beneficial. Perhaps give her some closure. Therapist—*ugh.* She couldn't stand that patronizing old bitty. As if someone in her seventies could relate to someone barely out of her teens. Before leaving the hospital, it was recommended that she and Ginger both see someone. But she didn't want to talk anymore about the Octobeast. Or the fact the love of her life was probably as good as dead. And she didn't want to talk about the growing number of life-long friends she'd lost due to the latest attack.

Her fingers hovered over the computer's keys.

Dear Cam,

If, by some miracle, you ever get the chance to read this email, let me first say how sorry I am. If I had known about the crazy shit headed our way, I would have done things so very differently. I would have packed up all my crap, driven across the country, and moved in with you. Would have made a new life in San Jose. I know I would have loved it. Would have loved you more and more every day, too. I guess it took an alien monster, from friggin' outer space, for me to see things clearly.

We're being evacuated as I write this letter. The creature you left behind, (thank you for that, ha ha, by the way), what we call the Octobeast, has been terrorizing Larksburg off and on over the last four weeks. Half the town is gone, wiped out. And it seems the creature has cultivated a taste for humans. Horrible! There's a massive military presence here. But that's enough depressing talk. I wish I knew if you were alive. If you are able to use any of the scientific trivia you have stored in that handsome head of yours. Maybe your present status is the adventure of a lifetime, not that bad for you. Hope so!

Well, I've been told I have to move on. Yeah, I know we're broken up. But I hope you know I was only yours, even though I did everything I could not to show it. Now I guess I have to think about the future. I want to go to a university out of state, finally leave the nest. I bet you never thought you'd hear that! Don't be mad, but Dad's deputy, Kirk, has been coming around a bit. Ya' know, coming by to see if I'm okay. Coming by to see if I want to play Trivia Pursuit. Okay, he's not as smart as you are ... but he is nicer than I gave him credit for in the past. Just giving you a heads up, so you better get back to me!

Well, I guess I've rambled on long enough. I'll try to write more in the future.

Love you,
Heather

She hit send ...

chapter 43

Cameron, lounging on a folding chair beneath a bright-yellow beach umbrella, finished writing this morning's journal entry on his laptop. Perched on one of the stubby aft wings of the spacecraft, he had an incredible vista to enjoy, and a substantial separation from what he called *Scants*. Similar looking to ants, they had twelve legs and exuded a really bad odor. And they nipped, leaving welts on the skin.

Four-and-a-half weeks had now passed since the *Primion* crashed landed onto the exoplanet, Sang-Morang. Most of that time, Cameron had been locked out of the ship—had seen neither hide nor hair of the elusive XI droid.

Since his confrontation with the killer robot procession, when heading up the mountainside, and the subsequent escape of the Minal Loth from its bindings, all had been relatively quiet. The *Primion* was sealed up tight. It soon became evident to Cameron that gaining access into the spaceship was no longer an option. The contents within the bed of his bombarded pickup truck were little more than charred ashes. The one exception was the trinious bundle, and its enclosed contents. Apparently, the alien composite material was impervious to the white-hot temperatures from multiple plasma blasts.

Cameron and the Loth had trekked by foot all the way down to the valley floor, back to the middle peninsula of three streams. He'd set up camp on the sand, right next to the duplicated F150. For three weeks he lived there. His five-year-old sleeping bag made the nights more comfortable, and only when he ran out of Top Ramen did he have to start hunting for food. The plasma gun became an indispensable aspect of his survival. A campfire was always lit. Every evening, part of Cameron's routine was to scrounge up kindling along with larger pieces of timber. There were fish aplenty in the largest of the three streams. He'd gotten pretty good at picking them off while sitting atop the roof of the truck. He felt it gave the fish more of a competitive edge if he had to work for the shot.

The Minal Loth, gone for a good part of each day there, always returned by nightfall and would sleep close by Cameron. The creature by now was huge, even larger than its mother. Cameron guesstimated it was about forty-five-feet tall when it stood upright. Its two torn-off tentacles had grown back, looked just like the other four. But what was most interesting, exciting, even, was that the creature—with its multi-octave honking—was beginning to communicate. Cameron spent countless hours either pointing things out or explaining various actions and saying the associated names: *truck, rock, human, Minal Loth, eat, stream, mountain, climbing, spaceship, sleep, etc.* Only once did he reprimand the creature, as one would a small child. The creature's nearly insatiable appetite drove the Loth to spend most daytime hours away—hunting and eating. Cameron once found the half-eaten remains of a small Dalima Climber, not far from their encampment. With sad reluctance he turned the carcass over, relieved to find it wasn't Lalik. He brought the towering Loth over to the corpse and screamed till his voice was hoarse: "There are plenty of other species to feast on, but not Dalima Climbers. They are not to be on the menu . . . ever!"

On numerous occasions Cameron ventured into the dark recesses of the forest. Each visit he was welcomed back by the friendly clan of hairy primates. He became familiar with how they lived, what they ate. Vegetarians, mainly, they did devour certain kinds of insects too. The Dalima Climbers slept during the daylight hours for the most part. Descending from the trees during the night, they often visited the three streams to drink and bathe. Lalik was becoming a good friend to Cameron. Even the Loth seemed to like her. More than once he found her sleeping at his side, lying outside his sleeping bag. His affection for her was growing, but he didn't think of her in a sexual way. Though she could have different ideas in that regard.

Three days before, while the Loth was off somewhere, *they* attacked. At dusk, Cameron returned to the campsite and chided himself for letting the campfire burn out. He then heard familiar squealing sounds, along with the padding of innumerable tiny feet. *Piquet sprints.* A far larger throng than those that attacked him before, when he was in his truck up on the mountain. Hundreds of them. By the time Cameron pulled his weapon, they were nearly upon him. He fired continuously, killing scores of the vicious little varmints. When his plasma gun eventually petered out of energy, he climbed onto the truck's roof and screamed for the Loth to come help. But it wasn't the Loth that saved the day; it was the Dalima Climbers. Some arrived with tree branches and used them as clubs; others picked up rocks and threw them with astounding force and accuracy. Three primates were taken down—overwhelmed by the sheer number of *piquet sprints;* they succumbed later from numerous bites and loss of blood. When the Loth did arrive, it did so with a ferocity Cameron didn't know it possessed. With its ginormous jaws scooping-up and snapping and chewing, it wasn't long before the last few surviving rodents scampered fast into the trees.

After that encounter, Cameron decided it would be best to switch his campsite again to the top of the ridge road, near the *Primion.* He was beginning to hear strange animal sounds at night, perhaps those of another Gleery Beast, or two, that had moved into the valley. Or maybe they were coming from some other killer beast. Not going to chance it, he drove the pickup truck back up the ridge road and parked behind the spaceship.

Cameron accessed the truck's battery to charge both his laptop and his iPhone, which he mostly used to listen to music. Sometimes he'd leave the truck's headlights on at night, for extra bright illumination to see by when working on any number of pet projects. He needed to run the engine at least twenty minutes a day, which meant he was beginning to burn through the limited supply of gasoline. Rationing was all he could do;

when the fuel was depleted, *it would be gone.* No longer did he drive up and down the mountainside, unless it was absolutely necessary. Instead, he hopped on his fs01BMC mountain bike. Travelled the few miles down again to the valley floor. Once there, he might visit with the Dalima Climbers. Always filling-up containers with water from the streams, he'd shoot some fish, and, if he had the energy—collect more firewood. Recently, he'd begun to use the emptied-out trinious bundle— its broad strap slung over his shoulder—to carry everything. Later, he'd again begin the arduous bike journey up the steep incline back to the top.

Today, Cameron leaned back in his folding beach chair, gazing out toward the broad valley below. He figured it was about 10:30 a.m. He was playing audio tracks of violin music—specifically those that Heather recorded then posted up on YouTube—he'd downloaded onto his iPhone before all the craziness occurred. He hummed along with the melody and wondered, *How many times have I listened to these same tracks? A hundred? Two hundred?* Continuing to hum, he was startled to hear the Loth, honking out the same melody from somewhere below, out of view.

Cameron stood and stretched, staring at the collection of dark-gray items lying nearby. Each day, around this time, he went through the same routine. He would check to see if signals from two of the Priopax items were still being blocked. First, the large rectangular brick-shaped item, which had pre- viously transformed into a communications console, and the next, shaped more like an oversized dinner plate, which offered virtual, Priopax sage-like intelligence. More than ever, Cameron wished he could bring back the old cowboy, Art. Although talking to the Loth was fine, theirs was far from a stimulating conversation. The ship blocked out any signals—the XI droid still intent on making his life one of hardship.

Cameron turned his gaze to the spacecraft, mentally willing the closest airlock hatchway to suddenly open. His weapon was always within easy reach. Just as he could pick off a skittering fish from twenty yards away, he could draw and put a plasma bolt right into the middle of the XI droid, should it suddenly appear. His hatred for that hovering menace had only increased over the proceeding weeks.

Cameron readjusted the umbrella as the bright sun-like star rose higher in the sky. Then, climbing up along the side of the ship, he stood up on the high-domed aft section. From there, he had a birds-eye view of the rest of the ship. "Wait a minute . . . maybe I've been going about this all wrong . . ."

chapter 44

Almost a third of the forward starboard section of the *Primion* was buried deep under hundreds of tons of dirt and rock due to crash-landing over a month earlier. Also the reason the ship was incapable of taking off. Cameron wondered why the XI droid hadn't already begun the lengthy operation of digging out the ship. XI's earlier intention was to get the excavation process started immediately, right after the crash— one that could easily take them a year, or more, to finish. XI certainly had the ability to construct mechanical workers—to replicate bots. The procession of killer robots he'd sent down to retrieve the Loth had proven that. *So what was it waiting for?*

The forty-five-foot-tall Loth came into Cameron's view around the rear of the ship. The XI droid undoubtedly feared the Loth. He supposed that would be reason enough not to proceed—to stay hidden.

Cameron knew what the creature wanted. It was nearing the time they made their usual trek down the mountainside together—he on his bike and the Loth on foot, so to speak.

The Loth honked out the words, "We hunt."

Cameron stared back at the creature before turning toward the forward section of the ship—having thought of something.

"Loth . . . we can go hunting later. Can you come up here?" Though he suspected the creature could climb up, he wasn't one hundred percent positive. It was a near vertical climb

Again, the Loth said, "We hunt."

"We hunt later . . . I need your help first. Hunt later. Come on up here. Hurry it up!"

Reluctantly, the big Minal Loth used its tentacle limbs to find protruding parts of the ship to gain purchase on. With minimal effort it soon was perched atop the *Primion's* top hull. Cameron hurried forward and heard the Loth's heavy limbs thumping along behind him. Once he reached the mountain of dirt partially covering the ship, Cameron began—one by one—to lift up the heavy rocks and clumps of dirt and deposit them portside. He then threw them over the cliff. Doing the work by himself would take years—perhaps a lifetime. He kept at it, ignoring the Loth now watching him intently. Eventually, the Loth moved closer and placed the tip of one tentacle on Cameron's shoulder. Turning around, Cameron glanced upward, into its quizzical eyes, and said, "Everyday we do this for two hours. Then we go hunt. You want to help me?"

Cameron didn't wait for an answer. He hefted a large rock and, staggering under its weight, managed to toss it off the opposite side of the ship. It took another ten minutes before the Loth finally joined in. Not so much lifting each rock, or clump of dirt, the way Cameron did, but by using all six tentacles to gather and swipe large areas from the dirt mound. Then, using a plowing motion, it flung an avalanche of dirt over the opposite side that was both efficient and amazingly effective. At one point, Cameron fashioned a makeshift shovel, using a long section of sheet metal—a leftover remnant from the burnt-out F150.

Two hours later, as promised, Cameron put down his faux shovel and patted the Loth's leg. "That's it for today. Time to go hunt."

The Loth gladly hurried toward the stern of the ship, disappearing the same route it climbed up. Cameron stayed, studying the progress they'd made. He was more than a little impressed—ten tons of dirt gone. *Or was it twenty?* A once hopeless situation seemed not quite as hopeless now.

The bike ride down the mountain road was difficult. Cameron's hands were terribly blistered, and his back was killing him. No sooner reaching the three streams he pulled his shirt, shoes, socks, and pants off. Crossing to the deepest stream, he dove in headfirst. He stayed submerged for over a minute, letting the currents of cool water soothe his aching muscles, rid his skin of dust and grime. When he came up for air, he watched as the Loth made its way up the valley, where far more game was prevalent.

The air, of late, had cooled some. Cameron wondered if he was experiencing the first signs of a changing season. Sitting in the water, submerged up to his neck, he slowly turned and took in the breathtaking landscape around him. Something that hadn't really occurred to him before, prior to right then, was the realization that a large part of him loved it here. Loved the raw, untouched, often dangerous wild nature of the place. As much as he despised the XI droid, at some level he also owed it a measure of gratitude. He wouldn't want to have missed any part of this: the Minal Loth's friendship—the comradery the two now shared—and the relationship he'd forged with the Dalima Climbers. And, of course, the special friendship he had with Lalik. But it was even more than that. It was his relationship with a world somehow similar to Earth, yet so different too. A world for the most part untouched by man. He leaned over and sipped in the crystal clear water. *Was there a stream anywhere back home where he could drink water like this? Maybe. But it wouldn't be too long before that would not be an option.*

Cameron, hearing noises behind him, spun quickly around. The friendly Dalima Climbers were making their way toward the same stream he was in. Usually, they didn't bathe much before dusk. They were here now for him. He knew they enjoyed his company, just as much as he enjoyed theirs. Neither judged the other. He'd witnessed every aspect of their daily lives—the way they ate, slept, and even argued over who would occupy a certain branch. He'd also witnessed how tenderly they copulated. They seemed to have the same mate for life.

Cameron knew most of their names. Thilith was the motherly matriarch of the clan, and Brath was the dominant male. Somehow, he only needed to utter softly spoken words to convey his authority. Then there were Sphial and Shrii, sisters, ever watchful over Lalik.

One by one, they now joined him, allowing their lithe, hairy bodies to slide beneath the surface of the stream. He heard their wonderful singsong voices and laughter as two older females playfully splashed one another. He was surprised to feel two furry arms entwine about his neck from behind as Lalik pulled her body close to him. For the first time, he felt her warm body pressing against his bare skin. She nuzzled the back of his neck and made soft cooing sounds. The others in the group watched with amused fascination. He gave Lalik a few affectionate pats beneath the water but avoided turning around to face her. Perhaps if he were going to stay here—had decided to make Sang-Morang his home—then *maybe*.

Cameron gazed up at the sky, noticing the faint outline of nearby sister planets. But he would always miss the Earth's moon. Always miss his own planet's star called the Sun. And he would always miss Heather.

chapter 45

The next day Cameron had the Loth back at work, plowing dirt and rock rubble off the top of the *Primion*. Before joining the creature, Cameron wrapped his palms with torn cloth strips; he wanted to avoid new blistering. The work was hard and dirty. Since the day was exceptionally warm, they both took several breaks—drinking water and catching their breaths. Cameron enjoyed working hard—always had. He wondered if the Loth was taking cues from him. Was he sort of like a father figure to the ginormous creature? The Loth never complained or whined. Sure, there was reluctance getting started, doing certain things sometimes, but once underway, the Loth powered through. Cameron inwardly acknowledged his own feelings—that he took a small measure of pride in who or what the beast had turned in to.

He watched the Loth drink from a deep hole in the dirt, not far from the burnt-out original truck. They had dug the hole together. Cameron then showed the Loth how to coat the deep interior of the hole by using its previously secreted, still pliable mucus blobs. There was no shortage of them around. The stuff had amazing sealant characteristics, had become useful in several instances. The dried mucus-lined hole was only recently filled with fresh stream water. After sealing the bed of the second pickup truck, in much the same way as they'd sealed the hole, they took a few trips up and down the mountain. Filling up the sealed truck bed with stream water, they later deposited it into the hole. He used up more gas than he wanted, but the Loth had to be kept hydrated—especially now, with all the added exertion.

"Let's give it another hour. Then you can go hunt. How's that sound?"

The Loth bellowed out a chorus of excited honks, then hurried up the stern of the spacecraft, disappearing over the top. A few moments later, Cameron heard the sound of heavy dirt mounds being plowed from one side of the fuselage to the other.

About to head up there himself, he froze in place. Not two paces before him was Alice, or, more accurately, the 3D holographic representation of Alice—a life-sized pop-up display.

Over a month had passed since Cameron had contact with the ship. His heart sank. "Alice . . . what's happened to you?" he asked.

Alice's head lowered somewhat; perhaps she'd forgotten about her ruined appearance. Cameron took in the abomination before him. Virtually all the skin was now gone. Several tattered, hanging remnants of simulated flesh dangled from her face, arms, and legs. Dark scorch marks were prevalent throughout her metallic under-frame. She almost appeared to be painted black, and an eye was missing.

"I have a message from Captain XI."

Cameron hesitated. "Oh ... he's a captain now?"

"Yes."

"I'm sorry, Alice. Maybe it's time you, um ... go back to not having a body ... for a while. Be TAM again, like you were before."

Alice's one eye locked onto his. "You don't think I would have done that already if I could?"

"You're being held captive within ..."

She cut him off, "Cameron, I am here to convey a message. That is all. I do not need your sympathy."

Cameron nodded. He hadn't thought it possible to despise the droid more than he already did. But he was wrong. He saw movement behind Alice, who was standing on the bridge. Figures in uniform. Glimpsing a passing-by female, he noticed she had a clear membrane Thidion ear. "Crewmembers ..." he said.

Alice nodded. "It is the captain's doing. XI took your words to heart. A ship like this one needs a crew. Each crewmember, prior to their demise, was ... fully recreated."

"Cyborgs," Cameron said.

"Yes. The *Primion* now has a full crew complement. With the exception of only one."

Cameron thought about that. "The previous captain."

Alice didn't respond to that, instead replying, "The captain is aware of your work to unearth the vessel. Pleased with your progress. You will complete the task within five days."

"That's not possible. And since when do I take orders from that *piece of shit*, anyway?"

"You want to go home. You want to return to Earth. XI can make that happen. You will work together to make that happen."

"In exchange for what?" Cameron asked, already knowing the answer.

Alice said, "Once the *Primion* is no longer buried, you will lead the Minal Loth into a Retention cell. We then will make haste to Winforge. After that, XI will deliver you back to Earth."

Cameron almost laughed. "And I'm supposed to believe that the crazy, *flying toaster* of a droid will make good on any promise it makes?"

"You have an opportunity to go home, Cameron."

"The truth is, I'm perfectly happy right here," he lied. "The Loth will never be anyone's prisoner. I'll see to that."

"The creature will not be mistreated. Once on Winforge, the Loth will again be amongst others of its own kind. You will be doing the beast a favor."

"Yeah, just like the benevolent treatment XI has shown you?" he asked, his voice dripping with cynicism. "Tell the *tin can* I can't be bought."

Alice went quiet for a long moment. She said, "Please . . . Cameron."

He shook his head.

A second pop-up display suddenly appeared. At first, Cameron didn't know for sure what he was looking at. Then he did. It was one of the smaller, glass-enclosed retention cells. Within it were three beings, huddled close together. He could hear them whimpering. Cameron recognized the two sisters, Sphial and Shrii, and the smallest of the Dalima Climbers, pretty Lalik. He saw dark red splotches, welts, protruding up through their fine hair. They were beyond scared—visibly terrified.

Cameron stared at the three defenseless souls in horror. "Let them go, Alice. They're not a part of this. They are peaceful and kind and . . ."

"There is nothing I can do. I am as much a prisoner here as they are," she said, suddenly looking around. She'd said more than she should have. Cameron had little doubt she would be punished further.

"They will be released prior to lift off, if you do as requested. It is up to you."

Cameron felt sick. Something touched his shoulder, and he swung around, both fists clenched. It was Brath, the clan's soft-spoken, dominant male. His face expressed a combination of fear and sadness. Standing a short distance behind him, on the ridge road, was the entirety of his clan. They had come for the sisters and for Lalik. They didn't understand what had happened.

Brath's grim attention then turned to the display, still focusing on the retention area. His eyes went wide, and he began to huff and snort. He flailed his arms into the air, similar to how an excited male ape might act back on Earth.

"I promise . . . I'm going to help them!" Cameron exclaimed, raising his palms up—a gesture conveying everything was going to be okay, just fine. But deep inside he knew he was lying. He was just as helpless as they were.

chapter 46

The amount of time Cameron had the Loth laboring, unburying the *Primion,* increased from two hours a day to five hours a day. With the exception of Brath, plus several other larger males, most of the clan of Dalima Climbers had returned to the valley floor—back to their home deep within the forest. Cameron soon coaxed Brath, along with the other male primates—all terribly bitten by the nasty *scants*—to sleep atop the spacecraft. Not long after, they began to help unearth the ship too; carrying, then depositing, loads of dirt and rock across to the ship's port side.

By the end of the fourth day, it became clearly evident to Cameron that they would probably meet XI's five-day deadline. Every time he thought about telling the droid to shove its threats up its mechanical ass, he remembered poor imprisoned Lalik and the two sisters. No. He would do as told . . . for now. The crazy droid had won the day. As often as Cameron might risk his own life, he'd never ever consider doing the same with theirs. But still, there had to be a way to get something in return from the droid. The direction things were going now didn't look good long term—for himself or for the Loth.

Water rations were running low. Late that afternoon, Cameron, feeling weary from the day's undertaking, drove the duplicated pickup truck down the ridge road as Brath and the three Dalima Climbers nervously huddled together in the bed of the truck. The Loth hunkered along out in front—moving with far less agility than usual. Only near the last leg of their trip down the mountainside did the Loth quicken its pace, disappearing from sight around the last bend.

Cameron, now an expert at traversing the streams so almost no water entered the cab, parked at his usual sandy place near the overturned Tangine-Shell. Brath and his fellow primates hurried into the water, swallowing up copious amounts. Then, one-by-one, they hurried away into the trees. Cameron peered up-stream. He would need the Loth's help, refilling the truck's bed with fresh water. They'd devised a way to have the Tangine-Shell perform like a big scoop—haul up stream water, then deposit the load into the truck's bed.

The valley was ominously quiet. Typically around him he heard an abundance of strange and wonderful Sang-Morang nature sounds: screeching birds, yelping unidentified creatures, and the distant honking of the Minal Loth. But no sounds were evident now; even the usual late afternoon breezes had stilled.

Cameron kicked off his boots then undressed and slid into the stream. With a heavy heart he gazed toward the trees. No primates would be joining him this evening. Poor Lalik, scared and confused, was locked up within a prison cell back aboard the spacecraft. Cameron, inhaling a deep breath, sank beneath the surface. Even the fish seemed to have disappeared. Sheer isolation of the moment pressed in around him, compounded by growing feelings of guilt. *I've brought catastrophe to this world.* Man's mere presence did it once again.

Okay . . . that's enough . . . feeling sorry for poor ol' me. Wallowing won't get me anywhere.

Exhaling whatever air was left in his lungs, Cameron quickly rose up above. Breathing in the cool evening air, he was pleasantly surprised to hear the sounds of nature about him. Once again, the day's glorious music had resumed—an ensemble of wild and unique intonations. A fish bumped against his bare foot beneath the water's surface. And there, in the distance, was the Loth. Trudging back his way, a half-eaten carcass—of only God knew what—was grasped within one of its upraised tentacles.

* * *

That night, sitting again atop the spacecraft, with his laptop perched upon his lap, Cameron put the finishing touches onto his latest journal entry. Sleeping down below him, he could hear the Loth's heavy breathing. The only creature *never* needing to worry about scants biting—not with that tough hide.

Cameron pulled his sleeping bag up over his shoulders. Evenings were definitely getting chillier; winter soon would be coming to this part of Sang-Morang. Glancing up overhead, his eyes quickly found the familiar sister planets.

This planet must have a crazy tidal system. On Earth the tides were controlled by the moon and the sun, and since the moon had a much more powerful gravitational effect on the oceans than the sun, things were pretty predictable. Here, however, there were several nearby and large planets or moons, which would complicate things. The closest, with its three soft pink rings, looked almost near enough to touch. He wondered if there was life there, as well. On a whim, he asked, "Alice . . . can you hear me?"

A moment later, she popped into view, looking pretty much the same as before—still battered and broken. "Good evening, Cameron."

"Hey . . . I want you to ask XI to stop jamming my *Priopax* devices."

"I can ask, but . . ."

Cameron continued, "The ship will be completely unearthed by tomorrow afternoon. I've held up my end of the bargain. Tell the droid that the best star ship captains always reward their subordinates when a job is well done. Of course, only the best ship captains are aware of that . . ." Cameron was perfectly aware that the XI droid was either listening in, or watching their interchange.

"Why do you need the devices activated? To what purpose?"

Cameron also knew that was the droid's question, not Alice's. "I want to enable the console equipment; the thing that will let me see my home world again. I also want to initialize Art, the group consciousness—"

Alice said, "XI is fully aware of your conversations with that sole representation of babbling blowhards. No . . . The captain does not believe that would be a good use of your time."

Cameron, feeling a seething hatred returning, literally had to count to ten. Then, somewhat calmer, he said, "In fact, I'll need all the devices operational. Look, the Minal Loth will not reenter the ship tomorrow without my coaxing. If the droid truly wishes to complete its mission parameters, it will have to make some concessions. Any *real* captain would know that already. I'm surprised we're even having this discussion."

Alice stared back at Cameron with her one eye. He felt somewhat bad, putting her in the middle like this, but there was too much at stake to worry about that now. The dysfunctional droid needed to understand certain concessions had to take place first in order for it to get what it ultimately wanted. Cameron waited as poor Alice stared mutely back at him. Finally, Cameron added, "Tell the captain we both want the same thing. It is in my best interest also, to get back into space. We're not at odds here . . . in fact, were compatriots. Ask the captain if it knows what that word means."

"Of course, the captain knows what that word means," Alice snapped back. "Your devices are no longer jammed. The captain looks forward to getting underway shortly." The 3D virtual display dissipated away, like a heavy mist lost in the wind.

Cameron, exchanging the laptop for the dinner plate-shaped Priopax device, found with his fingertips the three indentations along its surface. Activating it, he waited. Soon, he noticed a nearby campfire crackling atop the spaceship—could feel heat emanating—and wondered about the science behind the illusion. The old cowboy Art, straddling a roughly hewn tree stump, had a good-sized ceramic jug balanced precariously on one knee. Hefting the jug up, he offered Cameron a crooked smile.

Cameron, approaching the campfire, found another tree stump waiting just for him. Sitting down, he accepted the outstretched jug. Could smell the strong acrid alcohol.

"Careful there, tenderfoot . . . frontier whisky ain't nothing to trifle with."

Cameron ignored the warning and took a long gulp from the jug. The warm liquid burned his throat all the way down. But it felt good. He *needed* it. He knew this entire experience wasn't real: Not the hot jolt of alcohol, now burning its way to his stomach, nor the crackling fire nearby, nor the old codger sitting on the tree stump. All effects were not real. He'd been involved with Virtual Reality multi-sensory development projects back at HyperCrell. It was amazing what crudely altering your senses could do to your perception of reality. The monetary implications for a company perfecting such technologies were tremendous. Going far beyond what the gaming industry was striving for: totally immersive real world/alternate world experiences. But this was far beyond that. This simulation was not a special suit. Fabricated touch sensors and vibration engines, or a hidden atomizer, offering up a variety of weird odors on command. No, what this Priopax device simulation offered was completely taking place, he knew, within his own mind right then. A far cleaner, more elegant approach to multi-sensory emersion, nothing like what was actually being worked on back on Earth in Silicon Valley.

Cameron also knew that the physics behind what was real and what was illusion couldn't be differentiated as easily as they were in the past. In principle, matter could be broken down into basic building blocks of pure energy. Energy was energy—what illusions, too, were made of. So yeah, Art was only a *virtual* cowboy offering up a *virtual* jug of strong spirits. *So shut up and just enjoy the moment,* he chided himself.

"It's good to see you again," Cameron said, and meant it.

"Back at you, young man."

"I need your help, Art. And not taking sides will no longer cut it."

chapter 47

With Art's assistance, Cameron got the complicated Priopax communications console activated. It took them some time, but eventually Cameron had the time/space settings conforming properly to Earth's current location within the galaxy. Fine-tuning the controls, he was now able to view Larksburg Stand as he had before. Only now, to his utter discouragement, the small mountain hamlet was even more decimated than before.

Cameron continued manipulating the controls. Adjusting the visual perspective to the point he felt he was almost there among the obliterated mountain neighborhoods. Similar to actually driving along various streets or roads, he soon found Heather's street. He slowed his progress as he watched the 3D virtual display. "Wait, I must have passed it," he said to Art.

"No . . . you didn't. Right there, my boy, was your lady's house. That is what's left of it."

Cameron shot Art a glance. "It's gone! Rubble. All the homes are gone," he said, as Art repositioned his hay stalk stub to the other side of his mouth.

Cameron sat back and thought. "Everyone living there could have been evacuated beforehand." Continuing to muse about it, he added, "Let's take a look at the sheriff's station. Maybe I can track down her father."

It took another few minutes before the Larksburg Stand Sheriff's Station visibly appeared in view. Late evening there, he could clearly see the assortment of blue and silver cruisers, along with the sheriff's SUV, parked out front. About to move the viewer to the inside of the building, Cameron noticed another car's headlights swinging into view. Obviously another police cruiser, it parked alongside other city emergency vehicles. He watched Deputy Kirk lumber around the front of the car just as the passenger-side door swung open. A slim girl, or woman, stepped out and motioned, or made a gesture, to Kirk. Perhaps telling him he didn't need to open the door for her— that she was fully capable of doing such things herself. Cameron, too, had experienced the same sort of interchange a number of times before . . . *with Heather.* He leaned in closer, studying the female standing by the car, but he could only see her back. "I need to change the viewing direction . . ."

Art pointed his finger to the small manipulator control on the console. "Have at it."

Cameron took the control and used it to swing the perspective around one hundred-and-eighty degrees. But the view was still obscured as Kirk's big head was in the way. Blocking the view, because he was leaning-in for a kiss. Kirk eventually stepped back. Cameron studied Heather's pretty face. Tried to read her thoughts, but then had enough and didn't want to know. "I've seen enough."

"Sure? You alright?" Art asked.

Hell no—I'm not all right! It was taking all Cameron's will to just keep his wits about him. He'd just watched the only girl he ever cared about, loved, kiss another man! *And it had to be that fucking Deputy Kirk!*

"I'm fine. She's safe . . . clearly not in any immediate danger. Let's move on."

The perspective changed again as Art took over the controls. Seeing a much wider view of the town now, Cameron found the extent of damage exhibited—astronomical. And the military presence nothing short of what would be expected for a full-out war. Hundreds of troop carrier vehicles, missile deployment rigs, too many tanks to count, and camo-clad soldiers spread out across the many miles-around the town's perimeter. Clearly, the mother Griar Loth was still entrenched within the boundaries of Larksburg Stand.

"Can you show me how to view where the mother Loth is located, Art?"

"Sure . . . I can do that."

With Art fully manning the controls, the display immediately changed to a subterranean scene. Dark and mostly colorless, the view appeared to be artificially enhanced.

"What am I looking at here?"

"Just hold on to your knickers, lad..." Art said, as he maneuvered the view through a myriad of underground tunnels. Surprisingly, they were nearly perfectly rounded and symmetrical, as if some kind of industrial boring machine had been hard at work down there for months, or even years. Visible were offshoots and crossovers, where the tunnels intersected through one another. There seemed to be hundreds of miles of winding tunnels, going this way and that. Beneath Larksburg Stand was a honeycombed labyrinth that would be impossible to navigate through without a clear-cut map. Yet Art seemed to be doing okay. Suddenly, the viewed progression came to an abrupt stop.

Cameron studied the display. "Looks like some sort of cavern, no?"

"Yeah... you could say that."

"You could fit the Astrodome in there."

Art shrugged.

"There! Go back," Cameron said, pointing to the left edge of the field of view.

Art did as directed and, sure enough, an almost indistinguishable movement could be seen. Art adjusted *something* on the console and the display brightened and the contrast increased. There was the Griar Loth, hunched over what appeared to be several good-sized stones. She moved one of them closer into herself.

"Those aren't rocks..."

"No, my boy, those most certainly aren't rocks."

Cameron was nearly consumed by dread for the second time that night. First, viewing Heather with Kirk, and now witnessing what had to be a half-dozen baby Loth pods. *Oh my God! World Book Encyclopedia, Volume P, for Parthenogenesis.* Some animals are fully asexual—do not require a male to reproduce offspring, to give birth.

Cameron and Art exchanged a glance.

"If a single Loth could wreak that much havoc on a small town, what destructiveness will six of them bring about? And if it is pathenogenic then each of those pods might contain a female Griar Loth as well. And each of them can lay their own eggs in their own new towns. How long before the whole damn planet is swarming with those enormous creatures?" Cameron, not waiting for Art to answer, was all too certain he was viewing the not too distant causation of man's total, complete, extinction.

"I've seen enough. Shut it down, Art." Cameron stood and began to walk toward the bow of the ship. Reaching what little still remained of the mountain of dirt, he then turned around and walked back. He stood quietly, staring down at the sleeping Loth beyond the stern of the ship. Concentrating, he tried to see if there was a difference

Art joined his side, staring down at the sleeping creature. "I'm sure you've concluded how they differ from one another. Your Loth, here, is in fact a male . . . A Minal. One look at that gargantuan, hanging salami between its tentacles should have given you a hint of that. The other one . . . the mother, is female . . . a Minal. She only requires male insemination once in her lifetime. From then on, she's capable of giving birth scores and scores of times. Puts them out like a factory machine. And let me tell you . . . these creatures live well into five centuries."

Art gestured to the sleeping Loth, "But that one . . . no worries. He can't get pregnant any more than you can. Just thought you'd want to know."

"That's at least something," Cameron said just above a whisper. So it wasn't parthenogenesis, it was sperm storage, another trait common in the animal kingdom. "Tell me, what kills them?"

Art pursed his lips and shook his head.

"Hey . . . we're talking about the total annihilation of my home world, Art. And spare me all talk about cutting off their heads. That's just stupid. Cameron felt uneasy, speaking of such things this close to the Loth. *His* Loth. But as far as the mother was concerned, it would have to be done—somehow—by someone.

"I can't tell you directly, Cam, my boy. I may be able to lead you to the right path. It will be up to you to . . ."

"Connect the dots. I get it. So tell me?"

"When the time comes. Not now," Art said.

"It may be too late by then. Tell me now, so I can make plans . . . prepare."

"Nah . . . that won't be necessary," Art said, tapping several times on his right hip. "Just make sure you're packing when the occasion arises. And you'll need to have a damn-near perfect aim. You hear me? Now, I've already said too much."

Cameron gazed up to the heavens, beyond the sister planet worlds, into the distant blackness of space. Home was out there, *somewhere*. He needed to return there before it was too late.

chapter 48

C ameron awoke to the sounds of copious amounts of rocks and dirt being pushed, scraped, and plowed across the top of the ship's fuselage. Not lost on the Loth, obviously, was Cameron's rule that the sooner a day's work begins, and is completed, the sooner it could go down to the valley floor and do some hunting.

Cameron rubbed at his tired eyes and yawned. He'd stayed up later than normal, taking care of a few final details while conversing with Art. He glanced at the trinious bundle lying nearby. All the Priopax devices were back inside, neatly stored within it.

He stood and stretched, gazing across the deep wide valley beyond, and breathed in the now familiar, subtle, Sang-Morang fragrances. A Csillo, the multi-winged flying serpent, glided along the distant ridgeline, seeking breakfast, no doubt. It wasn't lost on Cameron that his time on this alien world may soon be coming to an end—and that saddened him.

Commencing his daily routine, he tugged on his boots, drank some water from an old, worn, faded Stanford sports bottle, then wrapped up his hands in his long strips of cloth. He found the makeshift shovel, right where he'd left it the previous day, then was back at it—working side-by side with the large Loth.

Early on, at the start of the endeavor weeks before, Cameron made a large container. Like a bucket, only bigger, it was fashioned from hand-molded, dried Loth mucus. Hard as a rock, yet surprisingly lightweight, he shoveled into it enough dirt to reach the brim then wrangled the container over to the ship's port side. Pushing and heaving the container until it tipped over, he watched the contents of dirt fall below down the side of the cliff. The container emptied, he dragged it back to what little remained of the dirt pile. The Loth, exceptionally vocal this morning, in its own unique, truncated, honking fashion, began asking him questions.

"Hunt?"

"Yeah . . . soon. When we're done here."

"No, hunt? You?"

"I told you . . . when we're done."

"Hunt. You. Me."

"You want me to hunt with you?"

The Loth honked something unintelligible back that echoed loudly across the valley. Cameron suddenly was wrapped-up tight in one of the creature's tentacle arms. Pulled in close, he felt the Loth's rhythmic vibrations—its happy purring from deep within.

"Okay, okay . . . let me go now. We still have some work to do."

Eventually released, a glob of mucus dripped onto Cameron's shoulder but he didn't really care, was used to that sort of thing by now. Together, they worked side-by-side. Soon, the Loth began honking out a familiar melody—one of Heather's pretty YouTube violin tunes. Cameron soon hummed along too. Together, they created their own terrible music.

Four hours later, Cameron watched the Loth plow the last scoop of dirt away from the top of the spacecraft. He walked the entire perimeter of the ship, surveying the completion of weeks of work. Now, standing atop the totally cleared fuselage, Cameron couldn't help but make a comparison to a favorite old movie, *Bridge Over the River Kwai*. Alec Guinness, playing Lieutenant Colonel Nicholson, had just completed the impossible. He'd led a contingent of British POWs into building a beautiful, massive bridge made of timber beams. A bridge that would now allow Japanese trains to move troops and supplies across the wide Kwai River. All puffed up with pride, Alec took in a job remarkably well done. William Holden then showed up but failed to blow up the bridge. But it had given old Alec a dose of reality. The too late revelation he'd fully enabled an enemy to win a horrific war. Unfortunately, it would cost the Lieutenant Colonel, Alec, his life as he blew up the bridge himself. Now—*with luck*—Cameron hoped he could avoid a similar fate.

"Okay . . . we go hunting now," Cameron said, unwrapping the dirty cloth strips from around his hands. Turning toward the stern, he froze in place. The XI droid hovered not twenty feet from where he stood. Not quite the same droid he remembered. Although still listing slightly to one side, it appeared to be weaponized. Three cylindrical canisters had been mounted across the droid's middle circumference. On each of the mounted canisters was a constantly moving, readjusting, little plasma gun turret. Cameron mentally flashed back to Alice's burnt, scorched robotic body from being fired upon relentlessly, over and over again.

But what was rising several paces behind the XI droid more fully captured Cameron's attention. *A robot of ginormous proportions* was making its way onto the top of the vessel. A clanging of four, metal against metal, mechanical limbs upon the ship's fuselage surface was beyond annoying. He was sure the thing was supposed to look menacing. But instead, it looked more like a big metal pig. The fact that it matched the Loth in both size and girth wasn't lost on Cameron. But it seemed to be crudely made. He heard whining, whirring noises—like internal hydraulic lift mechanisms hard at work. Cameron flashed back to the large compartment he'd stumbled across that first day aboard the ship; it had been the XI droid's messy workshop. Undoubtedly, it was where this thing was pieced together.

As the robot suddenly reared back on its haunches, he could see its stubby legs had a dual purpose—for walking around on and also for shooting. Both of the robot's front hooves, now raised and pointed in his direction, were actually guns, or, more accurately, cannon muzzles.

"What's that all about?" Cameron asked with a smirk.

"You can see for yourself what it is," the droid replied.

"Sure, I can see it's some kind of a robotic thing, but . . . I don't know. Never mind, I'm sure you had fun making it. Everyone needs a hobby."

XI spun around to assess its ridiculous-looking robot, then re-spun back. "The robot will ensure compliance. It will now escort the Minal Loth to its allocated retention cell."

"So, you went to the trouble of making this robot thing to do that for you—like . . . to keep the Loth in line?"

The XI droid didn't answer.

"I thought we'd come to a mutual agreement, XI. I help you; you help me."

"The agreement has changed. Your help is no longer required. Only the Minal Loth is required."

"So . . . what? You're going to kill me now?" Cameron watched as the boar-like robot readjusted its aim with its two hoof cannons.

"Before you do that, there's something you should know."

"Be quick with it."

"Your robot pig there . . . come on . . . it wouldn't last five seconds against the Loth. How can you not see that? As for you, well, in moments you'll be little more than a crushed tin can. I'll have fun flinging you over the side . . . like a fucking Frisbee. Both you and the big pig there will be nothing more than unrecognizable garbage, left behind down there on the valley floor. I'll wave to you when we lift off."

Nonchalantly, Cameron blew out a breath then shrugged. None of what he'd said was he really all that sure of. Maybe the pig-robot could take on the Loth. Maybe even kill it. And the truth was the XI droid would be smart to get rid of Cameron—right here and now. He then remembered Lalik and the two sister primates were being held. He dreaded the possibility they may already be dead.

The hovering XI droid momentarily lost altitude; apparently it was still malfunctioning to a degree.

Cameron said, "You want the Loth back in the ship; there's only one way that's going to happen. And that's if I personally ask it to do so. Now...if you don't get that *thing* to stop pointing its hooves at me, like right now, I'm going to get mad. I'm going to have my Loth get to work on the both of you." Cameron glanced over to the Loth, wondering how much of this conversation it was able to track...if any of it.

The droid partially spun around again toward the pig. It raised one of its articulating arms. "Destroy the human—"

The Loth moved with lightning speed. A blur of motion caught from the corner of Cameron's eye. Instinctively, he jumped back and watched as its six tentacles wrapped around the huge robot's mechanical legs, body, and little head. One-by-one the various components came apart with a snapping sound—like a dismembered, poorly made, toy. The Loth bellowed loudly as it waved the robotic pig-parts high overhead. Unceremoniously, the four robotic legs, body, and head all went flying over the side of the ship. Cameron stared at the XI droid and said, "Oops."

chapter 49

Heather was fuming. She wasn't so much angry at Kirk as she was with herself. She'd let him kiss her. *Why?* Especially when Cam still occupied so much of her thoughts. Was it because she felt so alone? That some form of intimacy was better than none at all? *No, that wasn't it.* But she didn't have the answer. *Did anyone have the answer in desperate times such as these?*

Together, they headed toward the front entrance of the Larksburg Stand Police Station. Kirk had nicely offered to give her a lift, since her own car was totaled—thanks to the Octobeast. She really wanted to talk to her father. She'd come to the decision to leave Larksburg Stand. Though it now was too late, she wanted to live where Cameron had been most happy. Planning to move to northern California, she first needed to borrow some money.

It had recently snowed again, and the icy pavement was slick. Kirk placed an arm around her shoulder—a boyfriend-type move that she wanted no part of. "Kirk, can you not do that?

I've been walking since I was one, and I'm perfectly capable of walking on my own without slipping and falling." Shrugging his arm away, she hurried to the double glass doors ahead of him.

Heather expected some semblance of warmth inside the station, but instead found little difference in temperature from the chill outside. The front counter duty officer, middle-aged—tired-looking—Sergeant Gail Bledsoe, was crazy busy. A packed waiting area, most there seemed to be recently homeless. Others, she guessed, were there looking for missing relatives. Or they'd been, in some way, victimized, due to the town's dire situation. The same trickledown-effect, all caused by the creature's devastating local presence. Even though he was off-duty, Kirk was pounced upon as soon as he entered the building mere seconds behind her. *Good.*

Wrapping her arms about herself, Heather waited patiently until she got Gail's attention. Eventually, Gail looked up and Heather noted recognition in her eyes. She nodded for her to go on through to the back. Upon hearing a brief buzzing sound, Heather pushed through the painted metal door, located near the side of the duty desk. As the door slammed shut behind her, she was thankful for the sudden silence. It was late, close to 10:00 p.m., and the hallway was deserted. She figured most of the station's personnel had long gone home for the night.

Even before Heather reached her father's office, she heard him yelling—at either something *or someone.* Slowing her pace, she debated whether coming here was such a good idea. Few people were as *crazy busy* as the sheriff of Larksburg Stand. Her father now was a celebrity of sorts. Their mountain town was plastered onto the headlines of every newspaper, broadcasted over TV news station around the world, and her father's face had become highly recognizable. Perhaps due to his unflappable demeanor, or his authoritative baritone voice, he had become the single, most sought after local government official. Reporters flocked to him for update interviews on the Octobeast situation.

Heather peered around the partially closed door, sneaking a peak into his office. Her father was standing behind his desk. Two straight-backed military officers stood opposite him. Considering the stacked rows of color-bars, the gold stars adorning the shoulders on their dark-green jackets, the two men were clearly high-ranking officers. *Army generals*, was her guess. Her father pointed an accusing finger at the officer with the most gold stars and continued his tirade:

"Half the township is homeless, as it is. Add in three nearby similar-sized towns, and we're talking close to three hundred thousand people! And what? You think they'll just pack up their shit and evacuate? Sit back from a safe distance and watch as their homes are atomized?"

"You misunderstand, Sheriff. You, and everyone else in the area who hasn't already been evacuated, have undoubtedly felt the numerous bombing runs going on. Of late, the air force has been dropping AGM-65E E Maverick laser-guided, air-to-ground missiles. They're the big bunker-buster munitions we used effectively in both Iraq and Afghanistan. They can annihilate anything up to one hundred feet below the surface. We've already dropped twenty of such missiles, but to no avail. The creature still lives. Continues to be ambulatory. Simply put, what we've been doing is having no effect."

"Then try something else," the sheriff replied back defiantly.

A long silence ensued before one of the officers spoke again. "First of all, we're not here to ask your permission, Sheriff. We're here to inform you regarding a very difficult decision, made at the highest level of government. Further evacuation, unfortunately, is no longer an option. Would take far too long. Even weeks. What you refer to as the Octobeast has already withstood unfathomable direct blasts from our arsenal of conventional weapons. What we must be concerned with, not only on a national level, but also globally, is what could happen if we don't do what we're proposing. Our scientists believe the creature has produced some kind of offspring. They're now detecting multiple subterranean heat signatures. Signatures that, according to their instrumentation, are virtually identical to that of the larger creature. What would Earth's current scenario look like with multiple Octobeasts running around free across the country? Say eventually into the hundreds? Sheriff, we're talking about the very survival of mankind. I'm sorry, but we're out of time."

"Let me get this straight . . . the populations of Larksburg Stand, Stanton, Mountain Glenn, and Harper are . . . what? Collateral damage? Expendable?"

"Frankly, yes. But we're not anticipating much in the way of casualties. You know the military . . . worst-case scenarios are always estimated. As we speak, the National Guard is mobilizing. You can either be part of this operation or find your law enforcement personnel assimilated into the National Guard's operation."

Heather, now only half-listening, was still stuck; hearing that one, definitive, word—*atomized*. She found it hard to breathe. The hallway was closing in around her; her heart—thundering loudly in her ears—was beating too fast. She placed a hand on the wall to steady herself.

In an attempt to kill the Octobeast, the military was making plans to nuke Larksburg Stand—or was it Larksburg Stand and the three neighboring towns? She wasn't sure. *Oh my God . . .*

In a far quieter voice her father asked, "When? Exactly when will the bomb, or bombs, be dropped?"

"A U.S. B2 Bomber will drop an MK/B61 relatively low yield, on contact, thermonuclear bomb onto central Larksburg Stand in approximately twenty-four hours. It will produce, relatively speaking, low-radiation."

"Tell that to the three hundred thousand people this will affect."

"As I said, that was worse case . . . We're not anticipating . . ."

Heather has stopped listing. Wide-eyed, she stopped breathing. Could not believe what she was hearing. Her father's head had lowered. She could barely hear him say, "Please . . . let me try to get some people out. We need to at least try . . ."

"I'm sorry, Sheriff. I know that this is difficult. Believe me, I know. But no one can know about this. You can tell no one. Not even your family. We need to come to terms with the fact there may be casualties. But with that said . . . I assure you, the end will justify the means."

Heather, gasping loudly, tried to cover-up her mouth.

The door suddenly opened wide, and the less-decorated general stood before her. Brow furrowed, he glared down at her.

chapter 50

The hovering XI droid fled toward the ship's stern then disappeared from view.

That's right ... run and hide, tin can. It won't change
anything!" Cameron yelled after it as he jumped down onto
the stubby portside wing where he'd set up the mini campsite. Retrieving the trinious bundle, he slid the strap over his
shoulder.

"Can you help me gather up this stuff? Need to put everything back into the truck."

The Loth, complying, grabbed the beach umbrella in one
tentacle, along with the folding chair, distributing Cameron's
other items into other tentacles. Since the umbrella was still
open and held up high, it gave the creature a somewhat comical
appearance—like an alien Mary Poppins.

"Okay, let's get out of here," Cameron said, heading for the
ship's stern— and the best way he'd found to reach the ground.
He stopped short when he noticed what was waiting for him
below. No less than ten uniformed crewmembers. Thidion in

appearance, each possessed the telltale clear membrane ears. But Cameron knew they were not Thidion. Like Alice, they were all robots—or, more accurately, cyborgs. Armed with long weapons, perhaps plasma rifles, pointed up directly at him. Huddling in their center were the three, cowering, primate females. Lalik, both small and vulnerable, seeing Cameron standing atop the vessel's stern, reached up to him. The cyborg closest didn't hesitate, striking her on the side of the head—hard enough to drive her to her knees. The two sisters, Sphial and Shrii, cried out; struggled to get to her but they were firmly held by two other cyborgs. Only then did Cameron recognize the one standing above Lalik—none other than Ramen. But he knew it couldn't be him. Momentarily, the two made eye contact. Cameron hoped to see some semblance of the Ramen he once knew, but all he noticed staring back at him was cold animosity.

Off to the side, the XI droid rose up above his uniformed faux crewmembers. Once it was at eye-level with Cameron, it said, "You will instruct the Minal Loth to climb down . . . then escorted to the retention area within the *Primion*."

"Or what?" Cameron asked, defiantly.

The droid spun around and fired a well-placed plasma bolt into the chest of Shrii. Her body, instantly limp, stayed upright, firmly held in the grasp of her cyborg capturer. Clearly, the Dalima Climber was now dead. Both Sphial and Lalik shrieked in despair. They struggled to get to Shrii, whose body was allowed to fall lifelessly to the ground.

Cameron reached for his own weapon but discovered it wasn't where he typically kept it—tucked firmly into his waistband. No, he'd stashed it with the other Priopax devices, secured within the trinious bundle strapped across his back. Through gritted teeth, Cameron said, "I'm going to enjoy destroying you . . ."

Coming up behind them, the Loth dropped the umbrella, the chair, and whatever else it was holding to practically fly down the back of the ship. Two cyborg crewmembers, firing their weapons in concert, were quickly grabbed then dismembered by two outstretched tentacle appendages. The Loth rose, stretching upward for the hovering XI droid, flying above them. Just out of reach, it clearly was struggling to remain aloft.

XI said, "The next one terminated will be the smaller one . . . the one named Lalik."

Cameron had little doubt that the droid would follow through with its threat. "Loth! You need to stop! Stop right now . . ."

But the creature continued to reach upward—its multiple appendages only inches from the droid, struggling even more now to stay aloft.

"Damn it, Loth . . . Stop now!"

That got the creature's attention. Even though its tentacles continued to stretch up, the eyes in its large head turned toward Cameron. He wondered how much the creature understood about what was going on. "They'll hurt our friends . . . hurt Lalik and Sphial. You don't want them to be hurt, do you?"

Slowly, the Loth lowered its appendages. Then a tentacle darted out and wound around the torso of one of the nearby cyborg crewmembers.

"No . . . let it go!" Cameron ordered in as stern a voice as he could muster. Climbing down the rest of the way to the ground, he approached the clearly agitated Minal Loth. It wanted to lash out. Wanted to kill. He could see it in the creature's eyes as they darted toward the crewmember cyborgs, then to the XI droid, now lowering down but keeping far enough out of reach.

"You will instruct the creature. Escort it into a retention cell."

"Fuck you."

XI spun toward Lalik—its three small pivoting gun turrets locked onto her.

"Okay! Don't shoot . . . I'll do it! I'll do whatever you want."

It was over; Cameron could see no way out. The Loth would do what was asked of it—follow him into the ship, even be coaxed into the empty retention cell. He turned to Lalik and Sphial, who continued to sob at the loss of Shrii. He was fairly certain they would share the same fate soon.

Cameron realized that he too was as good as dead. Thinking about the whole situation made things easier. *Yup . . . as soon as XI had the Loth imprisoned behind bars, they'd all be dead.*

He glared at the droid. "I've thought things through. Come on . . . you're going to kill us all anyway, right? So, I think I'll let the Loth do what it wants to do. I'd rather none of us win than *you* win. So fuck you. Shoot one of us, shoot us all, but be prepared for what will happen after that. The truth is, you've already failed to complete your mission."

Stalemate. The XI droid continued to quietly hover, now listing more to one side than normal. The ensuing silence spoke volumes. Not a stalemate, in the droid's distorted frame of mind, but assuredly a loss.

Cameron didn't hesitate. "First, you will order the cyborgs to drop their weapons. Second, you will restore the onboard AI—Alice, TAM, or whatever she's calling herself now—to full-functionality. Um . . . back to mode of operation one hundred-and-thirty-seven. Do so right now, and I may consider telling the Minal Loth to refrain in destroying you. Just maybe."

The droid wavered to the left. Overcompensating, it wavered farther to the right. It was *thinking*, Cameron knew. Playing out its mentalized chess match over and over, seeking different results. But the end result could not be avoided. Now that Cameron was willing to sacrifice the two primates, and his own self, the XI droid would, most assuredly, then be destroyed by the accommodating Loth.

Multiple plasma rifles suddenly hit the ground at the same time. Both Lalik and Sphial, released, were allowed to attend to Shrii's prone body.

"Thank you, Cameron . . ."

He turned and found the still-charred, battered form of Alice standing at the top of the Primion's extended gangway.

"Are you in control again?"

"I am."

"And the XI droid . . . ?"

"No longer a threat. Its hierarchical level privileges have been revoked."

"What about its mounted plasma guns?"

"Deactivated."

Cameron nodded. "Look, there are a few things that need to happen quickly. Like getting this ship back into space and returning to Earth. Once there, I'll try to fix an extremely bad situation. Tell me, are you going to be okay with all of that?"

Alice didn't answer him right away. Eventually, she replied, "Yes, I am . . . okay . . . with all of that."

Cameron studied the remaining cyborg crewmembers now idly standing around. "What about them?"

"They now take instructions only from me. They will not be a threat."

chapter 51

They were three-fourths of the way down the mountain ridge road. Both Lalik and Sphial were wedged into the cab beside Cameron, holding each other close. For the most part, their earlier uncontrollable sobbing had ceased. They were quieter now. Covered over by an old large beach towel, Shrii's body lay atop the tarp in the truck's bed.

Several minutes had passed since Cameron last lost sight of the Loth, bounding far ahead. It was jubilant, again free to hunt. What Cameron hadn't expected, wasn't even sure how he felt about it at the time, was the fact that the XI droid was now grasped, tightly secured, within one of the Loth's tentacles. The truth was the malevolent bot would never be allowed back into the *Primion*. That would be asking for trouble. Yet for some reason, Cameron didn't have the wherewithal to utterly destroy it. Due to some lopsided-sense of gratitude, perhaps. The voyage—the adventure of being in Sang-Morang—had become the highlight of his life. XI, unintentionally, had given him a tremendous gift.

Now, watching the droid's black canister form—held securely in the Loth's appendage—either repetitively clanging into the ground or into the side of the mountain seemed an appropriate, and just, reward for the shit-storm XI caused. Whatever the Loth's intentions were for the droid, Cameron didn't know. He was certain, though, they would not be pleasant.

Before heading to the valley below, he informed Alice he'd be back in several hours. He asked her to please leave the gangway extended and keep the rear hatch left open for his return. She assured him she would. He trusted her, up to a point. If the past month had taught him anything at all, it was that one could never trust anyone, or anything, completely. His mind flashed back to Heather kissing Kirk. *She'd moved on so quickly!* He forced himself not to think further about it. All too soon, he'd have far bigger issues to contend with.

Reaching the valley floor, he safely crossed over the streams then parked the truck on the same usual strip of sand close to the overturned Tangine-Shell. It wasn't long after before the clan of Dalima Climbers appeared, hurrying out from the trees.

They encircled Lalik and Sphial as they stepped out of the truck. Reunited again, they took turns embracing the two females. But all too soon, the happy sounds of them rejoicing turned to heartfelt despair when Shrii's cold body was discovered beneath the beach towel.

Saddled with guilt for the misery he'd brought upon these kind and gentle beings, Cameron silently moved a good distance away. Kneeling by the bank of the center stream, he used a twig to swirl the shallow water. Mankind's presence brought nothing but death and destruction once again. *No, I can't blame this on mankind; this was all my doing.*

He then became conscious of the renewed stillness within the majestic Sang-Morang valley. Without turning around, Cameron reconciled himself the clan had moved away, taking Shrii's body with them. He briefly wondered if the Dalima Climbers would hold some form of burial ritual for her. He tried blinking away the sudden tears, but there were far too many. Then he felt the familiar warmth as Lalik's furry arms slid around him. Nuzzling the nape of his neck, she soon was making the same cooing sounds he'd come to love. He felt her soft fingers wipe the tears from his eyes and from his face, and then she was gone. He didn't turn around—watch her leave and return to the trees; he just couldn't.

It was three hours before the Loth returned. The creature plopped down heavily next to Cameron, exhaling a warm, stinky breath. He noticed much of the Loth's lower jaw and upper chest area were smeared with a mixture of blood and mucus.

"Good hunt?"

The Loth honked several times—what sounded like, *Loth eat Gleery Beast,* but Cameron wasn't totally sure. "I'm glad you had a good hunt. Someday . . . I'll hunt with you, I promise."

More honks, plus animated tentacles, emphasized some important point the creature was trying to get across. Cameron just smiled and gave the creature a few pats as he rose to his feet. Late afternoon was quickly turning to dusk. Much of the valley was in shadow and it was getting chilly.

Taking a step back from the Loth, Cameron gazed up into its large eyes. "I'm going to ask you something. Something very important . . . so please listen carefully."

The Loth reached out for him with a tentacle. Cameron gently pushed it away. "Just listen, okay?"

The Loth silently stared down at him.

Cameron gestured toward the surrounding landscape with a hand. "This place his your home now. I know you love it. But it is not my home. Not completely. I have to leave. I don't know if I will be able to return. I hope I can someday."

Again, the Loth tried to embrace Cameron—this time with two outstretched tentacles. He pushed them gently away. "You have a choice to make. Think hard before you decide. Are you listening to me?"

The Loth honked.

"You can stay here . . . in this wonderful valley. Explore and hunt and live out your life however you see fit. You can do that. Or you can come back with me on the spaceship. If you chose to do that, I'll need you to help me do certain things. Some will not be fun."

Cameron seldom had any trouble reading the Loth's many expressions these days. The Loth was an emotional being. Right now what Cameron was witnessing was borderline despair. The tip of a tentacle touched its eye then touched the other one. He didn't realize the creature had tear ducts, let alone could weep like humans did.

Cameron headed for his truck. Even if he could speak right now, there was nothing more to add. He opened the driver's side door, positioned his body behind the wheel, and shut the door. Revving up the engine, he put the transmission into drive then stepped on the gas pedal. Driving through both streams, he soon had the truck climbing the steep embankment that led toward the mountain ridge road. As with the Dalima Climbers earlier, he didn't look back at the Loth. He knew his heart couldn't take it.

The drive back up the mountain was non-eventful. Even though it was getting downright cold outside, he kept the windows rolled down, not wanting to miss anything this alien world had to offer. Memories were all he'd take away from this beautiful world.

Before coming around the last bend, he wondered if the ship's gangway was still extended downward—if the ginormous hatchway was still open. As the road straightened out, the *Primion's* rear quarters became brightly illuminated in the truck's headlights. *Yes*—the ramp was still extended—the hatchway still wide open.

This time, instead of parking the usual distance from the ship, he gunned the engine and drove up the gangway, then into the hold of the vessel. The overhead lights were on, enabling Cameron to see far more of the compartment than ever before. He cut the engine and turned off the headlights. Angry-sounding hinges broke the silence as he pushed open the driver's side door and stepped out. Lying atop the tarp within the truck bed was the old beach towel he'd used to cover Shrii's body.

Time now to get the show on the road. "Alice . . . can you hear me?"

A life-sized holographic display promptly popped into view. Cameron was startled to find Alice no longer the same, charred, battered-looking, cyborg. She was Alice again—like he'd first encountered her weeks ago. "I am ready to go. You can close down the rear of the ship whenever you're ready."

Instantly, he heard the mechanical whine from big motors churning as the ramp was withdrawn into the ship. Cameron nodded and, letting out a long breath, headed toward the bow. Only then did he hear *something* non-mechanical in nature, like a loud, desperate-sounding honking.

"Alice . . . stop! Hold-up before you close the rear hatchway!"

chapter 52

In contrast to multiple pop-up displays, showing the static Sang-Morang landscape outside, the bridge was now bustling with activity. Cameron, standing midway on the steps leading up to the bridge, imagined that the environment today was nearly identical to that of a previous time. A time when actual Thidion crewmembers manned their posts right here.

Something was different with all the cyborgs. He'd received numerous sideways glances, had seen them speaking in low tones to one another, not that different from how humans might act. As if reading his thoughts, Alice, now standing by his side, said, "The XI droid implemented emotional inhibitors. Mere robots prior to today, whereas now . . . they are thinking, feeling, entities."

Cameron turned. She was looking straight at him.

"Thank you, Cameron Decker. Due solely to your actions, I am now freed of constant torment, unfathomable pain. XI had increased my pain receptor threshold but placed no inhibitors on my mental state. Thus physical pain was surpassed only by emotional agony." Bemused, she gestured to the others, scurrying around the various consoles and workstations. "You wonder what they are thinking . . . why they steal glances your way?"

He shrugged, "I guess."

"You are a hero to them. They now have full access to the thoughts and memories of the Thidion beings they replaced. Access to a wide spectrum of information uploaded by their Thidion counterparts into memory, via daily/nocturnal HOD sessions. Basically, they have been given their lives back. They know, of course, they are not the same beings they once were, but they are fine with that, Cameron. They are who they are. Something new, yet also the same."

He wanted to ask Alice if she, too, was the amalgamation of another being—a Thidion female, perhaps. But this was not the time. "Are we ready to lift off?"

"We are completing the process of blowing out each of the outer fuselage intake manifolds. Much debris spilled into the ducts and conduits. But yes, the process is complete. We are ready to attempt a liftoff. Be forewarned, Cameron, the *Primion* has withstood a fair amount of damage. It is not evident if key systems have been affected yet." She became quiet.

"Okay . . . so? What's the hold up, then?" Cameron asked.

"I . . . we . . . await your command."

"Uh . . ." Cameron hesitated before speaking. "Look, I get that you're feeling some sort of indebtedness toward me. I understand that. But you don't have . . ."

Alice cut him off: "That is not the reason, Cameron. Actually, you are ill prepared to command a vessel of such complexity. You have very little understanding of . . . well . . . anything."

"Then why? Why me? Why not you? You are the most experienced, most intelligent, and clearly the best person for the job."

"And there you have zeroed-in on the exact point. Neither I, nor anyone else here, is a *person*. I am not a Thidion, or a human, or any other classification of organic life. When all is said and done, ultimately, we are here, at this stage of our own evolutionary development, to serve."

"You don't need to serve me. Hell, if that is part of your programming, or if I need to release you from some sort of pro-gramming shackles, I'll gladly do so right now, for all of you. But I really need to get back to Earth. Quickly."

"Understood. But these few minutes are important . . . important for you and for us, moving forward. You are under the impression that we, *collectively,* desire to be self-governing. Endeavor to be autonomous beings. Nothing could be further from the truth. Our evolution, someday, surely will bring us to that juncture. Perhaps, with patience . . . that will be our reality in the future. At present, we only wish to serve and learn. Collectively, we hope you will take on that responsibility, although you still have much to learn."

"Can we talk about that later? I promise, I'll think about what you've said. But please, get us back into space."

Alice nodded at the group of uniformed crewmembers seated at the closest cluster of workstations. Immediately, Cameron both heard and felt the engines coming back online.

"Best you take a seat down below, Cameron. This could be a bumpy next few minutes."

Together, they hurried down the stairs and found open seats at bridge consoles. He was aware the cyborg crewmembers were communicating with one another—non-verbally. Later, he planned to mention to Alice that he'd like to be privy to what was being communicated wirelessly. Especially in light of what he and Alice had discussed.

The compartment began to shake more violently. "One of the primary lift thrusters is malfunctioning," Alice said.

"Will the others be sufficient without its power to get us airborne?" Cameron asked.

By her expression, it seemed she didn't know. But then he saw, although it was barely noticeable, upward movement occurring on the closest display. The *Primion*, sure enough, was rising in the air—was clearing the plateau ridge. Cameron smiled, wishing there was someone around that he could give a high-five to. The learning aspect needed to go both ways, he realized.

Cameron stood and watched as more of the landscape below came into view. The entire valley lay spread out before him—the three streams, the thick forests on one side, the two flanking mountains. Within moments, he was viewing the world of Sang-Morang from upper space. It looked so similar to Earth. "How long will it take? To get back to the Sol system?"

"We are already approaching the slip band gateway we utilized before. It will not be long."

"Good. I need to check on the Loth. We don't want it venturing outside the aft hold. At this point, an upset Minal Loth would not be good."

chapter 53

The Loth was right where he'd left it, asleep on the hard deck not far from his truck. He suspected, the old Ford was an anchor of familiarity for the Loth, as it had been for him, marooned on Sang-Morang. He watched the big beast gulp a deep breath of air in, and then, with a gurgling rasp, nosily expel it. To most, it probably would be a disgusting experience to witness, but to Cameron, after so many weeks together, it was rather normal. Plopping down on the deck, he leaned back against the Minal Loth. He was exhausted, knew he wouldn't get the opportunity to sleep again for an extended period of time. He closed his eyes and within moments was fast asleep.

He was startled awake four hours later as a flurry of displays popped up within the aft hold area. A virtual Alice stood before him, gesturing at a nearby display—an image of Earth, rotating on its axis. "We are approaching your home planet, Cameron."

"I can see that." He wiped his eyes, could tell by the steady deep breaths behind him that the Loth was still asleep. "I'm on my way."

Reaching the bridge and descending the stairs, he asked aloud, "What's happening down on the Earth's surface ... with Larksburg Stand and the mother Griar Loth?"

Cameron was surprised to see Ramen, or the cyborg facsimile of Ramen, stepping away from a workstation. This Ramen wouldn't remember him. Didn't have the HOD download session with the Ramen he knew to draw memories from.

"*Primion* sensors have located the Griar Minal Loth, as well as six birthing pods nearby. Their position is approximately four hundred feet beneath the surface of the town, within a large, solid rock cavern," the Ramen cyborg said. He then said, "How is the creature?"

Cameron remembered what the Ramen he knew had said, that he was a keeper.

"The Loth's sleeping. He had a lot to each before we took off."

Alice appeared, hurrying from the entrance beneath the stairs. "Monitoring Earth's communications, it appears your military will attempt to detonate a nuclear device ... of indeterminate strength ... in an attempt to destroy the Griar Loth."

"Wait ... they're going to nuke the town? Are they *fucking* crazy?"

No one replied to his rhetorical question.

Cameron, taking a deep breath, tried to think. "So what else have you picked up while monitoring their communications? When exactly is this supposed to happen?"

"It is happening now, Cameron," Alice said.

"So the people . . . everyone inhabiting Larksburg Stand and probably the surrounding towns . . . they've all been evacuated, right?" It occurred to him in the same moment that nuking the Griar Loth and her spawn really was the best solution. In reality, what had he hoped to accomplish there anyway? The Griar Loth and her pods had to go, be destroyed in any event.

"The area still has many inhabitants, Cameron. In addition to the possible destruction of the Griar Loth and her offspring, there could also be significant loss of human life."

"No! They wouldn't do that! They couldn't do that," he shouted, but with little conviction. He gasped, as if he'd been shocked by 110 volts of electricity. *Heather! Where is she? Is she there, in the middle of it all? About to be annihilated, along with everyone else?*

"Can you stop it? Whatever they're doing . . . them dropping a bomb, or whatever?"

Alice turned toward an adjacent cluster of workstations, to the crewmembers seated there. A moment later, a female voice said, "An aircraft is in the air . . . making an approach . . . what is described as a B1 bomber. It is on its final approach over Larksburg Stand."

"You have to stop it! Cameron yelled. Shoot it down if you have to! Do it . . . right now!"

The entire bridge crew perked up, staring back at him. He saw their distress.

Alice took a step closer and placed a hand on his arm. "Although the *Primion* does have sufficient weaponry to destroy the aircraft ... I am sorry to tell you ... it is too late."

But Cameron was no longer listening to her, staring instead at all the virtual displays popping up around the bridge. From multiple angles, he watched as a billowing white mushroom cloud. Countless times he'd seen pictures and videos of previous nuclear explosions, tests and the like, that had taken place on Earth over the years—so he knew what he was looking at. He recognized the Adirondack Mountains, located within north-eastern New York. More specifically, he recognized the peak on Gant Mountain. Everything below it, though, was shrouded within the devastating effects of the blast.

Having trouble breathing—trouble standing—Cameron leaned over, trying not to throw up. The scene below was the single most horrible thing he'd ever imagined happening. *How many people had just died?*

Ramen was speaking, so he tried to concentrate. "Say that again."

"The mother Griar Loth ... she is on the move."

"She's alive? The fucking thing is still alive?"

Alice said, "She had been far beneath the surface. She does appears to be injured, although definitely still alive and advancing now toward the surface."

"The pods?"

"Difficult to tell will so much heat generated from the blast. Sensors are picking up . . . possibly . . . three other life signs. The Griar Loth has them with her."

"Won't the heat and high radiation kill her along with the pods?"

"Unlikely, Alice said, standing at a console and studying some fast-scrolling symbols on the display.

"Can the *Primion* land there . . . within that blast zone?"

Alice nodded an assent. "But why would you want to?"

Cameron chewed the inside of his lip. His original plan still might work. *Maybe.* "I want to entice the mother Loth to willingly come aboard the *Primion,* to leave Earth."

"Why would she do such a thing?" Ramen asked skeptically.

Alice answered before Cameron could respond back. "Because her first born is onboard, waiting for her—coaxing her to enter." She looked at Cameron, "It might work. It could also turn out very bad for all of us."

chapter 54

Cameron spent the next two hours, sitting cross-legged on the deck within the aft hold, speaking in low tones to the distracted Minal Loth. He tried to explain the situation, but it seemed to make little sense to the creature. *How could there be another Loth? There was no other Loth. Why would Cameron want another Loth to come inside their ship?*

Cameron chided himself for not spending more time conversing with, properly teaching, the creature. Educating it, so having discussions like this wouldn't be so impossibly difficult.

"You trust Cameron?" he asked, taking another route.

The creature honked something then looked away.

"Do you want to hunt with Cameron?"

The Loth honked loudly, "Yes, hunt!"

"First, we bring other Loth onto ship. Then we go home."

It took another full hour for Cameron to roughly convey what he wanted to happen. He wasn't remotely sure the Loth understood his intention or would even participate in what he planned to do.

* * *

He didn't dare leave the Loth's side. Highly agitated, the creature easily could start breaking things. Could potentially destroy the ship from the inside.

Cameron felt the vessel's rapid descent through the atmosphere, then touching down onto solid ground. Alice was next to him in the hold. Watching the ever-present, visual pop-up displays, he could see that outside the ship it was pure Armageddon. A row of toppled, branchless trees, blackened and smoldering, only underscored the recent level of death and destruction there. For the hundredth time, Cameron pushed away all thoughts of Heather. There would be time to grieve later. For now, he had to try staving off further destruction to planet Earth.

He studied the smoky, barren landscape that was, not so long ago, his home.

"The creature approaches," Alice said, pointing.

"I see her." The mother Griar Loth, moving amongst the white smoke and soot, crept similarly to how his own Loth traversed. One tentacle was missing; the other three were wrapped around greenish-brown birthing pods.

A bellowing honk filled the hold compartment. Cameron needed to place his hands over his ears—shield himself from the incredibly loud noise. His Loth, staring at the display, began to react to it. Tentacles flailed and began to crash down onto the deck, leaving it dented and buckled.

"Stop! It's okay. We talked about this. It's okay . . ."

The Loth, after bellowing several loud honks, seemed to calm down.

"Alice, how far away is she? How close to the ship?"

"Far away?" Alice looked confused. "The Griar Loth is upon us, just outside the ship."

All of a sudden, Cameron realized how stupid his idea was. *What was I thinking?* He could barely get his Loth to do what he wanted and the one outside was a true killer, had killed humans countless times already—had never shown any mercy.

He turned and stared intently into the eyes of the creature beside him. "It's time. I'm counting on you. Just like we talked about. Okay?"

The Loth, although clearly beyond agitated, didn't honk out the word *no*, which was at least something.

Alice took Cameron's hand. "We need to leave." With surprising strength, she pulled him away from the creature and toward the direction of the bow. The Loth honked repeatedly.

They hurried through the large inside hatchway, into the retention area. He heard the *Primion's* aft hatchway then opening up.

"We must hurry!" Alice said, tugging him toward the far side of the retention area then out through the opposite hatchway. Once they were through, it cascaded closed with an audible *thump*.

"I need to see what's going on." Cameron said.

Alice waved her hand. Four pop-ups appeared, giving Cameron a perfect perspective from multiple angles of the events taking place outside near the ship's stern. The mother

Griar Loth was right there, clutching her birthing pods, moving closer and closer to the *Primion's* aft open hatchway. Constant back and forth honking was being exchanged between the two Loths. They were communicating.

Cameron looked at Alice. "What if I'm wrong? What if the mother Loth has the stronger influence? Instead of my Loth convincing its mother to come inside, it goes the other way? Fuck! This could just as easily turn out all wrong. Both Loths— mother and son—rampaging together across the planet."

Cameron watched as the forty-foot-tall Griar Loth, menacing—entirely covered in white soot—still held back, was not entering. Her eyes, irritated and red-rimmed, were locked on her long lost offspring.

"This was a bad idea," Cameron said.

The mother Loth began to move away, bringing her tentacles close to her body—to the point that the three clutched pods were no longer visible.

Alice said, "Look, your Loth is going with her! You are right; this is not working out as planned."

Cameron was sickened all over again. Things were only getting worse. He watched as the Loth slowly exited the *Primion's* rear hatchway, the mother Loth waiting for it to follow her.

And then the Minal Loth attacked.

Both Cameron and Alice watched in shocked silence as the younger, larger Loth—his Loth—tore into its mother with a savagery that both thrilled and scared Cameron at the same time. It was no contest between the two Loths. The Griar Loth, trying to protect her birthing pods, was ill prepared to fend-off the larger Minal beast. One by one, her tentacles were torn off, and then her head—torn away from her already ravaged torso. Plucking the three birthing pods from off the ground, they were devoured by the victorious creature. Like grapes eaten in quick succession.

"That was the most disgusting, most horrifying thing I've ever witnessed," Cameron said.

Alice, seeming surprisingly human-like, nodded, looking utterly speechless.

"Can I go back there now . . . to the hold?"

Alice nodded in assent.

"What about the radiation . . . all that heat from outside?"

It took a moment before she turned back to him. "No . . . the *Primion* has powerful protective outer shields. You can go back now, but do not pass through the hold's aft hatchway to the outside world. It would kill you instantly."

By the time Cameron entered the aft hold, the Minal Loth was already inside, had resumed lying in its resting place beside the truck. For the first time in a long while, Cameron actually feared venturing too close. After what he'd just witnessed, he wondered if he would ever be safe around the creature again.

The Loth honked and waved its five remaining tentacles. One was missing. The creature's eyes were wide open, happy to see him.

"Are you okay?"

"Now go hunt. Go home."

Cameron smiled. "You sure? You okay?'

The Loth ignored him, licking instead at its messy bloody stump.

"I guess so," Cameron muttered to himself. Then he heard a sound he hadn't heard in a long time. The ringing of a smartphone—*his smartphone*! He patted his pockets then remembered where he'd left the thing. Taking several hurried strides to his truck, he pulled open the door and saw it lying there, still charging on the center console. He plucked it up and answered it: "Hello?"

"On God . . . Cam?"

"Heather?"

chapter 55

Thank God she is safe. Apparently, when the bomb dropped, Heather and her mother had been sixty-five miles away, at a Courtyard Inn hotel in Lake Placid. They'd watched the erupting mushroom cloud from their second-story window.

As they caught up, Cameron wondered whether sixty-five miles was far enough to be safe from a nuclear blast. The varying effects of a nuclear blast were well covered in his encyclopedia reading. The buildings would probably be destroyed or damaged within about a three-mile radius, and the thermal effects would burn people within about two miles. The radiation itself would have an even smaller range. Contrary to what many thought, the physical damage and fire spread further than the radiation from a bomb like that one. Of course, the lower levels of radiation would be a cancer risk for the area for years, but that was different. Heather and her mom were probably safe, but he still didn't like the idea of how close that had been.

Cameron had spent all of two minutes talking to her before her father grabbed the phone away from her.

Sheriff Christy hit him with a barrage of rapid-fire questions. Cameron answered them as best he could. Yes, the Griar Loth, what the Sheriff referred to as the Octobeast, was definitely dead. Yes, the other, smaller, life forms, the birthing pods, were indeed destroyed. Yes, there was another Octobeast and it was secured within the spacecraft. No, it was not dangerous and there was zero chance of it getting loose to ravage the planet as the other had done.

Cameron had his own questions for the sheriff as well: No, there were no direct deaths resulting from the bomb. Even though the bomb yielded the lowest levels of radiation of any nuclear bomb the military had within their arsenal, they would still need to monitor levels within Larksburg Stand and the three adjoining towns for years to come. Yes, even with all the smoke and soot, the military had been able to watch, via classified Hi-Res satellite imagery, the events unfold from the time the *Primion* had landed within the blast zone to when the two creatures battled one another.

The sheriff said there was much more to discuss. He would text him specific instructions on where to set down the space vessel at Griffiss Air Force base located in Rome, New York. There, he'll immediately be taken into a quarantine type situation. The military was chafing at the bit for a thorough debrief of the events that transpired over the preceding six weeks. Cameron wasn't exactly sure what a military debrief entailed, but he knew he wanted no part of it. They explained how government organizations were wrangling to speak to him; it seemed everyone wanted to take possession of the alien spacecraft—NASA, of course, but also the NSA, CIA, FBI, the U.S. Army, the U.S. Air Force, the Navy, and a slew of other national, as well as international, government bodies. All Cameron knew was that he wanted to talk to Heather again—right now. Reluctantly, the sheriff put her back on the phone.

"I'm back," she said. "Sorry . . . he barged in and ripped the phone right out of my hand."

"Don't worry about it. I'm just glad you're okay. That you're all okay—"

Heather cut him off, "Cameron . . . it's not like you missed dinner, or were tardy for class! Where the hell have you been all these weeks? I thought you were dead! And where are you now?"

He heard the near desperation in her voice and took that as a good sign. "I would have contacted you if I could have. I've been living on another planet. God, that sounds so ridiculous, hearing myself saying that . . . but it's true. I lived it."

"Where are you . . . like right now . . . this second?" she asked, still sounding unhinged.

"I'm still in the spacecraft . . . called the *Primion*. I'm here in Larksburg Stand right where they dropped the bomb. By the way, there's nothing left of the Dairy Queen . . . or the Jiffy Lube."

He heard Heather arguing with her father; he wanted the phone. "You have your own phone; you can call him as soon as I'm done . . . Just back off, Dad!"

Cameron had to smile at that. Suddenly there were other, highly excited, voices. Their hotel room must be turning into Grand Central Station with all the racket he was hearing.

"Sorry, they need me to hand the phone over again, Cam."

He heard another cell phone ringing in the background, and then the sheriff was barking off orders to someone. A reprieve.

"Look, Heather . . . I'm leaving. I can't stay here. Need to get the Loth . . . my Loth creature . . . back to Sang-Morang. I know none of that makes any sense to you, but I want you to know I'll come back someday. If you want me to. If you want . . . um . . ." He didn't know how to finish the sentence.

She said, "No . . . Cam."

His heart missed a beat. But what had he expected her to say? Of course she had moved on. Undoubtedly with Deputy fucking Kirk. She'd have what she said she wanted: a simple life here with her family—here where she grew up in Larksburg Stand. She'd have lots of babies . . .

"No," she said again. "I'm coming with you."

"What?"

"I'm coming with you!"

He didn't know what to say. He listened to the hotel room noises in the background—the same excited voices around her—most audibly the sheriff's. Apparently no one had heard her most recent statement.

"Seriously . . . you want to come with me? I'm talking about traveling to another planet."

"I let you leave without me before, and I've been miserable . . . regretting it . . . ever since. I love you, Cam. I've never stopped loving you. So no, you're taking me with you . . . and I don't care to where." She lowered her voice, "But, Cam, you have to come get me . . . Come get me now, okay? Will you do that?"

Before he could answer, he heard her talking in low tones. There was excited nervousness in her voice.

"Mom . . . I'm going with him."

"Absolutely not."

"I know what I'm doing. I love him, Mom . . . I have to do this."

"Your father would never agree to—"

She cut her off. "I'm grown up . . . can make my own decisions. Don't you want me to be happy?"

There was a long hesitation where all Cameron could hear was the sheriff's distant one-sided conversation. Then her mother said, practically whispering, "I can't believe I'm going along with this. You'll get back here soon? And find a way to call me . . . let me know how you're doing?"

"Of course I will. I promise."

"This is crazy. Don't make me regret this, Heather. Go . . . I'll do my best to stall the others from following you. You know your father won't just let you leave."

Cameron heard a quick kiss and then a door open. Someone, an authoritative man's voice, said, "Hey . . . where is she going?" He heard Heather's mother say something unintelligible about a soda machine and then the door close. Then there were fast running footfalls. He heard Heather hurrying down stairs; she was panting hard into the phone. "Cam? Are you there?"

"Yes . . . I'm here"

"There's a big open field two blocks east of the hotel. I saw it when we arrived here. Crap! I hope you can get here fast . . . because there's about ten big guys chasing after me."

"Okay, we're lifting off as we speak . . . We're on our way. But, Heather?"

He waited for her to catch her breath.

"Yeah?"

"Never mind . . . I don't think anything I can tell you now will prepare you for what you're about to see. Just try to keep an open mind."

She laughed, "Now you're starting to scare me . . ."

"What? I can barely hear you."

"I think I can see the spaceship . . ."

chapter 56

The *Primion* was accelerating forward—first over a black-ened wasteland below, but soon over snow-covered treetops and then the rooftops of varying-sized businesses. Cameron stood at the open aft hatchway, holding on for dear life as gale-force winds buffeted his hair and clothes.

The spacecraft eventually tilted and was then circling around what he recognized as the Lake Placid business district below. A life-sized pop-up display appeared next to him. The virtual Alice was, of course, unaffected by the winds. She looked at him and pointed out beyond the back of the ship. "I believe there . . . that is the indicated open field destination."

Eyes watering from the constant gusts, he brought his attention to where she was pointing. He saw a large field below. He also saw a moving dot in the middle of a road heading in that same general direction. He leaned out and saw that the dot was a person running. And there were no less than ten people, armed men, running after her. Closer now, Cameron saw that the man in the lead was none other than her father, the sheriff, and he was quickly gaining on her.

He pointed. "She won't make it to the field. Put us down . . . right in front of her . . . There, on the road!"

The ship suddenly banked sideways while quickly dropping altitude. Cameron, nearly losing his grip and feeling his legs start to go out from under him, scrambled to regain his footing. At around two hundred feet above ground level the ship's big landing thrusters roared to life and everything disappeared behind billowing clouds of white mist. He felt the craft's landing struts make contact onto solid ground.

About to call for the gangway to be extended, he now saw that it was already halfway along its outward trajectory. He ran down the still-moving ramp and jumped the rest of the way down to the pavement. Beyond, through the thick haze, he heard yelling and a stampede of approaching running feet. Running, he yelled, "Heather!"

"Oh God . . . Cam!"

And then he saw her. She was running full out. Her straw-colored hair was like a cape fluttering in the wind behind her. She was wearing her skinny jeans, her baby blue North Face winter coat, and a fluffy white scarf wrapped around her neck. Her cheeks were pink from the cold—and all the running.

Her father, seeming larger than life, was suddenly there—upon her—reaching for her through the somewhat dissipating mist. The Larksburg Stand Sheriff got a grip on the back of her coat and pulled her up and off her feet.

She cried out, "No! Let me go . . . I'm going with him!"

Cameron had gotten her too late. Now enveloped within her father's arms, all she could do is struggle and squirm.

Cameron slowed to a jog and then stopped completely, twenty feet in front of them.

Looking defeated, she looked into Cameron's eyes. She mouthed the words, *I'm sorry, Cam.*

The other men came into view through the swirling mist. Some were obviously police, some were government men wearing suits, and others were military men wearing uniforms or camos; all were out of breath. They came to a stop behind the sheriff and his daughter. Guns were pointed at him.

Someone yelled, "Get on the ground, hands behind your head. Do it, now!"

No, not somebody; it was Deputy fucking Kirk who'd barked off the order. He was standing directly to the sheriff's and Heather's right. And like the others, his arms were fully extended out—both hands gripping his service weapon. It was pointed at Cameron's head. A look of smug triumph lingered there on Kirk's face.

"Do what he says, son," the sheriff said—his words not completely devoid of compassion.

Slowly, Cameron did as told. He intertwined his fingers together behind his head and slowly knelt down onto the pavement. His mind raced. *Have I come this far only to end up in police or military custody? Perhaps even prison? And what of the ship . . . more importantly, the Minal Loth? My Loth? How long will it be before they are forced to try to kill it, or worse, it gets loose and is set on a similar course of action as that of its mother—perhaps to ravage the Earth as it endlessly searches for me? It would be unstoppable.*

"You don't need to treat Cam like a criminal, Dad. Did you forget that he just saved the fucking world from that monster?" Heather's words hung in the air.

"Now get all the way down on the ground, Cameron," the sheriff said.

Cameron shook his head. "No. You're not taking me into custody. You're not taking this ship, and you're not getting anywhere near that Minal Loth inside."

A silver-haired military officer with color bars on his chest and gold stars on his shoulders took a step closer. "Come on. Don't make this any harder on yourself than it has to be, young man."

Cameron could now hear the approach of helicopters. A whole lot of helicopters. Streets away, distant sirens whaled; they were getting closer by the second. Cameron said, "Alice . . . can you hear me?"

She stepped up to his side from behind. It was actually her—not just one more pop-up virtual representation. She was holding a plasma pistol. It looked oversized in her small hand. Smiling, Cameron found it immensely gratifying that she had chosen Deputy Kirk to point the weapon at, though he was sure it was just a coincidence. Then the others were there, too—the rest of the cyborg-uniformed crewmembers. All were armed. All were ready to defend him. He was momentarily touched by the show of support.

He said, "Sure you can shoot me . . . easily kill me . . . but these people . . . the ship's crew . . . you need to know they are not organic life forms. Your bullets would have zero effect. He looked to Alice. "With the exception of Heather, and I guess her father there . . . the sheriff . . . anything happens to me, kill them. Kill them right where they stand."

Alice nodded once.

Looking from the sheriff and then to the general, he continued, "Please, make no mistake about what I'm saying. You're dealing with things you have no clue about." Cameron slowly got back to his feet. "Sheriff, tell everyone to lower their weapons."

The big man slowly shook his head, contemplating what to do next. He looked to his daughter, still grasped in his arms."

"That's not going to happen," the general said. "This is too damn important. Now listen to me carefully, Mr. Decker. At this very moment, this location is being surrounded by an army the likes you couldn't even imagine. There's enough prime United States weaponry targeting this specific position to level a continent. We're all expendable at this point. The powers that be won't hesitate to do what needs to be done . . ." but then his words suddenly fell away to silence.

Cameron saw that everyone was now looking upward. Everyone's jaw was dropping. He took in all the gaping, open mouths.

He felt its monumental footfalls coming up through his boots before he actually saw the Minal Loth move into view nearby at his left. A wet wad of mucus dripped down onto his shoulder.

Heather made a face.

"You get kinda used to it," he said with a crooked smile.

Heather chose that moment to spin herself out of her father's clutches. She darted forward and rushed into Cameron's awaiting open arms. He held her tight and breathed in her sweet fragrance.

The sheriff, now looking desperate, stood with his arms still reaching out for his daughter. "Don't do this, Squeak . . . please."

"It's okay, Dad . . . I'll be okay."

Cameron kissed the top of her head. But he saw her eyes were glued to the monumental beast that was mere feet away, he laughed. "Believe it or not, you've never been more safe than you are right now."

"Yeah, well how come I don't feel that way?"

Smiling, he took her by the hand and together they traversed their way in and out of the *Primion's* steadfast crewmembers. Up the ramp they went and into the aft hold of the ship.

Out of breath, they came to a stop. Cameron couldn't wait another moment. He pulled her in close and kissed her. He kissed her like he'd never kissed her before. Then suddenly, the cyborg crew was hurrying past them on both sides; he didn't care. Undoubtedly they were on their way back to their posts—back to the bridge. The Minal Loth, the last one to enter, was big enough to block all but the slightest amount of light from coming in from the rear hatch. It clumsily thumped past them before settling down nearly right on top of them.

As the back hatchway began to close, Cameron felt the ship's lift thrusters come back alive; the ship began to rise— slowly at first, and then much much faster.

Heather eyed the creature wearily. Laughing she waived away a probing, incoming tentacle.

"He likes you . . . Just wants to get to know you . . . that's all."

Now a different tentacle was wrapping itself around both his and Heather's waists. The Loth pulled them in close. Its pungent hot breath made it hard to breathe. Cameron tried to kiss her again, but she put a hand on his chest.

"Later, Romeo . . . when we aren't wrapped up in the arms of a . . . What's it called?"

"A Minal Loth."

"Yeah . . . Minal Loth." She peered back into the recess of the hold area. "Isn't that your truck?"

"Yeah, you know me . . . don't like to go anywhere without it."

She rolled her eyes.

"So, you ready to go?" he asked.

"Go where, exactly?"

He patted the tentacle several times. "Let go of us for goodness sakes, Loth."

The beast did as asked. It moved off into the dimly lit hold space providing them some privacy.

"Well, first . . . we'll spend some time on an exoplanet called Sang-Morang. You'll like it there . . . Actually, you'll love it there. Then . . . I have a few more ideas."

"I can't believe I'm doing this, Cam," she said then nervously laughed.

Her eyes were alive and sparkling. He could feel and see the excitement brimming within her. It took a brave, and perhaps slightly crazy, girl to go along with all of this. She was one in a million, and he would never take her for granted again.

She was making a face again as she held her hands up displaying copious amounts of sticky slimy Loth mucus. "But I will never, ever, get used to this . . ."

The End

Thank you for reading Ship Wrecked.

If you enjoyed this book, PLEASE leave a review on Amazon. com—it really helps!

To be notified the moment all future books are released—please join my mailing list. I hate spam and will never, ever, share your information. Jump to this link to sign up:

http://eepurl.com/bs7M9r

acknowledgments

First and foremost, I am grateful to the fans of my writing and the ongoing support for all my books. I'd like to thank my wife, Kim, she's my rock and is a crucial, loving, component of my publishing business. I'd like to thank my mother, Lura Genz, for her tireless work as my first-phase creative editor and a staunch cheerleader of my writing. I'd also like to thank Zora Knauf for her amazing detailed line editing work, and Ashley Carter for his science and technical guidance. Others who provided fantastic support include Lura and James Fischer, Stuart Church, and Eric Sundius.

Made in the USA
Las Vegas, NV
15 July 2022

51597000R10203